LENGTH OF DAYS – BEYOND THE VALLEY OF THE KEEPERS

A Novel

LENGTH OF DAYS – BEYOND THE VALLEY OF THE KEEPERS

Doris Gaines Rapp

The second novel in the Length of Days trilogy

Daniel's House Publishing

Copyright © 2015 by Doris Gaines Rapp

Daniel's House Publishing
P.O. Box 623
Huntington, Indiana 46750

This book is a work of fiction. Names, characters, places and incidents are either products of the author's imagination or used fictitiously. Any resemblance to actual events, locales or persons, living or dead, is entirely coincidental.

All rights reserved, including the right to reproduce this book or portions thereof in any form whatsoever.
For information contact: Daniel's House Publishing

Biblical Passages:
THE HOLY BIBLE, NEW INTERNATIONAL VERSION®, NIV®
Copyright © 1973, 1978, 1984, 2011 by Biblica, Inc. ™
Used by permission. All rights reserved worldwide.

Cover Art: Great Smoky Mountains from Morton Overlook
                © Jeremy Edwards/Thinkstock

                Gypsy Woman photo © Paul Hakimata/Thinkstock

Library of Congress Control Number: 2015902254

ISBN: 978-0-9915033-5-3 (paperback)
ISBN: 978-0-9915033-6-0 (eBook)

Contact Daniel's House Publishing at
www.danielshousepublishing@gmail.com

Table of Contents

Dedication

All across this beautiful, God given country of ours there are those you live in silence. Some live unseen lives. They see themselves as insignificant people who pass by others on the street like shadows. I dedicate this book to the hollow people, who feel empty and unseen, and the underlings who spend their lives under the feet of others. God intended you to make a difference. Today is the day to become fully alive.

Doris Gaines Rapp

Acknowledge

I give a loud shout-out and huge thank you to Debi Lindhorst of The Type Galley in Warren, Indiana for the beautiful cover. You took my ideas and made the design so much more than I could ever create on my own.

Thank you to Debbie Wilson and Vicki Borgman for reading *Length of Days – Beyond the Valley of the Keepers* and making helpful suggestions. I read what I assume is there and you read words as they actually appear.

I also thank my Reading Partners who took their time and read the book. I greatly appreciate your dedication to reading my work and giving feedback.

My photo on the back cover is by Bonnie Tobey Manning: website — www.printroom.com/pro/btmanning. Thanks Bonnie!

To my dear husband Bill, you are the first face I see in the morning and the last face I see at night. Thank you for sharing your life with me. It is truly, our life together.

Proverbs 3:1-2 (NIV©2011)

My son, do not forget my law, but let your heart keep my commands, for length of days and long life and peace they will add to you.

Isaiah 62: 6 (NLT@2007)

O Jerusalem, I have posted watchmen on your walls; they will pray day and night, continually. Take no rest, all you who pray to the LORD.

PROLOGUE
Capitol City, Central Zone, U.S.A.

Diary of Lady Christiana Applewait
December 26, 2112

The Blue Guard has been following us for days. We must stay alert every minute, but we are all so tired. I know I have been fighting to keep my eyes open.

I think I saw a strata car behind Silas's vehicle when we made that last turn onto the mountain road. Silas turned off his headlight. I hope the dark of night will hide us.

Even though I'm a legacy citizen, in line for a seat on the Council of Twelve, my position has not protected me from obsessive stalking by Chief Inspector Ward Stoner. But, we can't stop. We must place a Citizens' Referendum on the ballot at the next election to overturn the *Length of Days* law. If not, my dear grandparents will reach the age of extermination. They will enter the never-ending-sleep, thus ending their *Length of Days*.

Now, a few of us will try to erase that ghastly law. We will have to cross Zone borders, closed for many decades. Dawn will be coming soon. We don't know what lies beyond the mountains, and there is no road over it or pass at the top. Silas has assured us he knows a way to get past Howard Mountain.

Even though Christmas was banned a hundred years ago, just last night, Gifting Day evening, thousands of our people sang

Christmas carols they had never heard before while we marched on President Nathan Alexander's home. We delivered petitions, already obtained in the Central Zone. Judge Carl Brunner ordered a two-year stay on all final-sleep travelers. Now, we have just those twin years of hope to canvas the other three sectors of our country and secure the signatures, then, pass the bill and implement it before our time runs out.

We know no one beyond the Central Zone, but God will be with us. Like the wise men of old, we will follow the promise of Christmas hope. God will be our guide.

Lady Christiana Applewait

Chapter 1
Howard Mountain

Monday - December 26, 2112

Finally—safety! But, we must stay on guard. We had entered Howard Mountain cavern before the sun rose again in the East. We had to stay ahead of the Blue Guard, if they were tracking us. We couldn't risk it. I watched as the light wanted to break on the horizon but was reluctant to hurry the dawn. We had presented ourselves as the end-travelers did, through the big gate that Silas Drummond had opened. He met us in the darkness of the recessed door.

"We'll wait here for the sun to rise," Silas pointed to some chairs on the left of the entry.

We walked over and sat down like strangers on a train, lined up along the wall, all silently facing forward. My stomach growled and gnawed with anxious anticipation. We had fled to the mountain in the dark of night, now we waited for the light we had hid from.

"What is that awful smell?" Dahlia Zoobomba questioned as she cupped both hands over her nose and mouth.

"You don't want to know," Silas said. "That's the crematorium you smell." He got up from his chair and began to shuffle along through the processing area. We followed him deeper inside the huge cave. His gait was short, his step shallow and his pace like that of a banty rooster.

He scurried through the area ahead of us. I was amazed how a stooped man, whose feet didn't seem to lift off the floor, could move so fast. "I can hardly see where I'm going," I said as I pushed the brim of my hat back and brushed my hair from my eyes.

"I switched to the ghost lights just as you arrived," he mumbled but kept walking.

"I'll agree with that," Dr. Jason O'Reilly whispered.

"Why?" I too asked in hushed tones. "To reveal or hide the ghosts? How does that work, Silas?" I groped along the wide hall then realized what part of the cave we were in. I grabbed Jason's hand and clutched it to my cloak. "Jason, we're in the museum," I gasped. "Aren't we?"

"I think so, Honey," he spoke in reverence. The respectful silence was not for the museum that evil power-hungry Alister Bedlam had gathered over the years. It was for the abandoned subjects of his display who deserved our respect.

"Dahlia, don't look right or left, just follow me. The ghost lights may be dim enough to hide the glass cases." Silas said as he obeyed his own instruction and fixed his eyes on the hallway ahead.

I heard Dahlia gasp and moan as she hurried along, but she said nothing. When we got to the end of the hall, her tear stained face glistened with fresh grief. I put my arm around her and tried to sooth her wounded spirit. We hugged for a moment in silence.

"I had no idea," she choked.

"Bedlam has been exhibiting his human taxidermy subjects, the bodies of his enemies, like trophies in a case, after they have ended their Length of Days," Jason explained. "Even my parents are on display in this grotesque museum only he sees."

"Now what, Silas?" Jason questioned as we reached the end of the hallway, where the bare mountain face became the inner exposed wall. He wrinkled up his forehead and searched the ceiling of the cave and the surrounding rock walls for a way out.

Water dripped in a distant finger of the cave as snow melted above. It smelled musty, and I figured it must have been damp for a long time. Perhaps water had actually pooled around one of the down-sloping bends. I really didn't want to know. It just smelled bad.

Silas smiled mischievously. "We'll walk right through the mountain wall."

• • •

In Capitol City, Ward Stoner, ruthless Captain of the infamous Blue Guard, gazed intently through the floor to ceiling bank of windows that lined two adjoining corner walls of his office. He had been there all night. Bright red and green Gifting lights blinked from the garden below, but he saw none of it. "I will find you," he seethed through gritted teeth. "You think you are above my laws, the laws that everyone in the Central Zone must follow."

He rocked on his toes and back on his heels as he tried to imagine every place Christiana Applewait could be hiding. "I will release the entire weight of my fury on you ... on Dr. O'Reilly ... and anyone else who dares to side with you and your precious self-determined crusade. You think it's a mission for life. I will make it a fight to the death!"

It had only been two days since Dr. O'Reilly had saved his son from the horror of the Length of Days law. But, power-hungry hate remembers nothing of love.

Chapter 2
The Valley of the Keepers

"Martin!" Rebecca called from the house. "Ready for a cup of coffee?"

Martin Spires looked up from his work. Besides the rich smell of freshly brewed coffee that escaped through the open door when his wife spoke, there was something else in the air—an anticipation. The wind seemed to blow more sweetly and whistled down the valley more gently than he had experienced for quite a while.

"In a minute," he shouted back then smelled the air again. He smiled at his own foolishness and turned back to his work. He hadn't had a pre-event-knowing for a long time. *The wind blows wherever it pleases. You hear its sound, but you cannot tell where it comes from or where it is going. So it is with everyone born of the Spirit.* So it appeared in John 3:8 and so Martin knew.

With wide, rough work hands, he spread a deer hide across a wooden sawhorse and began removing the hair with a draw blade. It had been a big buck, an eight pointer. Martin always hated to see the majestic animals fall, but he knew the ways of life and said a prayer in thanks for the gift of the stag and all it would add to his family's sustenance. Besides the venison meat and deerskin hide, the sinew thread would sew winter boots with water tight seams. The December air was clear and cold, just the way he liked it. Dressing the deer was a great reason for enjoying the fantastic morning.

This is a beauty, he thought before he noticed that his wife had come out into the frosty air of the early hour. "It's a real looker, isn't it Sweetie Pie?" he boasted.

"That will tan out real fine, Martin."

"Several people have bid on the hide," he smiled. "Don't know yet if I want to sell it. It's such a good one. I only had to use one arrow to bring him down, so there is just one hole. With the small arrowhead that I used, the skin is nearly perfect."

"You're an expert hunter, Martin. But, I thought you were going to use the percussion rifle you invented for this hunting season. You told me there would be no hole at all with percussion," Rebecca observed.

"I nearly have the new rifle perfected. I'm still checking on any possible noise a percussive shot might make. In theory, there should be no sound, just a feeling of pressure in the chest. That is, if you aren't in the line of fire. If you're the target, you wouldn't be around to tell us what it felt like."

"I don't think I'd like to be downrange of The Whisper. I like what you're calling it."

Martin officially named it the Spires-C. But, he called it *The Whisper* because people wouldn't hear a thing. If struck, you would just drop over. The sudden compression would stop your heart. He ran his hand over the soft deer hide as if he were caressing the smooth wooden stock of the rifle and spoke with the confident facts of the inventor.

"I'm glad it's not dangerous to be near, Martin. With all the children running around here all the time, I don't think I'd like the idea that someone could get on the back side of a shot," she frowned.

"That's what's so great about the percussion rifle. The compression has a very fine focus. The down range danger is nil. It strikes with pinpoint precision on the target. It hits exactly what is in the narrow line of fire."

"Coming through," a small towheaded nine-year-old in a red striped hat and brown leather coat warned as he stumbled between Martin and Rebecca.

"Posse on your trail," pigtailed Virginia cautioned as she burst through the space between the husband and wife, with four other young deputies in hot pursuit.

"Enjoy yourselves while you can, Honey Childs. School will open again, soon after New Year's Day, you know." Rebecca laughed.

"Wouldn't it be great to be able to run wild like that?" Martin marveled then stopped when he felt a tremble beneath his feet. "Something is happening. Did you feel the tremor?" he cautioned as he watched the children disappear down the path that led to the village. "Maybe we should collect all of the children, just in case—"

Suddenly, the earth rumbled and shook. The ice that hung from the mountain outcropping above fell to the ground as the mountain shook. Dust from inside the rubble, filled the cold air and hung like fine gravelly sleet. The icy pebbles hit the earth and rolled down the tiny, dry arroyos that fanned out from the base of the peak. With a great gapping yawn, the mountain opened, as the huge stone that covered the mouth of the cave rolled to the side.

"Silas!" Rebecca called out as the small, wiry man stepped through the giant opening. With wide arms she hurried to greet the cousin she normally sees only a few times a year. On this side of the mountain, family is everything.

"Rebecca," Silas shouted as he approached. Bent over, he skittered more than walked. Behind him came three other people whom Rebecca did not know.

"Silas," Martin gasped, "we didn't expect you. When we heard the noise we were worried they had found us. But, now you have brought strangers into the valley. Why? Who are they? Are they seekers? You know how dangerous it is to reveal our lives to others." Martin clenched his fists, grabbed the back of his neck as if he were trying to rub out the anger.

"I understand your worry, Martin. But, I know these people." Silas Drummond turned to the travelers with him. In spite of the cold, he removed his hat as he spoke. "I'd like to introduce Dr. Jason O'Reilly and his nurse, Dahlia Zoobamba."

"Who is the other one, Silas? Who is the lady?" Martin squinted in the bright sunlight of the clearest morning in days and approached the small party of travelers. He couldn't believe that Silas had led adult outsiders into the valley. And, it was Silas Drummond who had breached the rule. He knew better.

"Martin ... Rebecca, I would like to present Lady Christiana Applewait, a Legacy Citizen, in-line for a position on the Council of Twelve." Silas stepped aside and bowed slightly as he presented a Privileged Citizen who called him "friend."

"My Lady," Rebecca curtseyed a little. However, her buckskin breeches didn't gather around her like the fine ball gown she would have worn to greet a person of such stature.

"Woman, get yourself up," Martin insisted. "We are all equals here in the valley." He approached Christiana boldly and extended his hand in friendship.

"Yes, Sir," Christiana replied. "We are all equal in the sight of God." She removed her glove and shook Martin's hand in friendship.

"You are from the Central Zone and ... you know about God?" Martin's jaw dropped.

Lady Applewait smiled as she replaced the black leather glove that protected her hand from the frigid air. "I know about God ... and I know God, Mr. ... ?"

"Martin Spires. Call me Martin, Ma'am."

"Only if you will call me Christiana," she smiled at her new friend. "Jason calls me Christy."

The middle-aged man with the long graying beard, looked at Rebecca and shrugged, then gazed with amazement on the small party. "I'll reserve my opinion about you all until I know more. Why are you here?" Martin asked.

"It's been a long walk. I'm tired," Dahlia gasped as she brushed some fresh snow from the edge of the porch and sat down. "Could I bother you for a glass of water? I am so thirsty." She bent down and grabbed her feet that stayed buried inside her winder boots. "Oh," she complained some more.

"We made it all the way from town in the darkened car, and then walked through Howard Mountain, on foot. We couldn't have done it without you, Silas," Jason marveled and slapped Silas on his shoulder in gratitude.

Silas smiled a sheepish grin. No one ever praised Silas and now he was included with a nudge to his shoulder. Even the twitter of the birds from the top of the nearby trees was more uplifting than anything he had heard in years. The ghastly cavern had been his only resting place. He couldn't spit out the awful taste of the place.

"You were the only one who knew the way, Silas. None of us had any idea that the valley was still here," Jason said. "The authorities said that the earthquake of the last century had totally destroyed the topography of the area. They said no one survived."

"Actually, we are all doing quite well," Martin boasted as he slapped his breeches with a deerskin glove.

They all laughed and cheered Silas's courage with new, adrenaline-laced energy as they looked out onto the sweetest valley this side of heaven. The morning sun was high enough to warm their faces and dissolve the images of the corruption inside the cavern under Howard Mountain.

"You are all welcome in our home," Martin smiled with a lingering hint of confusion. "Not to sound inhospitable ... but I will repeat, what are you all doing here?"

"Where is *here*, Martin? Silas didn't have time to tell us. He just said, 'Come! Hurry! And, we did," Christiana stated.

Winter birds sang back and forth from the tops of trees as if they would speak if the Squire would not. The more they fluttered, the more tufts of fluffy snow dropped from the branches and floated to the ground, a reminder that it was still December.

Martin studied the small party, but he couldn't take his eyes off the beautiful young woman in the green cape and red hat. Her eyes seemed as though they could see right through him. Then, he paused. He was unsure if he wanted to speak the words not heard in the valley in nearly a hundred years. There had been no need to speak of what everyone in the village already knew, since there hadn't been another traveler through the area in that time, except Silas Drummond. His other tiny travelers were not interested in such things.

"Martin?" his wife whispered. She went to the dear man and took the draw blade that remained in his left hand and placed it on the hide that waited where he had left it on the cross-beamed wood. The aroma of musk from the deer still clung to the air.

The great Squire of the forgotten hamlet beyond the mountain looked at his wife as if asking her for permission to speak. "It is your safety too, My Love," he said.

"Tell them, Martin," she said as she touched his hand. "Silas wouldn't have brought danger to us. You know that."

"You are basically ... nowhere," he began. "This valley was not buried like the outsiders thought, but, sealed off from everything except the passage through the tunnel. Since Silas was all alone and in charge of the despicable activities under Howard Mountain, he had discovered the exit during the long nights of anguish he had spent there."

"We know of the evil there," Christiana whispered. "We have seen it for ourselves. Each of us left all we've known in Capitol City to come here. What is this place?"

"This lovely woman in the leather pants and jacket is my wife, Rebecca. You have joined us in the Valley of the Keepers. All of us here are keepers of the history the ruling elite tried to erase after the great uprising of the previous century. For four generations, every man, woman and child in the valley have carried a verbal account of the history of this great nation. Different families have in their possession certain books and volumes which they have guarded and memorize in case the books are confiscated. We, the Spires family, are the keepers of the Bible, the story of all of us."

"You have never been discovered in all these years?" Dahlia marveled.

"We have skilled and learned people in many areas of life. Our communications people have been able to monitor the outside world without detection or tracking. We know of all of the world's inventions and innovations, and adapt them to the unique needs of our people who live invisible lives. We simply invent new ways of doing things that won't betray our location."

Rebecca smiled, "Like smokeless fuel. We don't even give off a heat signature. Look above you. You see blue sky, but we have produced a force between us and the clouds. From high overhead, the terrain looks like a rock pile in case anyone should fly too close. But, since the borders are completely closed, no one has drawn near for a very long time."

The Squire of Nowhere looked at the four and sighed. "We have been safe here, Christy ... for a long time. We are also Keepers in another way. We have sentries posted on the ridge beyond that far circle of the mountain." Martin pointed to where the outcropping had made a complete ring, which created the valley in which they live. "The guards watch and pray, every moment of every day. We are all watchers on the wall, just like in the days of Isaiah. We rotate duty on those outposts so no one is away from home and family for more than three months." He smiled and removed his broad brimmed leather hat with a bright eagle feather tucked in the band. "Now, I know your names, but ... who are you all, and why have you come into the valley?"

"Come Martin," Christy began, "if we can sit down someplace, I will tell you of a great commission, a miracle, a holy mystery."

Chapter 3
Chief Inspector Ward Stoner

Chalky Boone staggered to the left then to the right as she tried to stay out of Ward Stoner's way. His office was large enough for the Chief Inspector, except when he paced, which he did often. She carried a 281 Palm Device in her hand as she tried to keep up with his erratic movements. "Sir, if you would use the device—"

"Where are they?" he bellowed toward the outer office.

"I'm right here, Sir." Boone's smile was fading and inside, her anger was nearing its flashpoint. "If you would just use the 281, you wouldn't have to yell. I'm—"

"I want to talk to that little snippy Legacy brat or her doctor ... or someone!" The veins in Stoner's forehead bulged and his face grew crimson.

"Sir, you must—"

"I must what?" he demanded as he grabbed his communication device out of Boone's hand. "I do whatever I need to do. Right now, I need to find those two." He picked up his coffee cup, took a sip and spit it out. "This tastes terrible!" he yelled again. "It's cold."

"I know," she said as the liquid sloshed out of the passing cup and splashed on her arm. Boone brushed the droplets off onto the floor and sat on the edge of the desk as the inspector continued to swirl around her like a life-sucking whirlpool, drawing her into its vortex. "Sir—"

"Get me Applewait's parents' number."

"Sir, they have an unlisted number. You know that." She was growing weary of his unreasonable obsession with the Lady-of-position. Her shoulders drooped, crumpling her jacket. She stood up, straightened her back and shook the tension from her arms.

"I will find them. If you can't help, get out of my way." Stoner seethed as he dodged Boone's attempts to sidestep his every move.

"Sir, I am just trying to assist you. I'm your assistant," she reported back sharply but with a calm tone rehearsed over many years of working with Ward Stoner.

"Then assist!" he roared. "Find them."

"Inspector, it is 7:30 in the morning on a holiday." Chalky stretched as if to make her taller so she could meet his eyes with strength.

"What holiday?" he bellowed.

"Sir, Gifting Day was just yesterday. The medical center isn't open and the library, where Lady Applewait works, isn't either." Her shoulders slumped again and she eased herself down onto a brown engineered-leather chair.

Stoner paced with wide, pounding strides but said nothing. The room filled with the heavy air of his anger and frustration. He took three deep breaths and held the last one. Then, he let it stream out slowly. With contrived calm, he whispered, "Fine. We will call them both tomorrow at nine ... sharp."

"I'll be at my desk if you need me," Boone sighed softly.

Stoner only nodded once. Then, as Chalky left his office, he added with measured appreciation, "Thanks."

"You are welcome," she smiled weakly as she turned to leave.

"Tell me this," he spit out again, "why can't I reach that wretched little furnace tender, Silas Drummond? Are you telling me the Disposal Center isn't open until 9:00 a.m. either?"

"Ward," with carefully chosen words she outlined one more

time, "Judge Brunner issued a stay on all length-of-days terminations. The entire center will be closed for the next two years," Chalky reminded him.

"Well, there is no *stay*—no cease and desist order—in this office. I will find out just how that fancy pair plans on getting signatures from people outside this zone, when the law against travel is clear. They are forbidden to leave."

"Boss ... wouldn't a repeal of the Length-of-Days law benefit us all? Families wouldn't have to hide every accidental fall and each illness their children have. There would be no limit to medical contacts before their child is labeled *defective.*" Boone's voice strained with indignation. "And, people wouldn't enter the never-ending-sleep just because they lived a prescribed number of years."

"My son was spared a mark in his life chart the other night, I know. And, he recovered," he stated flatly as if it was because of his own doing. "Now, I will uphold every law of this land as long as those laws exist," Stoner insisted in spite of the blessing his family received. "And, those two are going to break the law and leave this zone ... somehow." His anger returned as he thought of Lady Applewait and Dr. O'Reilly. "I will catch them." Stoner stopped and looked out of the window on his town still adorned with Gifting Day lights. He felt no holiday cheer.

"Watch over your shoulders with every step you take ... you privileged ones. I will find you. I will stick to you like fear on darkness. The minute you step over the line, I'll be there."

Chapter 4
A Story to Tell

"Come on in." Rebecca invited us into her home with a sweep of her hand. On the other side of the rugged wilderness door, the frontier stopped. What was inside, revealed a century of advancements just miles from Capitol City, although a mountain away.

The room smelled of Christmas tree pine and warm, freshly baked biscuits. Holiday sparkle, bright colors, and dancing lights hung in swags from the stair banister and adorned a large tree.

She removed her jacket and hung it on a peg by the door. "Let me have your wrap," she said as she reached for mine. "My Lady ... Christy ... your cloak is beautiful. What is this fabric?"

"Thank you, Rebecca. It's manufactured wool, so dense that the wind cannot penetrate it. You don't get too hot in it either. It seems to breathe from the inside out, not the outside in," I said as I looked around. The warm room shone with a golden glow, as the morning sun bounced off the hand-hewn chestnut logs. "I have only seen beautiful, sprawling cabins like this in books, Martin. Did you build this?" I couldn't resist a temptation to touch the smooth log timbers, stacked one on the other and held in place like brick and mortar.

"No, my great-grandfather built this home before the earthquake. It was a mountain retreat for his family until they were sealed off." Martin reopened the door and shook the snow from his hat back onto the porch, then hung the hat on another peg. "Each generation has made their own improvements."

"Well, it is great," Jason marveled as he looked at every detail.

"Martin," Rebecca whispered with controlled excitement. "Did you not hear what she said?"

Martin eyed his wife like he was searching for a forgotten memory. "No . . ."

"Books, Martin. She said she had seen pictures of log homes in books. Find out more while I get some refreshments." Rebecca chattered with enthusiasm as she hurried into the kitchen.

"You have books?" Martin ushered the four of us to the couch and loveseat, then sat on the edge of the chair opposite us. "Books were burned many years ago. Of course, we have written and printed our own novels and non-fiction, but we haven't had access to any of the old classics or history books. The volumes that sat on mountain shelves are the only ones we have over here."

"I have a Post Graduate degree in Library Science." I thought for a moment before I went on. I had guarded my treasure for so long it almost felt painful to release the secret. "So ... I have access to the reference volumes in the public areas of the Library and ... the novels and documents in the back recesses, the locked area of the library that no one knows about except me and the curator, Marge Cummings."

Screech! There was a scratching sound at the front door and I froze. Had the Blue Guard caught up to us? I realized I startled easily and it angered me. I wanted to be stronger than a frightened child.

Rebecca smiled as she came back in with mugs and a pot of hot coffee. "It's all right, Christy. It's just Buddy." She put the tray on a table in front of the couch and then opened the door. A black and white dog of non-descript pedigree scampered in.

"They are friends, Buddy," Rebecca warned the animal that stood about twenty-eight inches tall from his toenails to the top of his pointed ears. "You go lay down." She passed the cups and filled them with the steaming brew.

The dog started toward his bed in the corner, then turned and walked slowly toward me. "I'm not sure about this," I said as my body stiffened. The squirmy little fellow sniffed at my shoes and rubbed his side against my leg. Then he rolled over and waited patiently.

"Rebecca, I can't believe it. A real dog? It's not a stuffy, look Dahlia. Isn't it beautiful?" I wanted to touch the little creature but I was afraid. I slowly leaned down and gently scratched his fur. "He's so soft. I had no idea. All we have are mechanical pets." Then, I opened my hand and let the new animal sniff as much as he wanted to. "I found a kitten a few days ago and took her in. As a legacy citizen, we have more privileges. I left him with my parents when I crossed the border. But, that is the only other animal I've ever seen." I smoothed his soft coat, from the space between his eyes to the top of his head.

I thought for a moment about what I had just said. "That sounded awful. Because of my name and birth, I get privileges others don't." With each day, I was learning things about myself I didn't like.

"Our new lives, without dulling chemicals, have allowed us to see what we hadn't seen before," Jason said. He smiled and watched the dog. "There may have been other animals we never noticed."

"Life is a process, Christiana. If you aren't growing up a little at a time, you're just growing old." Martin spoke with wisdom and then grinned. "Trust me, I'm still learning, aren't I Becca?" Then he paused and sipped his coffee as he watched Buddy warm up to us.

"Neighbors Buddy has known all of his life, he won't get close to, Christy," the Squire said with amazement. "He is a very good judge of character. Don't be too hard on yourself. You have passed the Buddy test." Martin chuckled and watched the dog make a new friend of me. Then he insisted, "Now, tell me about the books."

"Jason, you tell Martin about your books first," I urged.

"They aren't really mine," he admitted, then settled back with his hot drink. "Back in the old, closed section of the hospital is a library of novels and old magazines that patients used to borrow when they stayed several days while recovering from illnesses or injury." Jason leaned forward, placed his cup on the table and his hands on his knees. Then, he patted my leg and smiled. "Tell him more about your stash. They're better."

"They are all wonderful, Martin," I smiled as I thought about each book I have read. I could feel the texture of the paper and smoothness of the cover in my hands. My voice wobbled slightly with giddiness. "The Constitution and Bill of Rights ... all of it."

"That is amazing!" Martin's voice was low. He waited while Rebecca refilled each cup and passed around the creamer and sugar bowl. "But, let's get back to my question when we first met. Why did you four burst through the mountain and come into this valley?"

"It's a long story," Dahlia smiled with pride. "A few of us had planted a home-church. One of the members, Sean, had started a newspaper."

"Dahlia led the group," I added.

"We don't have a leader, Christy," she explained modestly. "They just meet in our building. At first, Sean's newspaper gave veiled descriptions about our activities. He doesn't use Christian words. It's a safety precaution in case someone found a copy of the paper. Upcoming events are coded into kitchen recipes."

Jason sipped at his coffee and smiled. "Christy and I are late comers to the church in the Indian River Apartments. We were totally unaware of the newspaper or any of their activities ... and Christiana lives in the same apartment complex. The work that Sean and the rest of them had already done has made our task possible," he added.

Jason set his cup down and took a biscuit from the plate Rebecca offered. The baking powder aroma was intoxicating. "With Dahlia's help, many of the younger people have gone through the detoxification process, like those in the privileged class. When a legacy citizen turns twenty-four, they start taking a small pill that washes out all of the drugs that had been added to the water supply, drugs that robbed them of their emotions." Jason tasted the quick bread and smiled. "That's amazing, Rebecca."

He began again. "The ruling class believed that people can be controlled better when they don't care about anything passionately. Dahlia passed out the detox pills to as many as she could without drawing attention to herself." Jason admitted, "If caught, Dahlia could have been in serious trouble. I'm ashamed to say that I wasn't the one to detoxify them."

"Jason, you saw that they were missing the joy of life. Don't berate yourself. You had forgotten what it felt like to be dull and unhappy all the time. You are Legacy too and were detoxed when you were my age," I explained. "That's been a few years back."

"Dr. O'Reilly," Dahlia gasped. Her coffee swished in the cup. "You're a Legacy Citizen? I've been your nurse for four years, and I did not know that."

"My credentials as a physician are more important to me than a position of privilege." He turned and smiled softly at me. "And, I might not have met you, Christy, if you hadn't come into my office with your bitty chip in your hand."

"Bitty chip?" Rebecca questioned. "What is that?"

"It's a micro-chip that is imbedded in a child's arm. It gives their entire medical history and pedigree," Dahlia said. She rubbed her index finger and thumb together as though she were holding one in her grasp.

"Pedigree? Like a prize race horse?" Martin put his hand to his mouth, but he could not hide the disgust and anger in his eyes.

"Yes, Martin. Just like a prize stallion or mare," Jason agreed. "As disgusting as it sounds, there was a positive outcome. That is how Christy and I met."

"A chip, like a dog-tag? That's disgraceful. So you have no privacy or sense of being an individual?" Martin sipped at his coffee and grew quiet.

I blew across the surface of my cup to cool the brew. The room was still for a few moments. It seemed we were all thinking about small children, tagged for future reference, for some distant advantage to the state. I had to think on something else. "Rebecca, where do you get your coffee beans?"

Rebecca's eyes snapped toward me and left the distant space into which she had apparently slipped. "We grow them in this valley. We're at a pretty high elevation."

I was amazed. "You do everything right out in the open here in the valley. Not like at home where it's all in secret. Sean moved all over town distributing his papers. No one knew what he was doing. It was all stealth activity. He also used his printing press to print petitions. In the Central Zone, they still follow the Length of Days legislation rigidly. People enter the portal to the never-ending sleep when they exhaust their worth to society, as measured by a pre-established formula. This Citizens' Referendum is vitally important."

"We have heard about the horrible policy," Rebecca stated. "It is the same in all zones, although there is a rumor that not all zones obey the law. Here in the valley, we are not part of a sector or zone. We live until the Lord takes us away. We have no limit to the number of illnesses or accidents we can have.

"At the time of the earthquake, there was a wonderful doctor on this side of the mountain vacationing with her family. She trained three additional physicians and so forth through the generations. We are well cared for here."

"That is amazing," Jason said and smiled. "Perhaps I can visit your medical staff. Do you have a hospital?"

"Yes, Dr. O'Reilly," Rebecca responded and then added, "Jason. I will call you Jason."

They all smiled and relaxed as the new trust continued to grow.

"My dear grandparents, Constance and Oliver Richly are members of the Council of Twelve," I explained. "They will be seventy-five soon. Their Length of Days comes up a few days from now. I couldn't let that happen. I had to do something."

"Absolutely. But, Christy, what could you do about it?" Rebecca asked.

"God led me to the home-church, to Dahlia, to Jason, and to Sean." Then, she smiled as she remembered. "And, Silas found me."

"We have all benefited from each other," Dahlia agreed. "It is a multi-pointed blessing."

I shook my head and stared at the hand scraped hardwood floor that shone from polish and care. "I rode that PT, Public Transit, every day. I saw Sean often," I said. I still couldn't believe it. "He had access to every part of the city, but no one paid any attention to him. As he walked around, he collected signatures on a petition. The petition was for a referendum to overturn the Length of Days policy."

"Overturn the law? Do you actually think it is possible?" Martin listened intently to the whole story.

"Jason and I were able to get the required paper work to accompany the petition." I took Jason's hand and squeezed it just to make sure it had all been real. If Jason were actually there beside me, on the other side of the mountain, then it wasn't a dream.

"Getting all that paperwork was very dangerous," Silas added seriously.

"I knew it wasn't safe at the time, Silas. But, getting caught wasn't in my mind. I guess I had been too sheltered to realize the real danger. Maybe, it seemed more like an exciting game when it happened. I'm happy to say, we had the petitions and the necessary paperwork when we marched to President Alexander's house to deliver the whole bundle."

Dahlia smiled and her eyes sparkled. "The entire town walked with us. They had found hope for the first time in their lives."

I sipped from my cup and thought about all that had happened. I added an explanation. "As you know, a Citizen's Referendum is the same as a legislative bill. It is voted on as it stands."

"Amazing," the Squire mouthed but no sound came out.

The dog began rubbing my leg and I thought of the miracle of life. Even dogs had value outside of our zone. "The amazing part of the story was the presence of the Lord with us all the way." I felt the warmth of the spirit rise within me. Buddy stirred some more and used my foot as his back scratcher.

Jason leaned toward Martin and Rebecca with his arms on his legs, as though he were sharing a mystery. "God gave us the ability to stay ahead of Inspector Stoner, the head of the Blue Guard." He almost whispered as he said, "We were nearly invisible as we slipped through the Capitol building after hours to get the required paper to accompany the petition."

"After hours?" Martin snapped to attention.

"With the blessing of a Judge—and his key," I reassured him and smiled. "We didn't break in."

Jason reached over and took my hand. His voice was soft, "The Lord gave Christy the gifts of convincing and healing. And, when Stoner tried to discredit her, more of her gifts were revealed by her grandmother, those of discernment and art."

"And the music, Jason," Dahlia added.

"Last night, with everyone gathered around, we sang Christmas carols for the first time in our lives. People who had never heard the songs, who had not even sung before, all joined in with one voice to sing, 'Silent Night, Holy Night', and it was a Holy Night."

I reached down and petted the furry one at my feet. His soft coat was soothing to me. "Judge Brunner declared a stay on all exterminations for the next two years. By then, the entire country, all four zones, will have a chance to sign a petition so the referendum can be put on the ballot at the next election."

"Silas got us this far," Dahlia reached across the couch and patted him on the back.

"We are depending on you and Martin, Rebecca," Silas burst out. He hadn't said much since we came into the house. Forgotten his whole life, he finally spoke out. "I got them this far. Can you and Martin get them out of the valley?"

"There are ways," Martin responded. "Yes, there are ways."

Chapter 5
The Hospital

"We'll go to the hospital first," Rebecca said as we walked along the brick sidewalks and wound our way past quaint businesses in the valley that time had forgotten. It was later in the morning, and the sun was bright in the sky. "Then, if you want to, we'll stop in for coffee. Unless you've had too much of the brew," she said and chuckled.

"There is never too much juice of the bean," I laughed.

Jason and I hadn't had much time alone and I needed to connect. I slipped my hand in his as I studied the architecture of the buildings.

"Look, what do these shops remind you of?" I marveled as I peered through each cross-hatched window.

"The Dickens-style boutiques and coffee shop near the hospital," Dahlia giggled.

"That's it," Jason chimed in.

"Our favorite place, right?" I agreed.

"The coffee or the shop?" Rebecca questioned with a smile.

"Both," all three of us chimed in together.

We all stepped off the curb into the street where patches of ice made a wobbly footing. I pulled my cloak around me more tightly as a light snow began to fall. I welcomed the new flakes that kissed my face. It made the little village seem more real.

"Are you warm enough?" Jason asked as he put his arm around me and massaged some warmth into my back.

"I think my blood is circulating again," I said as a child skittered past me with his coat wide open. "I guess the little ones stay warm by running around in circles."

"It's just here on the corner," Martin encouraged as we neared a large white building.

Silas stood back gallantly as we all passed through the revolving doors of Valley Hospital. Inside, the lobby smelled fresh and clean, not antiseptic. The aroma of freshly baked cookies danced on the air from the small oven at the greeting desk. A child hobbled by on crutches and joined other patients as they clustered around the cookie platter. The children and adults who sat on couches and chairs near the entrance to the examining room looked weak and ill.

"Next time," I heard a father admonish a child whom I guessed to be his daughter, "Watch where you'll land before you swing out over a frozen pond."

"I know, Daddy," the ten-year old responded with a heavy, audible sigh.

"They don't look like they're afraid," Dahlia said in amazement.

"Afraid?" Rebecca questioned. "Why would our children fear the hospital? They are made well here."

"In the Central Zone, each person is permitted only a certain number of accidents before they are labeled 'defective.' Defective human units are placed in the never-ending-sleep," Jason repeated in the mechanical voice he had learned. He paused. "I sound so callous," he admitted, as much to himself as others. "I'm not."

Our group turned to the right in the middle of the wide entrance with its leather covered chairs and approached the lift. The round, glass bullet-shaped elevator swooped silently from above, paused, and opened its doors.

"Kiersten, is everyone all right?" Rebecca asked with concern as a young woman stepped off. "You just brought the baby home a year ago."

The young woman with four little cherubs swirling around the hem of her skirt like a low-hanging halo smiled a patient smile. "Rebecca, good to see you. Little Hank stopped breathing and became rigid. The doctor said it was another febrile seizure."

"Another?" Jason asked as the rest of the children stepped off the lift and our little party got on. Jason held the door open with his foot while he finished talking to her.

"Yes, this was his third. But the doctor told me he should outgrow them by age three," she said and grabbed the hand of a particularly rambunctious child. "I'd better get these kids home so we can start to prepare for lunch. Children are creatures of habit you know."

"I am so glad everyone is okay," Rebecca waved as the doors began to close.

"We won't take a lot of time, but I really want you to see our surgery theater," Martin rubbed his hands together in glee. It was obvious he was proud of the advancements in medicine of these valley people, even though physically cut off from the rest of the world.

"We're not completely isolated here." He winked as he opened the heavy door to a completely white and totally soundproofed room with theater seats that faced a wall of windows. "Good, a procedure is going on," he whispered.

From our elevated position, we could see beyond the glass as they prepared a patient for surgery. First, the doctor and her assistants draped sterile cloths on the arm and upper shoulder. Then they swabbed a red liquid on the entire area of the surrounding tissue.

"Do they make an incision?" Jason appeared to be shocked.

"No, just a scratch" Martin said. They abrade the surface of the skin so the instruments can make perfect contact with the body.

They know, when they disturb the protective layer of the body, infection can get in. Just like the old days when the standard medical practice was to actually open the body, bacteria had mutated to the point that surgery was more dangerous than the condition that called for it." He put his finger to his lips. "Listen," he whispered as the sound of faint whirling came from below.

We watched the surgeon scrape the patient's skin surface and place another instrument, about the size of hand-held sander, on the prepared spot. With a slow firm motion she made small, ever widening circular patterns with the instrument.

"The dislocated shoulder will fall into place like the tumblers on a bank vault. Then, the torn rotator cuff will be fused by the sound waves emanating from the instrument." Martin sat back like he was well satisfied.

"Martin, you can be very proud of the advances you all have made, in spite of the lack of shared science with the other sectors. As a physician, I can say, this is impressive." Jason continued to fix his attention on the procedure that was happening on the operating table.

"I'm pleased too, Martin," I said as I tried to dig for information. "But, I am wondering if your isolation is as complete as you claim. You winked. In the books I've read, that usually means the person is not telling the whole story." I suspected that there had been travel between sectors in spite of what Martin had told us.

The squire of the valley paused as another observer came into the observation room. "Hi, Charlie," he said. Then he turned to us and added, "Let's continue our conversation over coffee."

Chapter 6
A Place to Begin

Silas led the way back out into the frosty air. It seemed to me his back was straighter, his stride was wider and his steps more solid on this side of the mountain. Something was very different about Silas. I could see it.

The village square was alive with people, but no one hurried. No one jostled or pushed. From what I could see, everyone had a pleasant expression. The smiles on their faces were a blessing to me. In the Central Zone, no one smiles because no one feels anything. Another thing that amazed me, there were young people everywhere, from the smallest baby to teens enjoying the remaining few days of their Christmas vacation.

"All of these kids, Martin, what about their education and college?" I walked past happy children who played in a sleeping flower garden in the center of the square. The little area had been transformed from dormant flowers into a bright display of lights and bulbs of greens and reds, all decorated for the Christmas season.

"Yes, of course. We have college and graduate school for all of our children." Rebecca said with pride. "Our children are part of our community, and we all participate in sharing the cost."

Suddenly, a loud noise I didn't recognize startled me. "What's that?" I gasped as a large chunky aircraft flew overhead. The noise caused my blood to freeze as cold as the ice that hung from gnarled tree limbs. Instinctively, I knew I should hide ... but where? Not knowing where to go, I slammed my body against the outside wall of the building beside me and tried to recede into its bricks.

"Christy," Jason saw my fear and quickly put his arms around me.

"No, no," I cried and pulled away. I didn't want someone to hold or restrain me. I wanted to feel the cold rough texture of the bricks that faced the building. It felt safer to hug the wall than to stand out in the open. "They've come! They've found us!"

"Who?" Rebecca questioned and tried to comfort me with her hand to my shoulder.

I recoiled from her touch and jumped into a nearby doorway. I sensed I'd be less visible from above if tucked in there.

"The Blue Guard!" I screamed. "I've seen helicopters in magazines I found in the library. Only the military have flying machines. The Blue Guard is here I tell you. They'll be all over this place in a few minutes!" My throat was tight, my voice reduced to a raspy whisper.

Dahlia searched the sky. "Christy, I can see the wavy grid. We're okay," she said.

"Christy ... Honey," Jason soothed and gathered me in his arms again. I finally let go and felt safe there. "Remember what Martin said," he reminded me. "There is a protective force field above the valley. We can see them but all they see are stones and boulders." He hushed my fears with his soothing voice as he whispered, "We don't have to risk our lives, going out into dangerous zones to gather signatures for the petition. You know that. We can go home. I don't want you to go through this trauma." Jason held me so close I thought I could feel the beating of his heart through my cloak.

"Grand-mère and Grand-père," I whispered. "I do have to do this ... for them."

We stood by the side of the walkway, up against the buildings that had reminded us of home. He rocked me in his arms as he spoke to Martin and Rebecca. "She is still terrified ... and exhausted ... and overwhelmed with the enormity of the job. We have been running for many days, chased by the Blue Guard. She hasn't been able to catch her breath."

"Oh, Sweetheart." Rebecca spoke gently as she patted my shoulder. "You won't be doing this alone. There will be many volunteers, including Martin and me. And ... God will be with us. Come into the coffee shop and get rested and refreshed. We'll have latte or cocoa. They also make the most wonderful pastries; pecan sticky buns and bear claws. Almost anything you can think of."

Suddenly, I started laughing. We had a life-saving mission in front of us, but it wasn't the enormous nobility of it that inspired me. It was sticky buns.

"Are you all right, Honey?" Jason asked cautiously. His eyes revealed his concern, and I didn't want to add to his worry.

"Yes, I'm fine now. I just realized what a paradise this is. On the other side of the mountain, they control and measure everything dispensed to us. Here, you can eat as much sugar as you want ... and we will still get a life changing mission accomplished." We all laughed as we entered the shop.

"Six please," Martin told the waitress as we removed our coats. A row of hooks and pegs hung on the wall, some in the shape of small deer antlers and others more like fancy boots and high-heeled shoes where the garment hung on the toe. I placed my red hat on the shelf above the interesting hooks.

Smiling faces were everywhere. It felt like their joy was re-knitting me from the inside.

We were led to a table in the back left corner of the shop. We worked our way back, past friendly laughing people. I was glad my chair faced the window. The freedom and energy of everyone I saw in the fresh wintery day was intoxicating. I slowly began to feel invigorated again.

"Our children?" Jason asked. "When we asked about further education, you said 'our children.' You have referred to them in that way several times."

"They are our blessing and our dilemma," Martin admitted. "We have limited space here. Our valley extends from Howard Mountain, across the fertile Valley of Hope, the Valley of the Keepers, to the watchful hills beyond."

Rebecca added, "We ... some ... have ventured beyond the far valley. We have for years. We know how to dress, what their customs are, and their laws."

"Rebecca," Silas gasped, "you never told me you have been to the other sectors. Which ones?"

Martin looked around for ears that might hear. "Some of our pilgrims have been to all of them. Rebecca and I have only been to the west, past the desert and all the way to the ocean. It is beautiful out there."

A small group of children swarmed into the café like a rabble of butterflies, obviously looking for someone, and interrupted our conversation. Then, with glee, they gathered around our table, like they had lit on a garden of flowers. Behind them was a lovely young woman I recognized.

"Mara, how . . .?" I was dumbfounded. I couldn't find the words to express my astonishment and my joy. The lovely young woman lived in my building in Capitol City. An injured leg had bothered her and continued to get worse until she could almost not walk. Her doctor recommended a "long rest." Unaware of the true outcome, she arrived at the mountain as an end-traveler just days before Gifting Day, to enter the portal to the never-ending-sleep. She was to end her life's travel at a very early age. But, now, there she stood before me.

"Yes, My Lady. It's me. Silas brought me here, just like he brought you." Her smile was sweet and peaceful. She touched the children who brushed by her, always aware, always loving.

"And your leg? It looks like you can walk again, Mara. How is that possible?" I was shocked and filled with joy for her. Getting her out of there was her salvation. Silas saved her from imminent destruction.

"The rest, My Lady," She chuckled softly. "I rested my leg like my physician said after Silas brought me here."

The children fluttered around Silas like they had found the last flower of summer. "Father Silas," they all squealed.

"Father?" I asked.

"Christ gave them eternal life," Martin offered and tousled a boy's head when he removed his hat. "Their first parents gave them their first life. And, Silas gave them their second life."

I was stunned and tried to make sense of what Martin had said. "Are you saying ... these children are some of the unwanted, discarded babies of the Central Zone?" My heart leaped in my chest.

"We are *the claimed*, Ma'am," said a gangly 13-year-old girl with silky brown hair and hazel eyes. "And Father Silas is our lead wayfarer."

A tear rolled down my cheek, only the second time I had cried in my lifetime. Detoxed only recently from the numbing chemicals, I had just begun to experience true feelings.

"You are beautiful," I whispered to the child.

"Thank you," she said shyly. "All are beautiful in the sight of God."

I looked again at the colorful streets, still adorned with Christmas sparkle. Laughing, playing children were everywhere. I wondered what it felt like to run with the wind in your face and inhale the aroma of life.

"How many children are here?" Dahlia gasped in amazement.

"They all look so healthy and strong," Jason marveled. "And these ... are the aborted?"

"No, I wish I could have gotten to them, too," Silas said softly. Then he turned to the children. "I'm very happy to see you again, kids. Now run and play while you're still on Christmas break."

After the children left, Dahlia whispered, "The aborted are born dead or are killed immediately after birth, aren't they?" The nurse's voice was full of shame. Jason nodded in silence.

Silas pointed to the happy young ones who waved when they got to the door, turned and bounded out into the snow covered grass. "These are the lucky ones."

Then Dahlia gasped and blurted out, "These are the third children, aren't they?"

"Oh my Dear Lord," Jason gasped. "These children are from the three-child-families who are forced to choose which child to abandon—making sure they are left with only a two-child-family as permitted by law," he paused.

Silas watched the happy children through the window. "The third child is sent to the ghastly furnaces for disposal." Silas shuddered. "They're length-of-days is aborted up to age two."

I felt ill. I couldn't believe what I had always suspected but to which I had chosen to close my eyes. "The parents can take up to two years to decide which two of their three children to keep," I realized out loud. My words fell like dead weights around me. I thought I was going to gag.

"Yes, that's true, Christy," Mara agreed." But, Silas started claiming them, years ago and brought the children here. Since I have arrived, I've looked after some of the smallest ones."

"That is why you need more space," I realized as I turned to Martin.

"My goodness, yes," Spires agreed. "At first, we tried to find homes for them here in the valley. Many people have included the little ones in their families, but we are outgrowing our space."

Rebecca added, "We have found homes for so many. We had also started finding placements in the Western Zone. Some of the children are ill, some have broken bones ... and we treat them in the hospital here before we send them on. Some children are here a year or much more."

I watched the hazel-eyed thirteen-year-old skate across an ice covered puddled. She threw her head back and giggled with glee. I couldn't ever remember feeling that free. Drawn back into the café, Martin was still talking.

"We have to stop the third-child destruction at the same time we do away with the Length of Days law." I was determined that senseless death would stop.

"Besides the need for larger homes for those families who have taken in as many as six claimed children," Martin smiled as he also looked through the window to see the children play, "we also need larger schools, larger farms and greater acreage on which to graze cattle."

"Then we have come in time," I said, "for you and for the discarded ones."

"Not discarded, Christy," Rebecca corrected gently, "claimed."

"That's right," Martin offered.

"Yes, the *claimed ones*" I agreed and added. "Your work, Silas, has given me the hope I have been seeking. I can see it is possible to accomplish what our laws will not permit."

Jason added, "We have a huge mission ahead of us. After meeting all of these happy children, I can see how our job will help even the youngest among us as well as the oldest. Dahlia will go back to the city and establish a ruse about my absence. She'll say, I'm at home, studying a new medical procedure."

"Jason and I will infiltrate into the three other sectors," I explained. "We hope to recruit volunteers to canvass their own zones and secure names for the additional petitions that we require."

"We have contacts in the Western Zone, Christy. People will be there to meet you, and they'll have a network started for you," Rebecca assured me.

"That will be wonderful! We hope to set up the structure for the volunteers to follow when we move on to another zone," I explained. "We have to have enough names on the line to get a referendum on the ballot at the next election. Then we will be able to meet our two-year time table."

Rebecca patted my hand. "You don't have to do it all alone. That wouldn't be possible. The volunteers will actually do the door-to-door canvassing." She gave my shoulder a little hug.

"So let me get this right," Martin asserted. "A referendum—is a citizens' bill, right?"

"Right," Jason agreed. "The citizens create it just like a bill drawn up by Congress."

Martin clasped his hands together. "Then we'll make sure that all of the citizens have a chance to sign it."

"We've gotten this far. I look forward to meeting your friends out there on the west coast. Will anyone here be able to guide us into that unknown territory beyond the Valley?" I asked with anxious hope in my heart.

"Rebecca and I can't go, but we will have someone for you," Martin answered. "We'll call on friends to lead you west until we can meet you in the East."

"The East, Martin? You and Rebecca will come to the city?"

"That's our plan. The Eastern Zone will require the most volunteers."

"It will?" I heard what he said about that zone, and I also heard the tone in which he said it. "Have you heard something about that sector? We know nothing," I admitted. "We are venturing into the unknown."

"We know you must feel like that, Honey," Rebecca said.

I smiled because, she seemed to understand. "It feels like a large hatch is opening, and we are stepping out of a space ship onto an alien planet."

"You asked about the Eastern Zone, Christy. We have heard information, but we haven't been there. So, we don't know first-hand how accurate the perceptions are," Martin said. "But, we can say with confidence, you will be able to trust your contacts there. In each of the three remaining sectors, we personally know, through face-to-face contact or long threads of communication, the people who will shelter and guide you." Martin spoke with confidence.

Rebecca had been quietly listening. "So ... you are the ones we have prayed for," she spoke in awe.

"You have waited for help? You have wanted to overturn the law all along?" I was amazed. Rebecca's words were the cement for the layers of assurance Martin had already laid.

"I'll be honest," she replied. "Because we haven't been affected by the Length of Days law, we hadn't thought about fixing it. I would like to say that we weren't aware that it was a problem. But, we knew. Look at all of these children in our valley." Her eyes lowed and revealed the emotion she felt.

The waitress hurried around the room, serving other tables. Dishes rattled and happy voices greeted and laughed, and shared stories with one another. But, there seemed to be a respect for those at our table and others gave us space. Certainly they must have recognized that Jason, Dahlia and I were strangers in the valley.

Rebecca covered her face with her hands. "Actually, we were just selfish I guess," she said as she then leaned on one elbow. "If the law gave the power to shorten, or take away lives, we certainly should have tried to stop it. And, for that I apologize to all of you who have lived under that evil system. The truth is, we have just wanted to get our lives back ... to restore our country. All of it. We want to repeal unjust laws and stop the madness." Rebecca then tapped her finger sharply on the table. "We just didn't know where to begin. Many layers of corruption piled precariously on top of each other. Like Pick-Up Sticks, we couldn't find the right piece to remove so we wouldn't cause the whole pile to tumble. Now we know."

Chapter 7
A Pause in Reckoning

Tuesday - December 27, 2112

"All right, you uppity pair, Gifting Vacation is over. I will find you and stay on your coat tails with every step you take." Ward Stoner seethed as he maneuvered his strata car through the early morning streets of Capitol City. Since most citizens had no personal transportation in the Central Zone, the roads were nearly empty. He slowed at each stairway entrance to the upper platform of the public transit, or PT.

It was eight a.m.

Snow swirled across the pavement and blew icy chills into the air. People walking to the PT-stop held their heads down to shield their faces from the bitter cold. A woman pulled her coat around her as she slipped on the frozen steps. Everything was white, the ground, the sky—everything.

"Hey, watch out," a man yelled as the women nearly fell into him as she jerked and slid again.

The woman grabbed the stairway railing to the upper landing and held on as the man pushed her in disgust. "Sorry," she gasped as her gloves stuck to the surface of the railing where the snow had melted a little in the morning sun. Her boots protected her feet but there was no one to shield her from the unnecessary rudeness. Her breath hung like a crystal cloud, and she shivered a little in the cold.

Stoner could hear her apologize to the man for what was more his fault than hers, and he thought of his own mother. She was like that. Today, she planned to take his son shopping for school clothes with some of his Gifting Day money.

"Phone home," Stoner spoke into the empty air around him. The lights on his 281 device flashed on. "Mother? You and Christopher had better stay in today. It's very slick."

"I think you're right," Mrs. Stoner answered. She sounded a little relieved. "We'll see you when you get home. Christopher would like to have a game night tonight."

"I should be home in time," he said. "End call," he commanded the 281.

Suddenly he heard yelling behind him. He checked his rear facing mirrors. The same man was now slipping and sliding as he struck the same woman again and again. The Inspector spun the vehicle around and raced back.

"Hey, break it up," he shouted as he leaped out of the strata car and charged at the mob that had gathered. The woman was on the bottom step and still braced herself with the railing. Three men were pounding on the one who had struck her. Stoner grabbed one of the three and tossed him to the side like he was shoveling dirt from a wheelbarrow.

"Okay, okay," one of the three sputtered. "We were just helping her," he bellowed and drew his fist back. Then he stopped abruptly when he saw the Chief Inspector's angry face glaring at him.

"Stand down!" Stoner gasped as he grasped the man's arm with one hand and held off the remaining two with the flash of his Blue Guard badge.

The man struggled and babbled as Stoner held him in his grasp. "Let go of me! You have no right! I am a citizen. I have my rights."

"You have the rights I choose to permit you to have," Stoner growled. The veins in his neck bulged. "What's wrong with you?" He opened his grasp and slapped the man across the face. Astonished travelers on the platform above heard the crack and peered over the railing. "I'm the Chief of the Blue Guard! I write the rules!"

Then he turned to the crowd and ordered, "Be about your own business."

The woman, attacked and trembling, grabbed her scattered packages and struggled to her feet. "Sir," she reached out to the Inspector as she tried to regain her balance.

"You look fine woman. I have no time for you. Now, I have to take this fellow into headquarters. If you had stepped aside and let him pass, I wouldn't have to drag his sorry carcass into the station."

"But Sir," she protested.

"Do I have to take you in too? What kind of trash are you?" The chief kicked at the snow in front of her in disgust. "Get to work!" he commanded.

She said no more. She gathered up her bags and limped up the steps.

"You will regret crossing my path this morning, Mister," Stoner warned with a sneer. He shoved the man into the back of the strata car and slammed the door. "Now, I'll be behind schedule," he muttered as he walked around to the driver's side. "Don't you worry, My Lady Dearest, I will catch up to you yet this morning."

Chapter 8
Morning in the Valley

Tuesday - December 27, 2112

Martin and Rebecca had three birth children and four claimed-children. Our small party of travelers from the opening in Howard Mountain had benefitted from the Spires' large family and home. Now grown, with families and homes of their own, the children's rooms were all vacant. The extra space, used for grandchildren's sleep-overs and Sunday afternoon scavenger hunts, provided the space the extra four of us needed.

I awakened in the fluffy white feather bed in the front bedroom where light streamed through the window and danced across the floor. I watched with childish glee as bright beams waltzed along the walls. Even the sun seemed freer on this side of the mountain. I dressed and went downstairs. As I crossed the living room, I could hear Rebecca singing in the kitchen. "Rebecca, your song is beautiful," I said as I entered the heart of their home.

"Some say, 'Whistle while you work.' I either hum or sing. Can't whistle worth a tweet. I hope I didn't bother you," she said with a smile as she kept on working.

"It's wonderful! In the Central Zone, singing was forbidden a hundred years ago," I reminded her.

"Not here," Rebecca said. She sounded surprised. "Why would anyone ban singing?"

"Years ago, the government thought the people would be better controlled if they were stripped of all their emotions, no more anger, rage, passion, just flatness," I told her as I sat down on one of the wonderful painted green kitchen chairs. I wondered if Martin had made them. Rebecca had pointed out some of his beautiful wood working craft the evening before. The aroma of crisp bacon and steaming coffee filled the room. My stomach turned a summersault and suddenly I realized how hungry I was.

"But, what does music have to do with it?" she asked as she turned back to the cast iron skillet.

"Good morning. Sorry to interrupt," Jason said as he came in the room then stopped. "This must be heaven. At least it smells like you're cooking food fit for angels." He breathed in deeply and closed his eyes. Then he added, "You asked why no music. If emotions are to be killed, the things that stir the emotions, like music, need to be silenced too."

"Well, I never," Rebecca breathed in.

"You never what, my dear?" Martin asked as he came in the back door.

"I never heard of such a thing. Martin, did you know that music is not permitted in the city?"

"No. I guess that doesn't surprise me. They practically ban love," he added.

"Martin!" Rebecca blushed and pulled her large, country apron up to her face. She turned her attention to the stove and giggled.

"Good morning," Dahlia beamed as she came in, followed by Silas. Her large brown eyes looked happy and she was light of foot.

Silas yawned and rubbed his eyes as he stumbled to a kitchen chair. He folded his arms across the table and allowed his head to flop down on top of them. "Sorry, I'm fine," he said as he looked up again. "I slept better last night than I have in years. Guess I could have slept even longer ... maybe a year."

"Come on, Sleepy. I have a nice breakfast for you all." Rebecca brought a skillet full of scrambled eggs to the table and set it on a hot pad that looked like a Santa face, complete with rosy cheeks and nose. Christmas decorations still dominated their home.

"Help yourself to some bacon," Martin offered as he passed the platter. "There's a stack of toast made from Becca's homemade bread and her scrumptious strawberry jam. We have a huge strawberry patch alongside the garden on the west side of the house."

"Shall we pray?" Martin began without waiting for an answer. "Papa God," he began. Then he thanked God for the blessing of our presence, our health, our souls and our safety.

It seemed we all buried our forks in eggs, up to the handle, at same time. It wasn't just how good the food tasted ... and it did ... but my appetite even seemed greater on this side of the mountain. The others were also experiencing the relaxation that comes with freedom. We chattered all the way through our meal then carried our white and wedge-wood blue plates to the sink. With the breakfast dishes cleared and the last of the coffee drained from the pot, Silas spoke the reluctant words.

"Dahlia, we'd better be getting back." He spoke slowly and fumbled with the toothpick dispenser on the table. Suddenly eight or ten of the little slivers of wood tumbled out and rolled across the table. "Sorry, Martin, I know you hand-make all of these."

"You make your own toothpicks?" Jason gasped in surprise. Then without waiting for an answer he added, "I've decided to go back with you, Silas." He spoke to all of us but his eyes met mine.

"Jason, no," I was shocked. "I can't do this without you." I grabbed his hand, hoping I could keep him by my side. And, it was more than that. Jason and I had been inseparable for weeks. I liked it. I no longer felt alone.

"I'll only be gone a few hours," he assured me. His eyes flashed and locked with mine. "I'll come back this evening." He turned to Silas, "Can you get me through again tonight?"

Silas seemed skittish but willing. He made no eye contact, but retreated inside his emotions. "Yes, after it's dark."

"Why?" I still saw no reason for Jason to return to Capitol City. "What if you see Inspector Stoner?"

"You will," Dahlia mockingly shook her head. "He's everywhere."

"Old Tombstone Stoner?" Martin quipped as he tapped his fingertips together.

"You've heard of him?" Dahlia laughed.

"Silas tells us all the happenings on the other side." Rebecca admitted.

Jason spoke in the comforting tones I loved to hear. He traced out his plan with his fingers on Rebecca's festive red and green table cloth. "We can't cross into the western zone until tonight anyway, Christy. And, I want Stoner to see me in the city. I thought about it half the night. It will be easier to establish our story if the Inspector sees me while he hears of my planned absence. It won't seem like we have just disappeared."

●●●

The falling snow fluttered down like angel-wing feathers kissing the ground. Voices of happy children from blocks away floated on the crystal clear air. I wished Jason and I could bundle up in Rebecca's feather comforters and sit on the porch for an hour but it was time for the three of them to leave.

Jason lingered at the mouth of the cave a few seconds after the other two went through the mountain wall. "Christy," he slowly brushed the hair from my forehead that stubbornly stuck out from under my hat. "I promise I'll be back tonight after it gets dark."

"I know." Tears welled up. I couldn't look him in the eyes. If I did, he would surely have seen the fear that was rising within me.

"But?" He continued to press.

"But," I choked on the emotions that caught in my throat. "But, I'm afraid," I admitted.

"You are the bravest person I know," he soothed my fears as he played with a curl near my ear.

"Well, thank you, even if you are full of Irish blarney," I teased.

Jason grabbed me in his arms and kissed me tenderly. I felt at home with him, safe, loved. "I'll be back in a few hours," he promised. Then he slipped past the bolder and disappeared into the mountain.

As soon as Jason left and I was alone, fear flooded back in. I felt abandoned. Silas, Dahlia and now Jason had all left me behind, on the valley side of the mountain.

"Come on back in the house," Rebecca coaxed. "The north wind is starting to blow again."

"Will that keep us from traveling beyond the valley tonight?" I asked as we went back into the warmth of the log home.

"We should be all right. The snow and wind might keep others inside. That could allow us to travel pretty far with little interference. Gray Fox will know the best route," Martin assured me.

"Gray Fox?" I hadn't heard of Gray Fox.

"Gray Fox will be your guide. His wife, Little Feather, will go too. They'll be able to get you through anything. But there's a problem," Martin warned.

"What problem?"

"There is a snow storm coming in. We have a small window of time to get you through the pass across the far hills and on your way," Martin said. "It just came across the wire."

"What wire?" I hadn't heard that term in reference to incoming information.

"We have to be very quiet here in the valley. We must make sure we don't draw attention by smoke, sirens or let the outside detect communication devices."

"Then how?"

"Gray Fox sends messages over an old telegraph machine. He uses an ancient Navaho language. Tribesmen in the Western sector pick up the message. Even if someone were to stumble across the signals, they wouldn't be able to understand it. Gray Fox and Little Feather will get you there and safely back. Like I said, there are ways."

Chapter 9
Through the Mountain of Tears

"Hurry," Silas cautioned as he led Jason and Dahlia back through the deep recesses of Howard Mountain, past the ghastly museum, owned and seen only by Alister Bedlam.

"Right behind you," Jason assured him while leading Dahlia through the maze of human relics. The people-statues were all that remained of the elite of the Central Zone who had gone through the deadly portal to the never-ending-sleep.

"Let me know when I can open my eyes," Dahlia whispered as she stumbled blindly behind him.

"We're nearly past," Jason said. "You did it before when we went into the valley. Just a few steps more ... okay you can open your eyes, but don't look back.

Jason saw Silas tremble as they passed the third furnace on their way out of the cavernous cave. The area still smelled of burnt flesh. He wondered if Silas could hear the cries of people from beyond the flames in his sleep.

"Hurry, just hurry," Silas continued to mumble. The man who stood so tall in the valley beyond the mountain, quickly morphed back into the stooped, dejected, shuffling shell of a man he had been before the fresh air of the valley filled and cleansed him. He slumped even more as they neared the exit to the mountain.

Jason grabbed Silas's shoulder before exiting the cave. "You, Silas, are a good man. You broke the silence and made us all aware of the lies of this place. Hold your head high."

"But I was—"

"That's right, you *were*, but you aren't anymore," Jason said as he felt the warmth of the winter sun on his cheek as it filtered through the small window in the door. He had forgotten it was still morning with all the darkness of the cavern and its contents around them.

"Let's hurry to my car before we're seen. We have to arrive in Capitol City early. Those going to work will be there by now. Maybe there won't be too many people still out." Silas burst through the heavy wooden door and nearly ran to his car.

The three piled quickly into the small car and rushed to the gates where Silas entered a code. Slowly it opened like a medieval castle entrance. Then, they turned toward Capitol City.

All three of them sat in silence as they sped along the isolated road that led back to the city. Jason watched the passing fields with steady gaze. "One good thing about all this snow, it's white. We'll be able to see everything that comes upon us from any direction."

Strange, few in the city had personal transportation: the Blue Guard, medical personnel of high rank, the Council of Elders and judges ... and Silas Drummond who kept the furnaces blazing at the Mountain of Woe. He was never to let the fires die out. And now, the coals were cool and the furnaces black and cold. They would remain so, until the people voted on the referendum in support of the abolishment of the Length of Days policy. Jason was determined, there would be a vote!

Chapter 10
The Pretense

"Thank you, my friend," Jason spoke quickly as Silas pulled up in front of his office. He scanned the street from the north and to the south. It was still early, even though the first wave of workers had already cleared the sidewalks and PT stations. "I can't thank you enough for all you have risked by taking us to the valley and back."

Silas hung his head and didn't meet his gaze.

"Look at me, Silas." When the man looked up, Jason said, "You are a good man. You are the hero of our time. You spoke up when no one else knew the truth. That makes you a hero. That's the flat out truth." They shook hands and Dahlia kissed his cheek.

"I'll be back the minute the sun goes down," Silas reminded the doctor. "I'll be right here in front of your office building."

"Good. I'll not go home. I won't take anything with me. I'll just— be gone."

The three continued to search the street for trouble. It was still empty. Jason and Dahlia hustled out of the car and entered through the glass front doors. No one stirred in the wide entry hall. Their shoes echoed as the heels tapped across the floor. Since many people who worked in the medical office building were still on Gifting Time vacation, the lights only lit the hall. Beyond adjacent office windows and doors, the suites were dark and vacant.

Jason pulled the elevator key from his pocket, and he and Dahlia road up in whispered silence.

"If no one is around, how will you establish your presence today? No one will see you," Dahlia asked.

"I'll make some calls on the communication device in my office and check on a few patients. Monitored conversations and their content are stored in the data retrieval and storage facility at the central repository. Even if no one sees me, there will be a record of my presence in the city today."

They stepped off the lift and it immediately went back to the lobby. The old style floor indicator above the elevator door registered that the lift car was ascending again. Someone was coming.

"Run!" Jason commanded as the two darted through the outer doors of his office and past the waiting room chairs and tables piled with pamphlets and stacks of government literature that outlined: the expectations of a civil society; the beauty of a two child home; what to think and what to do.

Dahlia dashed through the inner door, snapped on the lights as she rounded the corner and slipped into the chair at the entry desk.

Jason hurried into his office and grabbed the white coat that hung on the hook on the wall to the left. He could feel his heart pounding in his chest. The medical jacket was more than a piece of clothing. It was a symbol of all he had worked for, of all he had sacrificed—his future position on the Council of Elders, his birthright—for the awesome privilege of practicing medicine, of binding up the broken and curing the sick. Before labeled as *unfit for life,* he could see each citizen a handful of medical contacts.

Slowly, he turned the used clinical jacket right-side-out as he breathed in its essence and exhaled through his mouth. "Calm, calm," he reminded himself and was still buttoning the garment when he walked with measured steps into the nurse's station.

"Dr. O'Reilly," Stoner growled as he burst through the office door.

"Yes, Inspector," Jason looked up casually from the pad of paper he had just picked up.

"Oh ... you're here," Stoner's expression changed from "Got ya" ... to surprise.

"Yes, but then, you came to see me. Did you expect me to not be here?" he challenged.

"Well, it is still the holiday."

"Yes, it is. How did you happen to stop by on a day when you thought I would be out of the office?"

"You and the Lady-girl caused quite a ruckus Gifting Day night."

"Did we?"

"Where is she?" Stoner glared with a piercing narrow gaze. "I'm not here to play games with you."

"If you mean Lady Applewait, she was going to stay with family for a few days." Jason handed Dahlia the piece of paper he had been writing on.

"I'll take that," the Chief Inspector growled as he grabbed the piece of paper out of the nurse's hand.

"Sir, this office has a strict confidentiality policy," she snapped as she tried to grab the slip of paper back from his hands.

"I said ... I'll take it." He ground his teeth in rage.

Stoner turned the small notepaper over and read the words out loud. "Out until December 1, 2113." The officer crumbled the paper in his hand and threw it back at Dahlia. "What's this all about? What do you mean *out*?"

"I'll be studying a new procedure—the non-invasive approach to joint replacement."

"Joints? You have no specialty in orthopedics." Stoner gritted his teeth and his nostrils flared.

"No, you're right. I will be studying at home and at friends' houses as I prepare myself for an internship at an orthopedic hospital." Jason explained calmly and confidently as he met the officer's eyes blink for blink.

"Where, exactly ... where will you be studying?" Stoner demanded shrilly.

"Well, I can't actually tell you that because I will be in many places, depending on my mentor's requirements and my own study needs. I will be checking in regularly with my nurse, Miss Zoobomba. She'll be able to take any messages. Feel free to call her."

"No, Mister, you will contact me regularly! Not some flat-shoed nurse."

"I'm sorry, Inspector. I just can't do that. I will require long periods of uninterrupted concentration. Just call and talk to Nurse Dahlia. She will be in the office each day to handle questions and non-critical matters. She is an independent practitioner you know."

"Didn't you hear me? I said ... you will contact me!" The veins in Stoner's neck bulged and his eyes were large and menacing.

"I did hear you say that, Inspector." Jason's voice was even but his heart was pounding so loudly, he feared the officer might hear it. "I understand your need to make sure a physician is nearby." Jason looked deeply at the angry man who stood before him. "But, I'm sure your son will be fine now," he said. "You may not require a doctor on call." Then he added, "Judge Brunner has included Christopher in the stay on the Length of Days policy. Medical contact events will not be counted during these two years either."

Jason faced the man with his own authority. He knew that Stoner had secretly contacted a doctor about his son's accident and subsequent coma the day before Christmas. If he had taken his child to the hospital that day, it would have affected the child's length of days by one less year. Jason knew, because he was the doctor that Stoner had called.

The Chief Inspector said nothing. He stared at Dr. O'Reilly but neither of them flinched. Finally, Stoner pounded his fist on the reception desk with a loud thump, turned and stormed out of the office.

Jason and Dahlia exhaled loudly. "Well, hopefully, he has been appeased for now. It was for this very moment that I returned to the city. Stoner completed his own little charade. Then, he played his part well in my little script. He made it all happen whether he knows it or not. He validated my presence, and the reason for my absence."

"The Lord made it happen whether *you* know it or not," Dahlia reminded him.

"You are absolutely right. I actually gave credit to Stoner, that wretchedly sad little dictator, when the miracle belongs to God."

"What do you want me to do here, Doc?"

"Let's organize the office so you can manage it in the months ahead. You put together new job descriptions for the rest of the staff. I'll look it over when you're finished. While you're doing that, I'll sign drug orders, look through the files and go over policies which will protect you while you practice. Also, you'd better not give out any more detoxification tablets since a few people will abuse the drug just as they had recently. The city will begin to purify the community's water supply as they gradually pour in fewer and fewer chemicals. Some may experience depression because they have been drinking the drug-laced water since they were small. I'll place an order for an increased supply of anti-depressant medication for our pharmacy here in the office so you will be prepared."

"All right, but how will I contact you since Stoner will check our communication lines every day?" Dahlia asked.

"Use the regular lines to send innocuous questions and comments. But, contact Sean for the serious stuff. Silas will bring guarded messages from me to print in the newspaper. You can read my coded words there and ask questions that I will answer ... again, on the pages of the newspaper."

"It will take longer, waiting for the newspaper to be delivered, but okay, we'll make it work," Dahlia paused then jotted the word, Sean, on the pad of paper in front of her.

"No, Dahlia," Jason warned and tore the paper into tiny pieces. "You cannot leave a paper trail. The Blue Guard could come in at any time and confiscate our records. Verbalize your comments and questions directly to Sean with nothing written down except his final news sheet."

"We can do this," Dahlia asserted. "Nothing on paper, but the new structure of the office. It's possible. As Martin said, *'there are ways.'"*

Chapter 11
Later That Evening

"Okay, where is she?" Stoner barked as he burst through the door of the Indian River Apartment building.

Dahlia had just sat down in the large first floor gathering room, just off the entry. She carried a book Christy had given her, a forbidden novel. The clever nurse had put the jacket from a fact-based book on the subject of residential apartment building rules around the novel. The story was about a woman and her four daughters who lived during the nation's Civil War. Authorities had banned the book along with other books of fiction.

"Is there any romance in that book, Dahlia?" Tayton Braxton, a new resident asked as he sat in a facing overstuffed chair.

"Hey!" The Inspector shouted at the two as he stormed into the sitting room. "Can't you two hear me?"

"We can now, Chief," Tayton drew out in his southern drawl.

"Then, answer me! Where is she?" The vein in Stoner's forehead bulged and his cheeks flushed.

"She? Who?" Tayton questioned with a calm voice.

"That one knows who I'm talking about," he sneered as he pointed at Dahlia.

Dahlia had closed the book casually and laid it, title page up, in her lap. "I'm sorry Inspector. Can I help you with something?"

Ward Stoner pulled off his gloves and smacked them across his hand. "Do you want to answer my questions downtown?"

"Sir," Tayton addressed the inspector as he stood up and stretched out to his full six foot six inch frame, "we will be glad to help you if we can."

"Don't I know you, Mister?" Stoner turned to the much taller and more muscular man in front of him.

"I've just transferred into your precinct. My name's Tayton Braxton, Sir. My former Chief, Walter Collier, had written you last month, and I arrived today."

"You're on my team?" Stoner questioned with a mistrusting expression.

"Yes, Sir," he reached out his hand to greet his new chief.

Stoner ignored the gesture of friendship and continued to slap his leather gloves into the palm of his hand. "As I remember it, you asked for the transfer because you didn't like some of the orders old Walt handed out."

"Well, Sir," Tayton wiped his hand on his pant leg, "Chief Collier wanted us to push people around and work outside the law."

"Oh, really," Stoner drew out in mocked surprise. "And you're too good for that?"

"No, Sir," he paused. "Well, yes, Sir. I like to think I'm fair."

"Fair are you?" he paced back and forth across the lounge carpet. "You live here in this building or are you just keeping company with our esteemed nurse here?"

The new man in town blushed. "I would consider myself privileged if Miss Zoobamba would like to spend some time with me," he winked at a stunned Dahlia.

"Okay, okay, I'll call your bluff—"

"Bluff, Sir?"

"I don't know what you know of Miss Zoobamba here and the company she keeps, but if you live in this building, I have a special assignment for you. You stake out this apartment complex," he spit out. "You'll tell me where Lady Christiana Applewait is, when she leaves, where she goes, and when she comes back. You got that, Mister?"

"That sound like a good assignment, Sir."

"Good is it? You are to be rude, aggressive and violent if necessary to get the stiff necked people in this building to bend. And, they will bend," he snorted. Stoner said no more. He jerked his gloves back onto his hands and stormed out of the Indian River.

"Is it true?" Dahlia asked. "You are really a member of the Blue Guard? They are as corrupt as they come."

"I know," Tayton said as he turned back to her.

"If you know, why did you transfer?"

"Sean is an old friend. He asked me to transfer into this precinct so I can protect you and Christy and this mission you're all on. I can run interference with Stoner. But, I will have to fit in with the other guardsmen. You may hear rumors about me and think I'm one of them. If you do, know that I have fixed whatever I have broken."

"Why do you care what I think, as long as you protect Christy?"

"Because, I do. I was there on Christmas Day evening. I heard the speeches and saw the crowd. I'm more one of you, than one of them."

Dahlia eyed the man in front of her. There was something that gnawed at her, in a good but surprising way. Something she had never felt before. Deep down where her new emotions felt giddy, she bubbled a little.

"And, the other is true too, Dahlia."

"Other, what other?"

"You were here. You heard what I said to my new boss."

"Tayton, I feel strangely uncomfortable with this game you're playing." She looked down and tried to hide the blush she felt on her cheeks.

"Dahlia, it's called flirting ... and yes, I told the truth to the Inspector. I do want to spend some time with you ... if that's okay with you."

She looked away and tried to hide the smile she could not control. "To your first question, Tayton, yes, there is romance in this book."

Chapter 12
Gray Fox and Little Feather

Buddy pulled himself up from his comfortable bed at the side of the hearth. The large, thick dog cushion, stuffed with Martin's aromatic cedar chips, made the perfect mat. The dog found every excuse to lounge about all day. Now, he pointed his tail and pricked his ears. Something had stirred him from his usual nap.

Dusk had fallen in the valley so Rebecca had turned on the house lights. Martin strategically placed logs in the fireplace to build a fire and quickly ignited it into flame. "That should provide a steady burn this evening," he said as he straightened and proudly reviewed his backwoods talent. "I'd better check on the meat," he explained as he left the room.

The firelight danced across the golden logs of the huge cabin and created interesting shadows on the walls. I sat on the couch and watched the display of amber and light as it moved about the room.

"Do you smell that wonderful meat baking, Buddy?" I asked as I watched the dog sniff the air.

"That's not it," Martin cautioned as he came back into the room and silently pulled down the rifle that hung above the fireplace.

"What is it, Martin?" Rebecca asked from the kitchen doorway.

"Don't know yet," he said as he listened to the night beyond the cabin.

The three of us sat motionless and waited. We held our breath in anticipation. Yet another danger had found us. When would it all stop? It was hard for me wrap any measure of understanding around my doubt. Did God actually place us in this moment as I thought he had? Why couldn't he have made it easier?

"Could be a wild animal, Martin," Rebecca said. "Many still roam around. Especially here in the valley."

"Wild animals?" I didn't like the sound of that. "Is that a problem here? We have no animals at all in the Central Zone," I offered. My heart pounded.

My question fell by the side when I heard footsteps on the porch. Animals don't wear boots. I sat on the edge of my seat as Martin went to the door. Fear mounted within me. Would Blue Guard troopers force their way in? Rebecca motioned for me to hurry to her side and step into the shadows behind the open kitchen door.

Martin hoisted the firearm to his shoulder. With one glance over his shoulder toward Rebecca and me, he jerked the door open. A snow covered Jason O'Reilly stood in the gathering darkness of the porch brushing the freshly fallen snow from his arms and shoulder. Silas stood behind him. He removed his hat and shook the white icy powder onto the ground beyond the house.

"Come in, friends," Martin laughed as he lowered the rifle and held the door open.

"Jason," I sighed in relief. "You're back." I went to him and threw myself into his embrace.

He wrapped his arms around me and pulled me into his snowy jacket. "You'll get wet on my damp coat," he warned me but didn't let go of his grasp.

"I'll dry in front of the fire," I said and stayed in his arms. When I had refilled my need for him, I unbuttoned his coat and helped him out of it. Together, we sat in front of the burning logs.

"Did you have any problems on the wide-open road out to the mountain?" Rebecca asked her cousin.

"We saw nothing," Silas said as he removed his outer coat.

"The roast beef will be ready shortly. You can relax, Jason, before you and Christy set out on your quest. Gray Fox and Little Feather will join us in a minute." Rebecca went back into the kitchen.

I pulled myself away from Jason for a few minutes and followed her. I hoped to get a few more answers to sooth my fear. This whole mission had developed so fast, my mind couldn't keep up with it all.

"If you go across the ice, you will have to watch every step," she said as she checked the kitchen clock again to time the meat. "Gray Fox is never late. They will be here shortly."

"You said we might cross the ice. Is that safe?"

"It's been frozen for six weeks. The ice is thick enough to walk on or even drive on if you wanted to. Still, I have seen men with their eight-toothed draw-saws this afternoon. They cut holes in the ice so they can fish during the winter months. Many will have small tents over their little fishing site to protect themselves from the wind, but not all of them. Some will leave open holes down through the ice to the frigid water until they return in the morning. Be careful."

"It sounds like large open fishing holes doted across the lake is no real problem," I said.

"It isn't a problem ... unless you don't watch where you're going."

Buddy barked and wiggled as his toenails tapped on the hardwood floor. "Becca," Martin called from the sitting room. "Gray Fox and Little Feather are here."

"Wonderful," she sang out as she removed the large roast from the oven. "If you will grab the rolls and butter, Christy, I'll come back for the mashed potatoes and corn."

"Sure," I said as I turned and saw the large basket of freshly baked yeast rolls and a bowl with a large round ball of yellow butter in the middle. I picked them up as the rolls sent their heavenly perfume into the air.

"Jason, just smell these," I said as I waved the basket under his nose.

"Somehow, I don't think the health department of the Central Zone would approve of them."

"What possible difference would it make to eat wonderful bread if they're going to cut off your life at an early age anyway?" Martin questioned with a mocking smirk.

I turned and stopped. The last two guests to arrive came in, hung up their buckskin coats and entered the dining room. The man, Gray Fox, had long hair that shone as black as the marble in the capitol building grand hall. His skin was much darker than mine and weathered like the descriptions of Native Americans I had read about in books. Obviously, he enjoyed the out of doors. His face was strong and his bearing straight and tall. Little Feather was a bronze beauty whose smile was infectious. She walked with grace, like a deer, with her head held high. Her deep brown eyes scanned her surroundings.

"Little Feather," I smiled back as I extended my hand, "I'm Christiana Applewait."

"Yes, Becca told us all about you. We stopped by when you were napping." Her smile was genuine and friendly warmth poured forth.

"I'm sorry I missed you," I apologized.

"There is no need to be. You have had quite an ordeal." Little Feather touched my arm and made that connection that calls a stranger "friend."

"Come, let us sit and eat," Martin invited. We gathered around the table, Gray Fox, Little Feather and Silas on one side, Jason and I on the other. As soon as we had finished shuffling our chairs, Martin gave thanks to God for the food piled high on the platters, for friends old and new, and for our safe passage into the unknown zones.

"I heard Becca talking about the animals in these hills," Martin began. "Gray Fox, maybe you can fill them in."

Gray Fox took a bite of meat and thought for a moment. "In times long past, people of the Western Zone had a distorted sense of animal rights. In some cases, they thought the rights of a small speckled bird held more weight than the rights of man. Since they were no longer people of deep faith, they didn't know the natural order of nature, and thought of man as, not the holy protector and benefactor of all that God had created, but the predator. They passed laws that banned hunting and fishing. Then, in 2026, they carried their delusional thinking to the greatest extreme imaginable. They tore down all fences and opened all of the zoos so the animals were free to roam, to hunt and to seek their own comfort. Over the years, bears found their way back into the Northwest where it is cooler. Bob cats roam in packs nearly everywhere. Lions and tigers fought for their own territories and the large animals, like African and Asian elephants, worked again, in much the same way they did in the ancient villages from which they came. Monkeys can be the greatest nuisance. They forage for food wherever they can. They aren't in the trees of their ancestral home. They're in the backyards and on the playgrounds where our children swing and play."

"The health threat alone would be tremendous," Jason said. "Animal droppings would be everywhere and all the germs associated with it."

"The animal advocates didn't care. They believed that man was the menace, not roaming animals," Martin added.

"By the time the folks in the west came to their senses and found a faith in the one true God who ordered all things into their place, the animals were out of control," Rebecca explained.

"You mean the part of the country that gave us, *Do whatever makes you feel good*, now cradles a people of faith?" I couldn't believe what I was hearing. "I read about those who had rejected the morals of their heritage and embraced a freedom from responsibility."

Rebecca chuckled as she sipped her coffee. "The same women, who wore dresses with a neckline that plunged to their navel, now wear long dresses that reach just inches above their ankles, and high collars. The men wear button-up shirts and modest trousers, worn with a belt or suspenders ... or both," she laughed again. "Any male over twelve years old who is caught with their pants drooping down, is taken in to work in the gardens and orchards while wearing wide red suspenders."

"Then, we may find a lot of willing volunteers on the West coast. If they have changed their lives and now respect themselves and others, they may have a love for life that will help our cause." I thought about the task of canvassing the entire country, and I had hope.

"Animals and the empty ones must still be reckoned with," Gray Fox said. He broke his dinner roll in half and spread it with Rebecca's home-churned butter.

"I don't like the empty ones," Little Feather shuddered as she put her fork down and sipped water from the heavy tumbler.

"Who or what are the empty ones?" Jason asked. "Empty of what?"

The valley people looked at each other and then at Jason and me.

"The empty ones are those who are ... empty," Martin tried to explain. "Their eyes reveal no light or life within. They chose to believe the old lies. Everyone around them is supposed to make them happy ... and yet they feel no joy at all. They have no integrity, no steadfastness and no faith. They exist to take, to consume, and to serve their own needs, although they are unable to name the things that are important to them. They have no inner core. They have no spirit. They have no hope. They are very dangerous because they have nothing to lose. They are the hollow ones ... the lost."

Chapter 13
The Departing

Tuesday Evening – December 27, 2112

"Let's see how this one fits you," Rebecca said as she offered me a long, broomstick pleated, ankle length skirt with deep pockets. "Our daughter, Rachel, often wore this one when she traveled into the Western Zone. It's similar to the clothes the western women wear. She's married and doesn't travel much anymore."

"It reminds me of a gypsy skirt," I said as I thought about the Romani women with their full skirts that swing when they walk.

"You are familiar with the Roma?" Rebecca's eyes widened.

"Only what I have read, of course."

"The women in the west have adopted the dress of the Roma, or gypsies, because it seemed so practical for them. Cool, modest skirts, and loosely fitting peasant blouses that come up to the neck with a small collar, have replaced the scanty shorts and low hanging pants of old."

She thumbed through the hanging clothes and selected a white boxy blouse with blue and red needle art all around the edges.

"But you said the western zone had embraced their faith. Did they choose a pagan religion as the Roma had followed?"

"No. They went through several religions during the first decades following the collapse of their culture. They found them to be the same wishy-washy approach to belief that had contributed to their down fall. Now, they make no demands on others and what they believe, but they have chosen to rebuild their society on the old beliefs of the original founding fathers."

"Wow, how did all of that happen?" I couldn't believe it. "How did they hush the mocking laughter of non-believers, as surely there must have been?"

"Last question first. The public areas will still have Christmas decorations up, since that was the vote of the people many years ago. Various sections of the public parks will have the displays of other beliefs as well. None can be rude or insult the senses of others since they are all in public areas. No one can stop the visual speech of others."

"That is amazing, that they allow other voices to be heard. We can't speak at all in the Central Zone."

"Your other question: how did it happen? It first started as a movement by the evangelist, Francine, Franny Adams, a distant niece of the great Christian equalizer, Dr. Absalom Lucas."

"I've read about her ... Franny Adams," I remembered out loud.

"Then, you are the only one in the Central Zone who has. You may hear more about Franny when you get to the west."

"I'll listen for her name."

Rebecca looked at my shoe coverings and smiled. "Those won't get you very far." She stooped and pulled a pair of low-healed, high-top boots from Rachel's closet floor. "Your low-quarters aren't the best for this trip. Here, these boots are good for walking. They're warm for the desert nights and cool in the daytime. I'll get some socks from the drawer."

I quickly changed into the travel clothes of a Western woman and looked at myself in the mirror. How different I looked. Rebecca plaited my hair into one long braid and fixed it in place with a long piece of sinew.

"Why don't I keep your red hat here? You can get it when you come back through here. I have another one you can wear. In yours, they may spot you as the only cardinal in the woods."

I looked at her quickly as a doubt entered my mind. Rebecca saw my worried expression.

"Yes, Christy, you will come back this way. I know you will," she spoke with the conviction I needed.

I smiled and tried to hide the fear that could betray me if not buried deep inside. I looked at my reflection again in the mirror and hoped I looked different to any eyes that knew me. If I could pass as a Western woman to my friends, perhaps I could pass as a local to those who didn't know me. I checked again, and then stepped out of the room and into my new world.

Jason stood at the bottom of the steps resting his arm on the stair banister. His makeover was amazing. He wore pants made of blue denim material, a red plaid shirt, boots similar to mine, a split leather coat that was both rough and smooth in texture and a polished leather broad-brimmed hat. He smiled as I came down the steps and his eyes lit up my heart.

His hand felt strong when I gently touched it. He grabbed me boldly and pulled me into his arms. "We can do this, Babe," he whispered. "Together, we can do whatever God calls us to do."

I knew he spoke the truth but hearing his words out loud, buried the truth of them more deeply in my heart. I was new to faith, and I was still learning. With Jason beside me, he would be able to reassure me if I became confused.

"I love you, Christy," he whispered in my ear.

"Oh Jason, I love you, too," I responded and drew even closer.

"We must be going, Friends," Little Feather said as she reached for her coat.

"Your green cloak will be perfect in the Western Zone," Becca said. "Here is a smooth leather fedora. The lining pulls down to cover your ears when needed and folds back up into the crown when it's warmer."

"Thank you for everything, Rebecca."

Little Feather looked Jason and me over with a keen eye. "It looks like Rebecca and Martin fixed you two up really well. You won't stand out at all. Let's move out."

"Can we know the route we're taking—what we should expect?" Jason asked.

It had to be Jason to ask that question. Sadly, I usually follow as I have always done. I was no leader and yet everyone on Christmas Day evening called on me to lead them out of the Age of Silence. Truthfully, I would have gone anywhere with Jason O'Reilly, but I didn't know how to get there on my own.

Gray Fox looked at Martin and Rebecca. It was Martin who spoke.

"We met just yesterday, Christiana, Jason. I know you are stepping out into the unknown much like our pioneering ancestors did. But, they had more time to plan and I'm afraid, you do not. The reality is, you will see sights you have never seen. We don't have the time to tell you all of it. Simply stated, once you have cleared the hills, you will be out of the mountainous areas. Then we will cross the desert. Hopefully, the people on down the chain of contact will meet you and take you on by car. There is no time to tell you more. Sorry ... except to say, your mission is holy, and the Lord God will be with you."

Chapter 14
The Icy Trek

"We're nearing the lake," Gray Fox whispered as we silently followed a seldom used path toward the horizon where the sun had already slipped. We could see his silhouette by the light of a three-quarter moon, as he motioned toward the glassy icy that stretched out in front of us. The message was easy–"Watch your step."

We stepped out on the frozen surface of the lake. I thought of Grand-mère's story of Jesus walking on water and smiled. The water, frozen as solid as an old brick road, gave me a little confidence to venture out across it.

Little Feather was in front of me. I tried to walk in the exact footprints her boots had made on the snow. When her right foot slipped out from under her center of balance, she threw her arms out and bent forward as she tried to regain her equilibrium. I wanted to grab hold of her waist and help her, but I was afraid I would only knock her off balance even more and we would both go down.

We all stopped in the middle of the lake and watched as Little Feather tried to steady herself. I could feel my leg muscles tighten and ache as the tension of anxiety gripped me. Finally, she pointed to the other side. There was still ice in that area but there was no water underneath at the edge of the lake. I looked forward to the warmth of the desert that was somewhere ahead of us.

Then, silently we moved from the lake area to the rolling hills. Walking there was difficult. Ruts, buried beneath the snow, and cracks and dips in the ground could break an ankle. We stayed off paths and crept along untraveled areas so as not to draw attention to our movement. Suddenly, I held my breath. Some type of small animal was moving toward us.

I thought it looked like a dog my books called a German shepherd. As it got closer, I saw his bushy tail and froze. It was a fox, but it made no sound. The fox stopped in front of our guide, and fixed his eyes on his. Slowly, the animal stretched out his body to its full length. His tail was stiff, and he bared his teeth. Gray Fox didn't blink and maintained his gaze. Slowly, the sleek animal began to lower his tail until he tucked it between his legs. He turned his head down and slipped off into the night.

I couldn't move. I watched the fox until it disappeared among the frozen, leafless trees. Jason came up behind me and slipped his hand in mine. We walked as one. The snow and sludge were terrible on the upper slopes. My feet slipped backward with every step forward. I grabbed some nearby scrub brush and used it to propel me forward. On we trudged.

Little Feather had pulled her skirt up between her legs and had tucked it into her belt. It created a makeshift pair of pantaloons. I tried to do the same but was not as gifted at garment re-purposing as she was. As we reached the top, my skirt tail drooped to my knees.

We met our first challenge. We had crossed the Lake of Hope. Now, we would need to put the distant hills behind us. The walk was easier up the hillsides since the watchers had developed safe pathways with railings and carefully placed pull-rings to assist the hikers to the top. They had walked to the top for decades.

"Orville, anything happening up here?" Gray Fox asked as we approached the last outpost.

"Gray Fox, good to see you." He looked out to the west. "I have seen very little. There is something, miles away. I can see lights in my spy glass."

"We are headed that way."

"Watch your step as you approach the desert," the watcher cautioned. "There are always critters out there." He slapped Gray Fox on the shoulder and we moved on in silence.

Over the hill, the flat lands stretched out before us as far as we could see. On we walked, right foot, left foot, right foot, left foot. I watched the clear night sky out to the west ... and finally exhaled.

Chapter 15
The Pilgrimage Has Begun

7 a.m. - December 28, 2112

The plains spread out like a never ending table set with scrubs and switch grass. I could not imagine walking all the way to the desert but we would do what was required. I was exhausted. We had walked all night. I thought of the pictures I had seen on the covers of old western novels of dead cattle and chalk-white bony skulls of animals that had died in the blistering heat.

We had only walked another mile when Gray Fox and Little Feather sat down on their haunches and silently watched the eastern horizon.

Jason looked at me and studied our two guides. "Sorry friends. I'm a man, and I need a modicum of control over my life. What are we doing now?"

"Waiting," Gray Fox said with relaxed confidence

"I can see that. Waiting for whom ... for what?"

"For him." Gray Fox pointed to an old red stake truck that approached. It had to be more than a hundred years old.

The truck slowed down as it approached us then stopped. "Gray Fox ... good to see you," the driver said as he rolled down his window. "How did you know I would be coming along?"

"Because it is early Wednesday morning and I knew you would have been heading back from the ranch to be home in time to see your children off to school." Little Feather smiled. "I like that—up, overseeing the ranch for two days, then home for two days so you can see your babies."

"Little Feather, you know how old Alfonso, my *baby*, is now?" Armando laughed.

"I imagine he's older than I suspect," she smiled.

Armando crossed his arms and leaned them on the old window opening. "He is fifteen years old already. Marta is in college. She's going to be a teacher in a few years."

"That is wonderful my friend," she said.

"I wonder if you could give us a ride to the edge of the desert," Gray Fox asked.

"Of course," Armando agreed. "Two of you can ride up here with me and two back there." He pointed to the truck bed behind the cab.

"We'll ride in the back," Gray Fox answered quickly. "This fine woman is Christiana Applewait, Armando, and her friend Dr. Jason O'Reilly." He and Little Feather headed toward the bed of the truck and climbed over the stake sides.

In spite of Gray Fox's generosity, I would have been happy to ride in the back. But, he wanted to be gallant, so Jason and I walked around to the passenger side of the vehicle and reached for the door handle. It was a huge step up from the paved road. Luckily a long chrome hand bar was there for grabbing.

I slipped in beside Armando and Jason sat by the door. The view was wonderful, like that seen when riding on the Public Transit as it travels on the ribbons of steel high above the street in Capitol City.

"This is very nice of you," Jason said. "We're fortunate it's not out of your way."

"Your destination could not be out of my way," he said quietly.

"How far do you live?" I asked.

"About five miles down the valley," our driver stated.

"So, not far from the desert?" I asked. When I got no response, I asked, "How far is it to the desert?"

"Twenty-five miles," he stated warmly.

"Then taking us to the desert is out of the way. It's not on your way home at all," I said.

"The way of the Lord is never out of the way for his people," Armando answered.

"You are a believer?" I asked in surprise. Meeting so many who follow the Way is so very different than being one of the handful of believers in Capitol City.

"I am ... and my whole household is as well."

"It is so nice of you to take us," I said, not knowing how to thank him.

"I am privileged to be part of this great undertaking you and the doctor are on."

"Undertaking?" I questioned. How could this man in the Western Zone know of our secret mission?

"Yes, Lady Applewait. We heard of the great walk of the brave people in Capitol City on Christmas Day evening just minutes after your speech on President Alexander's front porch. You are going to get everybody in this whole nation to sign your petition so the Length of Days Policy can be overturned when it comes to a vote at the next election. To be a part of that miracle is a privilege, My Lady."

"Christy, Armando. Call me Christy ... please," I asked. It was important to me that I be equal to everyone else. If not equal, then I would be out of touch, out of reach. Those on a pedestal are very lonely and I had been alone enough to last a lifetime.

"I will call you Christy as you request, but I do so because a woman of God, a Crusader for Life, has asked me to. And I will respect that, My Lady." Armando kept his eyes on the road in front of us.

"But, how did you find out about our cause so fast?" I couldn't believe how quickly information travels from one zone to another.

"The Navajo telegraph," he said.

"Telegraph?" I asked.

"Gray Fox will tell you about it, My Lady ... Lady Christy."

I looked at Jason. The only life I ever sought was an afternoon curled up on the old brown leather couch in the back room of the library, reading a good novel from a century past. Propelled into a position of leadership and notoriety in only a few days? How was it possible? It was all too fast. I couldn't keep up with my own life.

"It's a privilege to live a miracle, Lady Christy," Armando added. "You can't know the way. The telling of it would take the same amount of time as living it. The time spent on your quest will be equal to the people and their stories you meet along the way. The pilgrimage has already begun."

Chapter 16
Revealed in the Desert

9 a.m.

The desert sand was warm under our boots as we stepped from Armando's truck and into the morning sun.

"The coolness of the night has taken some of the fire out of the sand." Armando assured us from his truck window. "It will be easier to walk on now. It'll be hot today." Armando looked at me with a strange expression on his face. He had tears in his eyes.

"Thank you, Armando, my friend," I said as I patted his arm.

"It is my privilege," he said softly.

"I'm honored to have met you," I added. "You have provided another link in our holy journey, and I didn't even get your story as you had promised I would."

"I'm just a humble rancher," he said as his voice cracked with emotion.

"You're the chariot driver who provided safe passage for these papers," I patted the side of the brown leather cross-body, buckled, legal case I carried.

"Those are the petitions?"

"Yes and the required cover sheets needed to legally file the petitions," I spoke softly and looked around the immediate area for ears that might threaten our mission. "Jason's briefcase holds the same. If we become separated or injured ... the other one will be able to carry on."

"You will be safe," Armando said. Then he reached out and shook Jason's hand as he came over to the window.

I offered my hand. Armando took it, kissed it and said, "My story is: my wife died two years ago. She fell from her favorite horse out on the ranch. She died instantly. I ran in and grabbed my rifle from my gun case and charged out with hate in my heart, bent on destroying the one thing Angelica loved almost as much as her family. My daughter, Marta, grabbed for the gun and it fired, hitting the side of the barn and grazed Alfonso's temple. I fell apart. My father had to manage the ranch for a few months and my mother stepped in to look after the kids. Finally, one day, Marta came into my room and said it was time I pull myself together. She needed me and so did her brother. She said that anger and hate only destroys the vessel that carries it. The object of our hate is only ourselves."

He paused for a moment and wiped his eyes. "I had to learn to lay the anger and fear aside and accept the responsibilities the Lord had given me. Now, Black Lightening is the finest stallion in our stable. I won't let anything happen to him."

"Thanks, Armando. Thank you for the ride. Thank you for your story and thank you for your encouragement. Bless you my friend."

"I am truly blessed," he responded.

I looked around our sand-barren surroundings. Emptiness loomed before us and the last promise of vegetation lay behind us on the plains. There on the edge of all that sand, a few yards from where we stood, was a small, long green building with a sign above the door—Ace's Place.

Jason took my hand and together we followed Gray Fox and Little Feather into the diner. The inside was everything it should be, or as I remembered from my many novels and history books.

"Over this way," Gray Fox led us to the back corner of the small restaurant where a turquoise and cream colored leather-like fabric covered the cushions of the booth benches. The table was clean but worn from all the elbows that had leaned on the surface. A lunch counter stretched across the opposite side with stools that spun the patron around and deposited him or her back in the isle when they finished their meal.

We took our seats and got comfortable. Gray Fox pointed to a back placard on the wall with white letters. "The specials for today are listed on the black board," he said.

I read the listing slowly, savoring the thought and possible aroma of each of the dishes. Food did not sound as yummy in the Central Zone.

Suddenly, a man entered the diner whose own energy was so vile I could feel his wretchedness from the back corner. The waitress froze when she saw the man and nearly dropped the coffee pot that now dangled limply from her hand. I was stunned and could not take my eyes off him.

"Don't look at that one," Gray Fox whispered. "He can't draw energy from your fear if you ignore him."

"Well, is it ready?" the empty one seethed.

"Yes," the woman said. Her voice was harsh with anxiety. She reached behind the service window and brought out a white paper bag. "See, it's all ready. Now, you go on."

She handed him the bag and before she could withdraw her hand, he grabbed her wrist and pulled her forward. She nearly fell over when she stumbled into one of the counter stools. "Raymar ... no! You're hurting me."

I saw it all and heard the fear in the woman's voice. I jumped to my feet but didn't move. The man, Raymar, snapped his glare in my direction and our eyes met. I didn't say a word, but in my heart, I prayed that anger would leave the man.

His eyes were empty. He appeared to be a shell of a man, with only basic animal instincts, like the need for food, still pulling at him. He could have just as easily been a growling bear.

Raymar didn't approach us, but tried to intimidate me with his fierce eyes and hunched attack-stance. Perhaps, it had worked the previous times he had intimidated others. Like a mad dog, he locked his eyes on mine and seemed to be trying to conquer me with fear.

I maintained my gaze on his hollow eyes. For some reason, the longer I maintained eye contact, the less I feared him. It seemed that God's warmth, love, peace and acceptance, all directed to the creature-man that stood bent over before me, were changing him. Suddenly, the man blinked. Then, his mouth opened as he inhaled a life breath he may have never experienced. He grabbed the bag and backed out of the diner, not out of intimidation, out of something else. It was like he could not stop drinking from the well of life. I watched him all the way out the door. Once outside, he ran out into the street, grabbed hold of the back of a passing truck, swung his body onto the vehicle and was gone.

"Not even the grandfathers of our community have been able to reach one of the empty ones," Gray Fox sighed with amazement.

"Who are you?" Little Feather asked as she looked outside to see if the Hollow Man was really gone.

"I'm just Christiana Applewait, as I said," I answered her.

"What she won't tell you and I just discovered in the last few days, is that Christy is a seer and a healer. She had expressed her *knowing* in artistic expression when she was a very young child. Now, she is only discovering her gifts as they are revealed to her," Jason explained as he put his arm around me.

"You are a disciple of the Holy One," Gray Fox acknowledged.

I didn't have to respond, and I was glad. I didn't know what I would have said. It seemed I was finding myself at the same time others were discovering me. Luckily, the conversation stopped when a man with shoulder length curly red hair entered, followed by a group of men and women who scattered throughout the diner. The curly haired man slid onto the bench beside Gray Fox and Little Feather.

"My friend," the man said quietly, and firmly patted his forearm.

"Good to see you, Rufus," Gray Fox spoke lowly as he touched his hat.

"These are your travelers?" Rufus asked.

"Yes, Dr. Jason O'Reilly," Gray Fox motioned toward Jason. "And, this is Christiana Applewait."

"The seer," Rufus lowered his eyes as if he were bowing.

"You have heard of us? Here ... on this side of the mountain," Jason asked in surprise.

"Word of Lady Applewait's gifts came to us through the Central Gazette."

"Sean's newspaper?" I couldn't believe how far Sean's circulation extended. Maybe getting the information out about the petitions and referendum won't be as hard as I thought.

"Yes," Rufus said as he smiled. "It comes by truck to my bus and I transport it west."

"Order some food, my friends," Little Feather said as a waitress approached the booth. "We have a long way to go. Make sure it is filling and nutritious."

We briefly scanned the chalkboard again for the daily specials and selected our choices. I chose something called meatloaf and Jason selected fried chicken. Jason and I chuckled over the concept of placing chicken pieces in sizzling fat and cooking it until the skin turned brown. Little Feather, however, assured us that our choices would be delicious. I had read about meals such as these in my books, but I had never eaten them.

"What is our destination?" Jason asked. "I'm still not comfortable with not knowing where we're going."

"Los Angeles," Rufus said. "The new Bible belt."

"Bible belt? Where? What do you mean?" I asked.

"The entire coast, from Baja to Seattle is the new cradle of belief."

"I imagine it's a patch-work quilt of all the world's religions," I laughed. "My books told me of all the many religions and cults that lived in harmony on the west coast, as well the vast number of unbelievers."

"All religions used to live side by side, except the Christian religion. They silenced the followers of the Christ, just like they have in the Central Zone. However, unlike your zone, when a balance returned after the collapse of society, soberness took over the people. Allowed to breathe again, the Christian religion blossomed and grew. While they don't defame the beliefs of others, the Christian religion is in the majority. About 65% are followers and roughly 62% attend church every Sunday. The people have found that accepting love and peace, forgiveness and grace, and eternal life is not a subversive, antiquated concept. It's a life-saving blessing."

"What will we encounter? What will be the dangers?" I knew in every good society, there remain imperfections.

"There is still a remnant of people who believe they hold truth in their hands. Oddly, some are rigid believers who believe they— and only they—are the people at the heart of God. They have been known to ostracize those who do not accept their beliefs or who speak out against Julius, the great Christian Evangelist of the year 2073."

"And Francine Adams ... what about her teachings?" I asked, remembering what Rebecca had said.

"Most people embrace her wisdom. So, those people will be with our cause. We don't know what to expect from the other groups; like the ones who are radical, free-spirits and rely on magic; those who are self-centered, self-importance, and believe in the concept of the self as God. They use crowd hypnosis and aggressive deception to attempt to win others to their way of belief. They and the Julius followers are dangerous and will require watching. If there is to be a return of freedom for all the people, we must try to keep the current balance in society but also bring in the outliers. We want to make sure we don't disrupt the distribution of power, while turning it up-side-down to include the hollow ones."

"Rufus," a woman with a round face and big brown eyes interrupted with an apology. "I'm sorry, but we must be going soon. Raymar may have gotten back to some of those in the caravan of dust heading west. They may try to stop these believers," she warned.

"Caravan of dust?" Jason questioned.

"As the hollow ones travel, their caravan kicks up dust when their wagons pull out. But, when they arrive, it's like no one is there. How can they be so frightening and yet so empty? I'm sure they have all found out there is a saint among you."

"A saint?" I questioned.

"You, My Lady," Rufus smiled. "We all know you have arrived."

Chapter 17
Rocky

We had been traveling for several hours when I woke up from a deep sleep. One of the children on the bus, holding a little stuffed bear, was hanging over the back of the seat in front of me. I smiled and closed my eyes. Suddenly, I felt a fuzzy fabric as it tickled my nose. When I opened my eyes again, the little boy was straddling the back of the seat so he could reach me with the bear. An impish smile was on his face.

"Hey, are ya 'wake? Talk to me," he teased with four-year-old glee.

"Well, I guess I could ... if you will tell me your name," I agreed.

"I'm claimed," he said as he wrapped the words around in his mouth. "I don't have a name."

"Everyone has a name," I said lightly.

The child's traveling companion turned and offered. "Hi, I'm Miss Granger. There are several claimed children on the bus." Then she added, "The family this boy was born into already had two children. They had until he turned age two to decide which ones to keep. This child turned three a year ago on December 15. His first parents kept him too long and didn't obey the law. When the Family Regulation worker discovered him, Silas hid the boy until he could be smuggled out of the zone. In the valley, a doctor treated him for an old spiral fracture of the arm and some problem with his leg. Now that he is doing well, I'm accompanying him to his new family in Santa Barbara, California."

"They'll call me, Rocky," the little boy beamed. "I got to name myself at Hope House."

"Rocky is it? I think you chose a very good name. It's solid."

"Like a rock!" Rocky shouted as he made a fist and showed his muscle.

"Do you want to play a game?" I asked the little man.

"I don't know. I guess," he shrugged, apparently eager to play anything just to pass the time.

"Okay," I thought for a moment. "Do you know your colors? I see something blue," I shot back.

"Sure, Ma'am taught me."

"Ma'am?" I wondered if the boy was talking about someone at the Hope Center.

"The boy's mother," Miss Granger explained. "That is often what the birth mother prefers to be called."

"I understand," I responded and I believed that I did. The first parents would not have wanted to develop an attachment to the boy. The sad truth is, as a baby, he would have had to attach, or bond, to someone in order to thrive and live.

"Blue, that's blue," he shouted as he pointed at the blanket on my lap. "My turn," he grinned and bounced on the chair. "I see something blue, too."

I listed several things in the bus that were blue, Gray Fox's shirt and the driver's ball hat but each time, Rocky threw his head back and laughed, "Nooo."

"I give up on that one," I finally had to admit.

"No, you guess," he giggled.

"I can't think of anything else. I believe I have named everything."

"The sky," he shouted.

"The sky?"

"The sky's blue."

"Yes, of course, but that's not in the bus," I protested.

"No, but it's blue," he laughed.

Chapter 18
The Western Zone

December 29, 2112

We had crossed the desert during the night and traveled most of the next morning. We made a few stops but took very little time to eat. Everyone seemed to draw food from their pockets, but mine were empty. I was getting hungry. My stomach growled and churned.

"As a physician, I diagnose your body sounds as symptoms of hunger," Jason leaned over and whispered.

Little Feather tapped me on the shoulder from the seat behind me. "It sounds like you're ready for another pressed food bar."

"Could you hear my stomach rumble from back there?" I was embarrassed. I had lived a life of privileged isolation. Now, I was close enough to people they could hear the growling of my stomach from several seats away.

"I am sure a legacy citizen's digestive system is well under control, My Lady," she said with poise and deference.

"Oh please," I moaned. "No elites can be found in God's kingdom, Little Feather. Everyone is equal in the eyes of the Lord. You know that."

"Yes, Christy, I do. I wasn't sure if you knew it," our guide spoke diplomatically. She passed two condensed food bars to Jason and me.

"Does the little boy in front of me have any food?" I asked Little Feather through the crack between the two chair backs.

"I'm sure he does, Christy," she assured me. "His handler, or guide, is seeing to his needs."

"Is Miss Granger his guide?"

"Yes, his traveling companion is his guide. Silas kept him safe at his sister's house where he stayed for several months. Then he took him to the mountain, hid him in a room behind his own, and then Miss Granger met him in the Valley of the Keepers several days ago."

Jason nudged my shoulder to get my attention. "Look at that wonderful sunrise, Christy." He turned and pointed out the back window. "Have you ever seen anything more beautiful than the sunrise over the desert?"

Together we watched the rosy glow of the sky as it blended with the morning clouds. The desert shimmered as the light danced off the hot sand. When the sun had finished greeting the day and rose firmly in the eastern sky, we turned and faced forward again and I smiled. We were on the last leg of the path that would lead us into the basin and on to the shining City of Angels.

"It is amazing, Jason. The ocean is far to the west, where the city meets the sea. I can almost smell the salt air, I've read about it so many times. It all seems so enormous when compared to the closed-in feeling in the Central Zone."

We traveled many more miles until we finally came to the erector-set creation called the highway system. "They haven't torn down the highways and replaced them with the public transportation system like we have in Capitol City," I observed.

Gray Fox, ever vigilant to all our needs, explained, "The Western Zone continues to enjoy the independence of personal transportation. They have an evolved energy system that produces no carbon," he said.

The nearer we got to the city center, the more it was obvious that the new positive and conservative ethic of the people of the western zone had painted and polished everything in the city, from the trimmed and point-tucked buildings, to the white wash on every rock.

We drove through the city streets and into the neighborhoods of Holmby Hills and Beverly Hills. It was in the latter sprawling community where we finally pulled into the gated drive of a gleaming home that stood tall and stately among the trees and gardens of the estate.

"Who lives here?" I gasped in amazement. "Not even the elite of the Central Zone live in mansions like this."

"This is listed as the home of film producer, Rachel Claudette. She lives on the main floor and the upper floor houses the offices of Claimed-International. Children stay here in the many rooms of the second floor, north wing while they await the arrival of the parents who have claimed them."

"How long do they have to wait?" Jason asked.

"There really is no wait. Call this a meet-up place. The new parents have claimed them before they leave the Valley of the Keepers," Gray Fox said.

"Do the claimed children go to other zones as well?" Jason questioned as he looked up at the massive structure.

"Not yet. C-I is investigating the other zones for their receptiveness to the idea of becoming claimed-parents. The Christian heart of the Western Zone still provides as many homes as we currently need. Some of the families welcome claimed children into their home where three to six other children already live. C-I has placed a few children out of the country, in Canada. "

"How can people with six children possibly parent each child effectively?" Jason shook his head in amazement and doubt.

"That is Central Zone thinking, Doctor," Little Feather stated boldly. "A family of six or seven children always has a place of belonging and safety. An only child may actually feel more alone and insecure than a child from a large family, especially if both parents work. I understand all adults are expected to be employed in your zone."

"Point taken," Jason smiled with the sheepish grin of a professional, educated by another.

"Let's go in before you're spotted," a resident from the mansion cautioned when she came out to greet us.

We entered through the massive, eight foot tall front door. Inside, the children from the bus streamed across the marble entry and into the huge dining room. There, a sideboard, filled with exotic breads, rich meat platters, and fresh fruit and vegetables of all kinds, awaited them. It even had varieties of fruits that didn't grow in the Central Zone. Citrus fruits that abounded in the West were nearly non-existent in the other zones since exportation across sealed borders was impossible.

"Ah, two travelers from Martin and Rebecca Spires, keepers of the Bible," the greeter smiled as she extended her hand in friendship and hospitality.

"You know Martin and Becca?" Amazed by how wide the little circle spread, like eddies in a pool, I followed the others inside.

"Lady Christiana Applewait, Dr. Jason O'Reilly, I would like you to meet Rachel Claudette, the blessed angel who shares her home with C-I," Little Feather said.

"If I cannot help C-I, Claimed International, with all the space I have here, I'm not worthy of the blessings I have received. I do share, with joy. With abundance, comes abundant generosity and abundant responsibility." She smiled and shook our hands.

"Some, who are blessed with plenty," Little Feather explained, "share what they have from an indifferent distance. They pretend generosity. Rachel gives up her own space and solitude to welcome the children and their guides into her own home."

Rachel smiled and turned modestly to the new travelers. "And, yes, of course, Martin and Rebecca are dear friends," she agreed. "During the Great Collapse, the books of the Western Zone were destroyed, as they were in the other areas. When the Evangelical Revolution happened out here, it was all by testimony, by word of mouth. We wanted a real Bible to verify our collective memories.

Martin and Rebecca were silent supporters of the revolution and they presented us with a complete copy of the Holy Bible."

"That is amazing," I said slowing. I wondered if I should admit that I had one too. Then I realized that I was past the mountain, through the desert, and in a forbidden zone. If I couldn't trust the people I was with, I was in more trouble than I realized. "I have one," I whispered.

"One?" Rachel questioned. "One what?"

"I own a Bible," I admitted.

"And, so do I," Jason confirmed.

"Two? Two more Bibles have survived?" Ms. Claudette's surprise was evident as her face lit with excitement.

"More than that," Jason offered. "The stash of books in which I found mine has many more bound scriptures."

"This is not the time to discuss a possible sharing of Bibles, since your mission has to be accomplished in a short length of time. Maybe, when all this is over, we can talk about sharing some scripture." Her voice was full of hope.

"And novels, history books, philosophy ... many of them."

"I have spent the last few years in the Library in Capitol City," I joined in. "The books were not destroyed at our facility. Many book lovers simply stored them in the sealed off back recesses of the building. If we can accomplish our mission, you will have more than earned an opportunity to participate in a real *lending library*."

I watched as the children filled themselves with the feast, prepared just for them. As people carried food to and from the kitchen, filling and refilling the serving dishes, I felt a beautiful sense of *enough*. Some fine-china dishes had sterling silver spoons to serve potato salad and mixed fruit. Beside the elegant china and silver display was a sturdy cleaned and stripped tree branch, the children used as a fork to stab an old fashioned hot dog. It appeared that Rachel Claudette used the tools she owned, not just displayed them like a victor's bounty, or evidence of wealth.

"Thank you Ma'am," a small one smiled with a tooth-sparse grin. "This is very good. I've never been this full before." His arms were thin and his face gaunt.

"I thank you, young man, for visiting me." Rachel bent down and met the child on his level.

"I bet you get lonely in this big house." The child's eyes scanned the tall ceilings with ornate moldings and center glittering light.

"I would be if children like you didn't come to stay with me for a short while every day," Rachel said.

"Kids come every day?" he gasped. "Are they all claimed-kids like me?"

"Every one of them," Miss Granger informed him.

"Wow! You have saved a lot of lives," he grinned in awe. At the end of the side board were platters of cookies and a giant chocolate cake, which now had a huge hunk carved out of it.

"Yes," Rachel laughed as she saw his longing gaze. "Of course you can have dessert."

"I've never had anything like that," he gasped.

"Just a small piece then," Miss Granger warned. "It will be very sweet and you aren't used to all the sugar."

As the boy walked away, Mary Granger said, "Many of the first parents don't give treats of any kind to their third child. Sugar is very scarce due to the ban on rich pastries, so they share their finest only with the first two."

As a cherished, only child, I could not believe the cruelty of some first parents. "Don't the children feel profoundly rejected?"

"Indeed they do, My Lady. See how thin these children are and how gaunt their faces. The opposite is also true, look at Starla over there. She is very overweight. She would sneak into the food storage of her first home and steal food at night, trying to fill the emptiness she felt. In the morning, her first parents would beat her, which made her need to stuff her sadness even more. She is four years old.

They had kept her longer than most because they liked to abuse her."

"Please," I begged as I turned my head to the window and the peaceful green garden that grew beyond. "I can't listen to any more."

"I understand," Rachel soothed as she touched my shoulder. "But, Christy, if you don't know, how will you recognize the wickedness of destroying a third-born child?"

"I have seen the evil under Howard Mountain with my own eyes. Those images will be burned in my mind forever," I shuddered as I remembered the ghastly private museum of Alister Bedlam.

"I'm sorry," Rachel apologized. "Now, please have some food. The new parents will be here in about two hours. By noon, they will claim their children. About one o'clock, the army of volunteer C-I board members I have selected will arrive and we can begin. The mission will continue."

My heart leaped within my chest. "We are actually beginning a task some have said cannot be accomplished. I'm as amazed as the rest," I said as anxiety gripped me and tore at my faith. "No, I choose to not be afraid. We will develop a team to canvas the entire country, a country that has its zones sealed. We crossed one zone border and we will, somehow, cross the others. I'm sure of it."

Chapter 19
Still Searching

That same afternoon, Inspector Stoner slowly circled through the streets of Capitol City, trolling for clues to the whereabouts of Lady Christiana and the doctor. Sure, Dr. O'Reilly had helped him when his son was injured, but if the man and his Lady had broken the law by escaping from the Central Zone, he would catch them and see they were prosecuted the same as any law breaker. "Where are you two self-important uppity elites?" he mumbled to himself. "I will have control over this city and that includes you two. I will not be stopped."

He wound around the tree lined streets of Oakwood, the neighborhood in which Christiana's grandparents live. The beautiful old Victorian homes glared at him from the other side of the sidewalk. "Why do two old people, like Oliver and Constance Richly, occupy a large four bedroom home all alone?" He coasted in front of the white house with the broad veranda, but no one stirred. The icy streets were glassy, which only made him grumble more.

"I would have thought the special-class would have had their roads cleared by this hour of the day."

The winter had been a particularly harsh one. A child from a house two doors down slid across the sidewalk like an ice skater on a pond.

"Hey you, kid," Stoner bellowed. "Why aren't you in school?"

The boy nearly lost his footing when the Inspector yelled. "It's still Gifting holiday," the child said as he froze to the spot.

"Go home," Stoner ordered.

"Mother said I could get some fresh air," the child protested. When Stoner glared him down, he turned to go in.

"Hey, kid," he called out as an afterthought. "Have you seen anybody around this house today?" he motioned toward the Richly home.

"No sir. No one is allowed to hang around in this neighborhood." He squinted at the Chief of the Blue Guard. "You just loitering, Mister?"

"What?" Stoner yelled and reached for the door handle.

"Anything wrong?" Oliver Richly asked as he walked out onto the porch. "So, we meet again, Inspector." He eyed the strata car and the man who commanded a vise like grip on the people of Capitol City.

"Nothing wrong. It seems that your granddaughter and the doctor are missing. Do you know where they are?" Stoner masked his nasty attitude with a vile-sweet smile.

"Of course ... in general," Oliver answered cautiously. "Dr. O'Reilly is taking a sabbatical while he studies a new procedure—"

"What *procedure* is so important he would be away from his patients?"

"I don't know what he is studying. The doctor is a professional who can take care of himself."

"And Lady Applewait? Is she studying something too?" Stoner grinned, the smirk of one who believes he has trapped another.

"Not that I know of. Her master's thesis has been done for a long time."

"Then where is she?" Stoner screamed.

"She doesn't live here, Inspector. She did express an interest in the history of the Great Collapse and the social changes in the aftermath of that tragedy."

"What changes would that be?" Stoner questioned.

"Well, now that would defeat her need to write the book. If it was all told before the writing, she wouldn't have to do the telling," Sir Richly said with a smile.

"You are required to tell me where she is," the Inspector growled as he jerked the door open and placed one foot on the snowy ground.

Oliver folded his arms across his chest and rubbed them. "It's getting cold out here. I can tell you this. Christy could be at her work in the library ... she would have the resources there to begin her research. Then, there's her parents' home, her own apartment, the little coffee shop she enjoys, and the many new friends she has been making lately."

"You will get me a list of all her acquaintances, immediately," Stoner gritted his teeth.

"I will do no such thing, Inspector. The Council of Twelve and those who will ascend to one of those positions, cannot be harassed, followed or investigated." He rubbed his arms a bit more and then added, "I think I'll go back in, Inspector. It's cold, and I have wasted enough of my time out here." Sir Richly turned and went back inside, leaving the inspector to shout at the wind.

"Something wrong, Inspector?" Guardsman Braxton said as he pulled his strata car along beside the chief's.

"Not with me, Mister!" he shouted. "But, there is everything wrong with these people who believe they do not have to follow the same rules as the rest of us."

"But, Sir," Tayton stumbled cautiously into the line of verbal fire, "they don't have to follow every rule. Special ordinances are in place to protect them and their privacy as well. They can't be vulnerable to possible blackmail if everyone had access to their private information."

"You know too much, Mr. Braxton," Stoner bellowed as he started back to the car. Then he whipped around, "But, do you know where she is?" he screamed.

"Well, I saw her late last evening when she came into Indian River Apartments," he lied. He maintained a sober face and added, "But, I believe she was gone by the time I left this morning." He continued to fabricate a story that would stall Stoner a little longer.

"You saw her?" Stoner smiled a sickening smile.

Braxton looked corruption in the eyes and did not flinch. "Yes, Sir, I am sure she is safe, if that's your concern. I will be happy to continue my surveillance assignment."

"Oh, you would? You'd be happy? Well now ... isn't that nice," he sneered as he jerked open the door and got back in his car. He clenched the wheel with fists of steel and gunned the engine. The rear tires spun and swerved on the ice, sending broken, frozen puddle shards into the air like an explosion of shrapnel.

Chapter 20
Chalky Boone in Pursuit

5 p.m. - Stoner's Office

"Boone!" The Chief Inspector yelled from his office in the direction of the squad room.

"Ward," Chalky responded with the tone of someone who has repeated herself many times. "If you will use the communication devise, I can hear you and you can save your voice."

"There's nothing wrong with my voice," he bellowed.

"I can hear that," she said as she closed the door behind her.

"I want you to go on a ... special mission."

"Of course," she agreed.

"I want you to go into the Western Zone ... and see if you can get a lead on Miss Applewait," he said her name with distain. "Braxton said he saw her but I think he's wrong. Someone must be impersonating her. I can feel it in my bones. She's no longer in this zone."

"Inspector, you know I follow your orders but ... it is forbidden to ... stalk a Legacy Citizen, especially one who is more likely than others to rise to a seat of authority. You heard the cheers and adoration of the crowd the other evening, Gifting Day Night. You can't—"

"I'm not going to, Boone. You are," he sneered defiantly.

"But Inspector—"

"You will follow that subversive brat. It may be illegal to stalk a Legacy," he screamed until the veins in his neck bulged, "but a sworn officer of the law can follow, in hot pursuit, someone as dangerous as one who would overthrow the government. If Braxton said he saw someone trying to pass as Lady Applewait, then maybe she's in danger. We need to protect her."

"Sir, where will I find her? The Western Zone is huge," she continued to protest.

"Boone, you will find someone who will know something. I can feel it," he said with certainty. He walked behind his desk and opened the drawer. Here," he said as he handed her a small packet.

"What's this?"

"That is your travel permit, the blue one is a border crossing authorization, and the yellow one is a permit to carry one of the new sting-ray laser wands you can conceal in the open, right in your pocket like a writing pen."

"But Ward—"

Stoner's eyes grew narrow and his jaw was tight and clenched. "I better not hear one more word out of you, except, 'Yes, Sir.' I'm not saying it will be easy, and you may not find a lead at all if she isn't there, but if I find out she has been in the Western Zone all this time and you haven't at least found a lead, you will be collecting fairs at a transit stop."

Chalky Boone looked at the man she had always respected. Suddenly she saw the bitter shell of the person he used to be. He had turned into someone else, a stranger. Like in the death of an honored statesman, Ward Stoner's flag had slipped on its mast.

Chapter 21
The C-I Board

5 p.m. - In the Western Zone

"In here," Rachel Claudette directed. She had led us past the grand entry, through massive, solid wood double doors and into an office of mahogany paneling, leather chairs, and the scent of peppermint. Rachel pointed to the large jar of wrapped red and white striped candy. "I try to keep a treat in here for the children."

"You are very thoughtful," I said as I took a chair beside Jason around a large conference able. It was good to put my satchel down. Jason and I placed our pouches on the broad polished table.

There was a faint knock on the door and Rachel's assistant entered. "The C-I board is here, Rachel," Kasamar announced. She stepped in and held the door for a group of nine, very different people.

I watched as Rachel introduced each member. A blond man with chiseled jaw and deep blue eyes maneuvered a chair with wheels silently through the door. I was shocked. No handicapped people lived in the Central Zone. The lame entered the portal to the never-ending-sleep immediately after diagnosis of the prolonged disability.

"Friends," Rachel paused as she introduced him to the group. "I would like you to meet Phillip Santiago, a professor of physics at the large Christian University in Berkley."

An echo of "Hellos" followed. Behind the professor eight other members filed in and introduced themselves to our small group.

Annabelle Rodrigues, a judge of the District Court, was a dark beauty with laughing eyes. "I'm pleased to meet you," she smiled. "You are Lady Applewait. We have heard about you."

"How is that possible?" I couldn't believe the story she was telling me.

"The church was praying for you on Sunday. We heard the message of the petitions, carried to the president of your Zone the day after it happened. The Western Zone does not uphold the Length of Days laws. We here die natural deaths. Most live to be one hundred-twenty-five or thirty. They maintain their beloved work as long as their body can do the job."

"A hundred-thirty?" Jason blurted out his surprise.

"Yes, of course. That is our life-expectancy now," Judge Rodrigues said matter-of-factly. "If the Central Zone had not killed their aging treasures, you too would have long life."

The next two people, Faye and Otis Augustine were obviously two of the treasures of whom the judge spoke. "They were both teachers and they retired at age one-hundred," Rachel explained. "They have been wise advisors to many not-for-profit organizations that serve children."

"Happy to meet you two," Faye offered with a strong, clear voice. "You are true patriots and national heroes. We will be happy to do all we can to organize a great citizens' movement to gather all of those signatures."

"Since our Zone doesn't obey the evil law of termination, we will be able to get many signatures and volunteers to cross into the other two zones," said an African-heritage man of mid-life age, about sixty-five.

"As the logistics coordinator of Outreach International, Hermon Lincoln, you would be just the executive to accomplish such a massive drive of people," Rachel agreed wholeheartedly.

Three of the other board members were Chief Zoning Engineer, Deborah Radcliff; author Stephen Seebring; and Young-Life Executive Director, Levi Liu. If nine board members were present, someone was missing.

"Rachel," Kasamar said as she opened the door again. "My father is here. Do you want to prepare the other board members?"

"Thank you. Ask him to wait a moment." She smoothed and stacked a few papers in front of her. "My friends, we have a new, perhaps temporary, board member to replace Shafer Digby who fell and broke his leg and will be out for several months."

"Surely, a mere break wouldn't keep someone down, with the sound wave fusion procedures we have now," Dr. O'Reilly stated.

"True," Mr. Lincoln agreed. "But Shafer is also a world class triathlete. He will have to get back into competition shape. There is an event in a few months."

"I am amazed by all you have accomplished," I admitted. "I feel like such a slacker."

"Indeed you are not," Steven Seebring bellowed, although I still didn't feel worthy of their praise.

"With your vote and permission," Rachel began cautiously, "I am suggesting that we fill the vacancy while Shafer is out, with ... Raymar Goring."

"How coincidental, I met one of the hollow ones whose name was Raymar," I remembered.

"He is the same," Kasamar said with a cringe to her face and a hesitant voice.

"Raymar Goring is a hollow man." Rachel informed the board.

"A hollow one?" each membered questioned in their own way.

"We encountered him on the journey here," Jason said with a puzzled expression.

"Yes, he has been living in the desert, for the past ten years." Rachel looked at Kasamar and stepped slightly to the side.

"Rachel asked me," Kasamar explained slowly, "if I thought Raymar might be willing to come to the coast and at least meet with you as a whole board."

"Why did you want Raymar?" Judge Rodrigues questioned angrily. "He and his kind have been through the courts more times than anyone can imagine."

"His kind?" I questioned. So far, I hadn't seen a display of discrimination in this loving zone.

"It is not discriminatory to tell the truth," Annabelle snapped.

"No, Judge it isn't," Rachel assured her. "And, I certainly know why you have informed the board of some of the facts of Raymar's life. It is not discrimination to point out the characteristics of a whole group of people, when it's true. Evil seems to ooze from the Hollow People. Their behaviors are destructive and their history of harming others is legion ... every single one of them ... including Raymar."

"What event happened to all of these people that changed them from being civilized to savage?" Jason asked. I had wondered the same thing but I didn't want to profile a whole group of people.

"The same event was a positive one," Kasamar said and then turned to Rachel. "If I may explain what I understand of them."

"Oh course. Who better to tell their story?"

"When the Evangelical Awakening happened, years ago," she began, "some people didn't accept the beliefs. In fact, some laughed and deliberately chose anything that was in opposition. They became more and more depraved until their soul escaped the evil body in which it lived."

"That was fifty years ago," Steven explained. "And children born to those people were born with no life inside. They breathed and functioned but Life was gone."

"But, I think you're wrong, Mr. Seebring," Kasamar protested. "I think they can be reached. I don't think they lost their soul. I believe it hid inside them, away from the horrible experiences the body participated in."

"What do you know about the Hollow People?" Steven questioned.

"A seventeen-year-old Hollow being would sit in the bushes beneath the window of the daughter of his master. There he would listen to the music the girl would play on her piano or her acoustic 723. Sometimes, it was classical and sometimes inspirational. The strains of the music reached inside the boy and rebuilt his soul with the vibrations of the notes. He and the girl secretly married and soon she was pregnant. When she died in childbirth, he abandoned his soul and slipped back into emptiness. Raymar was that boy and the girl was my mother," Kasamar whispered.

"Raymar is your father?" I gasped as I remembered the savage I had met in the desert.

"Yes," she smiled. "Rachel took in a homeless infant and I grew up knowing her as my mother. Raymar would visit me about once a month."

"He had clear rules," Rachel explained. "If he acted out in any way, he would be escorted from the estate and could not return the next month." Rachel spoke with the authority of a protective parent.

"He has moments of clarity," Kasamar insisted.

"What about moments of sanity?" Jason asked.

"He is not insane," she insisted. "He is empty." She smiled as she seemed to remember pleasant times. "Sometimes, I think ... if I had stayed with him, his soul would have returned."

"You couldn't be responsible for your father, Kassie. He was supposed to take care of you ... and he couldn't," Rachel assured her.

"Well, I still don't see what a Hollow one could offer. It would be dangerous to have him around," Judge Rodrigues snipped.

"Statistically, we need him," I chimed in. "I don't pretend to know any of the happenings here. In my library, I have access to the history of the Central Zone since it began. But, the history of the other zones was lost when the borders closed one-hundred years ago, prohibiting travel between zones." I thought of Raymar and how he had terrified the serving girl at the diner. But, other issues abounded. "Even if we are able to get the signature of every person in the religious majority and those who are in accord with those beliefs, we will still need a small percentage more. The Hollow ones would make up that difference," I concluded.

"Then I say, show him in," Hermon said with resolve.

Rachel nodded to Kasamar. She took a deep breath and opened the office door.

The man who entered was clean and shaven. His hair was combed but straggly. His clothes were old and wrinkled like he had used the back of a chair for a closet, but they were clean. He made no eye contact and kept his focus on the floor.

"Raymar," Rachel reached out her hand in friendship, "I'd like you to meet the Board."

Raymar said nothing, but cautiously stuck out his hand in an expression of friendship that seemed awkward to him. The judge sniffed indignantly, but allowed herself to touch the man.

"And, these are our visitors, Raymar," Rachel directed him in Jason and my direction.

"Raymar, I'm happy to meet you," Jason said as he smiled.

"Jason is a physician, Raymar," Kasamar explained. The man looked up and got a glimpse of us.

"Raymar," I soothed as I reached for his hand, then I patted his shoulder with my other hand. "I'm glad to see you are feeling better than when we first met."

His arm started to tremble and his face contorted as I touched him. What was happening? His expression was of pain, but I didn't know why. I took a step forward to steady him, but then everyone jumped to their feet.

"My Lady," Steven gasped.

"I'm okay, thank you. Raymar," I asked while still making physical contact, "am I hurting you?"

"Yes, yes," he cried as tears streamed down his face. I reached out and embraced him. I didn't know why. I just followed the urging of my heart. I could feel the rigid stiffness of his body as it began to relax. Suddenly, his knees started to buckle and I couldn't hold him up. Jason helped ease him into an empty chair but Raymar would not let go of my hands. I knelt on the floor beside him.

Deborah Radcliff and Levi Liu leaped toward him. Jason stepped between them. "Raymar," Jason ordered, "you have to let go of her hands."

"Please ... no," he begged.

I was on the floor at his side and I could see the tears drip from his chin. From within his grasp, I tried to wiggle a finger enough to sooth the back of his hand. As I stroked him, I began singing the only song I knew. "Silent night, holy night," I sang softly. Finally, Raymar looked into my eyes and inhaled a deep gulp of life again and again until he seemed to be full.

His entire countenance changed. The lines in his face softened and turned up. His trembling stopped as he looked deeply into my eyes, and gasped, like one seen for the first time.

"Raymar," I whispered, "God loves you and has been seeking you for a long time."

"Oh," he screamed from the depths of his being as if convicted for all of his crimes, "I am not worthy."

"That's all right, Daddy," Kasamar cried as she bent and wrapped her arms around him. They huddled together for a moment, rocking back and forth.

I took my seat and wiped tears from my eyes and blotted my cheeks. I felt completely drained, like a tea pot, tipped up and poured out of all emotion. Even the judge and fellow skeptics, for that moment, appeared visibly touched by Raymar's coming-alive experience. I wondered about what my eyes had seen. How could a transformation happen like that? Like a wadded up piece of paper, snatched from the trash and placed in reverse, Raymar unfolded from a life utterly destroyed, to one pristine and pure again.

"Raymar," Rachel interrupted quietly, "thank you for coming. We need your help."

"You?" He looked around the table of impressive people, his eyes wide, then narrow. "You need my help? Why?"

"You are aware of the despicable Length of Days policy, right?"

He looked at Kasamar and back at Rachel with a searching expression on his face. "What policy?"

"Each citizen is allotted a prescribed schedule of life-days. The more value they are to the whole community, the longer their length of days. Even very young individuals who provide nothing to the greater good, are sent to the portal of the never–ending-sleep," the Judge made the pronouncement like a sentence of death.

"That is why you have called me here?" Raymar's voice grew hoarse and faint. "You have decided I've lived long enough!" He jumped to his feet, turned right and left, as his eyed flashed like a trapped animal.

"No, Daddy, no!" Kasamar patted his chest to comfort him. "No, we need your help."

"We are a far more compassionate people than those in the Central Zone," Steven assured him. "We are conservative with everything, including the lives of our citizens. We want them to enjoy the most out of their years for as long as they can."

Phillip Santiago smiled and moved his wheelchair back and forth, like a little dance. He smiled reassuringly. "If they were going to get rid of you, my friend, they would have gotten rid of me a long time ago."

"You are an important link to the success of our efforts, Raymar," Rachel spoke quickly. "I told you, we need you and I meant it." She sat back in her comfortable chair like she had used all of her arguments.

"How? Why?"

"We are going to canvass the entire Western Zone," Jason began. "To be more truthful, we need you and many more of the people out here, to contact others and get them to sign a paper that says you all agree that the Length of Days law must be abolished, overthrown," Jason quickly added.

"We hope most of the population will agree with us and sign the petition. But, we need many more signatures ... and that means the Hollow People," Rachel explained.

Otis Augustine eyed the man with a piercing gaze. "I'm not a young man," he began, his head lowered. "I have been around the empty ones my whole life. I have never seen them amount to anything. But you, Sir, I must admit ... I don't know what to make of you."

Faye looked him over carefully, "Raymar Goring, you are a puzzle. We are supposed to vote on whether to include someone from the belly of the earth into our small group. To my knowledge, you people have lived in the mountain caves for decades. You come out at night and steal animals like a stalking fox. You attack anyone you think might have something you want. Am I correct?"

"Yes, Ma'am, but is it fair to profile a single example of a group? That is discrimination." Raymar protested.

"When I see a wolf near the hen house, I don't expect the wolf to act like a rabbit. I know it will act like a wolf. I get out my weapon and eliminate it," Otis stated logically.

"But, what if the animal has been mistaken for a wolf?" Raymar asked.

"Hollow people do not have your logic, Sir," Otis conceded. "What makes you think you are hollow?"

"My parents were the rejected of man—their parents and their parents. That makes me one of them. That is the way it is."

"But, your daughter is not," I smiled at Kasamar. "She is a lovely, educated woman. If my vote counts, I say Raymar is on the Board. He will be part of the canvasing team."

"But—" Judge Rodrigues began.

"And ... I would think some of you may feel better if Kasamar came with us and escorted Raymar around a world he has never experienced. We will see who we have here when he has new clothes and a haircut." I was sure his presence on the Board, and out in the field, would be a blessing to us and to him.

Rachel Claudette stood decisively. "Are we ready for the vote?"

Chapter 22
Boone in the West

Friday - December 30, 2112

Chalky Boone searched the ground below the chopper cruiser. The new silent-ride motors that turned the blades muffled the old sound of the blades above the cab. Still, the cab doors were open so she could lean out and view the space below. The rushing wind was loud. "I see nothing," she hollered as she turned toward the passenger in the back seat.

"I don't see anything but sand out the other side either, Lieutenant." Daniel Washington continued to stretch out the open door. He steadied his reach by holding on to the strap above the door. "We'll be out of the desert soon," he yelled.

"What?" Boone shouted. She smiled as she thought of Ward Stoner and his unwillingness to use the office communication device. She had tried to talk Stoner out of sending Daniel with her. The whole mission was distasteful to her. Following a Legacy Citizen was illegal.

"She is more than a fancy Legacy brat," the Chief had bellowed. "She is breaking the law if she has left the zone. I can feel it inside; it's gnawing at my innards. That Council of Elders wannabe thinks she's above the law." His jaw grew tight and strained. "I am the law! She will not cross me!"

"If she has left the zone," Chalky had said, "she has already crossed you. She's crossed the entire boundary." Boone felt a smirk on her lips and turned away from him. "But why do I have to take Washington with me? I don't trust him."

But that didn't faze Ward Stoner. Daniel Washington was in the chopper cruiser with her. He was the most dangerous Blue Shirt she had ever encountered ... and that's why he was along. While she searched for Lady Applewait and the doctor, he would break bones all around her to see that she got the answers she needed.

"We are entering the city's airspace," the pilot announced. "Close all doors. I will be receiving landing instructions."

They said nothing but sealed up the cab. The silence was louder than the wind. Her mind whirled like the blades. Daniel was brutal and charged many times. She had lost count of the offences. Sometimes reprimanded, his greatest punishment was a week's suspension ... with pay.

One day last summer, Washington dragged a woman into the station. "Help me!" she had pleaded. Boone was with the Inspector in his office at the time. Stoner didn't even look up.

Through the window in the office, Boone saw the woman fall to the floor. As she struggled to get up, the Blue Shirt terror kicked her in the side and then yanked her up by the same shoulder. "Ward," Boone yelled as she jumped to her feet, "that officer just accosted a woman." She started toward the door.

"Boone, mind your own business!" Stoner growled.

"Sir!" She couldn't understand why no one had come to the woman's rescue.

"All of my Blue Guards know the rules, and politeness is not one of them. Sit down."

She lost another measure of respect for Stoner that day. She lost even more respect for herself. She also did nothing. Now, Washington was to accompany her to the Western Zone, but this time he was under her authority. Would she have the steely backbone to keep him under control?

Chapter 23

Simza Bihari

Saturday - December 31, 2112

"Thank you for coming," A woman in a long shaysilk dress with butterfly sleeves said as she greeted Jason and me at the entrance to the huge church, but it wasn't Sunday morning.

"We are very thankful that you were able to contact and gather all the clergy so fast," I said and shook her hand with eager appreciation. "I'm sure those of the Black Robes would have been busy with their congregations. This evening is New Year's Eve, and I hope we haven't kept anyone from their celebration."

She leaned in closer and whispered, "There is a rumor that you have been followed."

"By whom?"

"A representative of the Blue Guard and her enforcer."

Shaken, I questioned, "What will we do? How had they known where to look for us?"

"They may have heard about the gathering of the Black Robes," Rev. Grace Small suggested. "It will be important for you to be able to speak but not recognized. Come with me. I have something for you to change into, a costume of sorts." She led Jason and me quickly into a small room beside the chancel. It had built-in closets all along the eastern wall. She opened one of the many doors and withdrew a garment. "Here you are," she said as she handed me a hanger with an interesting dress on it.

I took it and inspected the design. "Grace, this is something I've never seen before."

"I would think not. This is a Roma transformational dress."

"Gypsy?"

"You know of the Romani?"

"The traveling costume Rebecca Spires gave me was Romani but this looks nothing like that one, well maybe the lines are similar," I noticed as I held the outfit in my hands. The skirt was very full and flowed like a ballet costume. It had a high collared and long, tight sleeves.

"The clergy will be ready for us in a minute." She turned to Jason. "Doctor, I have a vestment for you. Hope you don't mind being a spiritual leader for a little while."

"I can think of worst jobs to do," he laughed as he put his right arm through the sleeve.

"You look very reverent, Sir," I teased. I looked at the skirt and top Grace had given me. "Turn your back, Jason. I think I'd better step out of what I am wearing." I unfastened the bright skirt and stepped out of it, then slipped into the long black silky matching skirt to the black, jeweled blouse. The top had a small capped hood attached.

"Now Christy, I want you to have an open mind." Pastor Small was cautious with her choice of words and I wondered why. "This veil is worn with the mourning clothes because if the widow goes out and doesn't wear it, it is said she will be shunned for up to a year as a provocative woman." She held the veil out for me. "Do you want to affix it yourself or shall I?"

"Please, I would appreciate your help."

"Two little buttons are on the hood," she said as she walked around and placed it on my head. "There they are." She draped the shimmering, sheer veil over my face below my eyes and let it drop to below my chin. Gypsy beads accented the hood and dangled along the bottom of the band below my mouth.

"Christy," Jason started to say then pulled back as he glanced over at Grace.

Rev. Small smiled softly. "I will leave you two alone for a moment. I know what danger you're in. I can only tell you that God will be with you. Perhaps you will want to decide if you are going to go through with this meeting. If you want to continue, we need to begin."

Jason smiled and waited for Grace to leave. "Christy, before we go out there, I want you to know that you are beautiful beyond words. The safe physician in me says we should stop this dangerous mission and slip back into Capitol City in the dark. We can resume our lives just as they were when we left—"

"No Jason, we left a life in which my grandparents would be exterminated soon." I looked at him, searching for the meaning under his words. I couldn't believe I was hearing what he was saying.

He placed his finger over my mouth and smiled. "I know. But, I hadn't finished. I started to say, that I know we cannot walk away from this. We ... you are called to such a time as this to follow the leading of the Lord and let our people live. And—"

"Oh Jason," I fell into his arms.

"And ... I want you to know how much I love you. I love you, My Sweet Lady." He held me close and I could feel the beating of his heart.

"Thank you all for coming." I heard Grace speak into the voice enhancer in the huge auditorium style sanctuary. "I am thankful to God that you were all able to make travel arrangements on such short notice. The church where Fanny Adams preached is open to everyone."

"We had better get out there," I said as we hurried out the door that led to the side entrance of the chancel. I slipped inside and slid onto one of the two large pulpit chairs. Jason followed.

Grace turned and gestured to me with a sweep of her hand. "I will turn the pulpit over to Mrs. Simza Bihari. She is a Romani and a real joy to us all. Like Pastor Adams taught us, 'Listen with your heart and the heart of God will draw near.'"

The gathered people of the cloth applauded me as I rose and came to the lectern. I would speak, but, what if someone from the Central Zone was present? Would they recognize me?

"Thank you so much," I said with a feigned raspy voice. "I hope you will all be able to hear me. I apologize for my laryngitis."

People smiled and nodded in understanding. I watched as they settled back in their seats.

"I am here this evening to present a great need—a need that affects the entire country. As you know, some zones do not obey the Length of Days Law, just as you do not here in the Western Zone. There is at least one sector that does."

A murmur rose up in the crowd. I heard whispers of, "What? How can it be?" One of the clergy jumped to his feet in protest. "That despicable law was overturned years ago."

"No, Sir," I corrected hoarsely. "It was never abolished. The people of the Western Zone simply did not obey it. But, our brothers and sisters in the other zones still must live under that evil law."

"All laws are to be obeyed, are they not?" a woman stood up in the back and spoke out critically. "Rev. Julius said that we must obey all laws. Are you saying he was wrong? His teachings are truth," she stated emphatically. "Do you know how dangerous it is to speak against The One?"

"Yes, Ma'am, I understand. We are not denouncing Julius's teachings. We are bringing facts into the light about an evil that is still enforced in other sectors. You in the West have been much more compassionate and faithful to the teachings of love, and did away with that law. Laws are intended to protect the people," I said as I tried to maintain my masquerade of one who could barely speak. It was harder now as I experienced gripping fear. I recognized the philosophy of the woman even though we had never met. She was one who belonged to those who believe that they have captured the entire mind of God. Only they know the truth. I couldn't show fear. Fear would have undone me.

"Our laws were changed about one-hundred years ago," I explained. "They no longer reflected the protections that citizens benefited from for so long. We, as a people, are responsible for re-writing laws that are detrimental to the citizens."

Rev. Small came to the lectern and leaned into the enhancer, "Thank you for the question. Those of us who have been clergy for many years know that this body has discussed this law over and over and tried to determine what we could do to over-throw it. We had agreed it needed abolishing, but we didn't know how. Mrs. Bihari has come to me with a solution."

"Will Mrs. Bihari remove her veil? I believe we could hear her better," a stranger in the back asked.

"I beg your pardon, Miss . . .?"

"Boone, Chalky Boone. I'm not from here in town."

"I would think not," Grace gasped. "If you were from anywhere in the Western Zone, you would know that a Romani widow woman must hide her face in respect for the death of her husband. If she doesn't, a year of shunning would be her fate. I know you wouldn't want that to happen to Mrs. Bihari. You may sit down and listen, or you may leave. You can make an appointment with my assistant for some time in the next few days. I will be happy to talk with you about the matter at that time."

The woman sat down beside a tall muscular man who seemed foreign to a house of worship. He hadn't removed his hat and his expression was taut and angry. I choked up inside. If these two were from Capitol City, the Central Zone, they would indeed have found the building and its sacred enhancements offensive. They had banned all religious expression and experience a hundred years ago in the Central Zone. But, I knew my silence was not possible. Hadn't Silas risked his life by revealing the despicable furnaces under Howard Mountain? I looked Boone in the eyes, squared my shoulders and began.

"We are here to start the process of liberating all of our people from extermination in the furnaces that have burned for one-hundred years. Their flames have never gone out."

I scanned the faces of the good people in front of me. I avoided making eye contact with Boone and her companion. "You, here in the Western Zone, have not adhered to that law, but it is still enforced in the Central Zone, the Mid-western and the Eastern Zones. I'm here to ask you to inform the people of your congregations of a petition we are circulating. We are gathering life-saving signatures." I watched the expressions on the people's faces. They were intent, but they nodded and followed my plea.

"With the proper number of signatures, this petition will permit a Citizen's Referendum to be placed on the ballot at the next election."

"What is a referendum?" One of the clergy in the front of the room asked.

I was glad for the question. I knew they were processing my message. "A Referendum is like a Congressional Bill, but in this case, citizens by-pass Congress and write the bill themselves."

The people of the cloth were following every word. "After your people have signed the document," I continued, "perhaps they will join us. They can canvass their neighborhoods for anyone who may not have been in church or who aren't church goers. We want to make sure we don't miss even a handful of adults. Our efforts are vital to the lives of everyone."

"I cannot believe you people would undermine the laws of our country," Boone snapped.

"We decide what is best for us, Miss," a man mid-way back snapped back at Boone.

"I thought all of you pray and ask your God to tell you what is best," the Blue Guard woman mocked.

"Many do. God has revealed Himself to some of us," the man smiled arrogantly. "Jesus said only a few will be saved. I am one, but

I'm sorry to say, you are not." He folded his arms and sat back, content with his self-serving beliefs.

"You are defaming the body of Christ," another clergyman shouted and pointed his finger back at the self-proclaimed righteous one.

"I am sure these would be good discussions for another time," I said as I felt my hands tremble. "For today's gathering, we need to stick to the topic of the Length of Days law. I'm afraid I won't have a voice left very quickly." I had to change the topic without raising suspicion. I feared that panic would overtake me like the waves of the western ocean and totally take me under.

I began again, "The Length of Days law was never part of the founding fathers' plan for a free people. We have received word from the Central Zone that they terminate each person before the time of their natural passing. Each one is assigned a prescribed Length of Days for their lives, depending on their contribution to society."

The people shifted restlessly with anger and repulsion, their faces drawn up in torment and grief. While in the back, the stranger with Boone smiled a crooked smile, crossed his arms and settled in with satisfaction.

I ignored the man who had spoken arrogantly and continued. "We have also been told that in the Central Zone, the people have already gathered signatures. They were collected in secret over time and were enough to fulfill the quota for that sector. They delivered them to President Alexander's home on Christmas Day eve, or Gifting Day as they call it. We now need full petitions from this Zone, as well as the other two, in order to make the referendum happen."

I heard eager responses. "Yes, we can do it." But, there were also murmurs and gossip back and forth about whom does she think she is?

"You ask who I am. I am a woman who has come to speak truth to lies. Will you help our effort?" Most agreed, and those that didn't, listened.

I paused. What I would ask next was risky. I needed people who would be willing to break the law. "Some of your number, or members of your churches, could assist us as we cross the borders into the other zones." I let that reality settle a moment. "You, my friends, are already an enormous body of people who don't have to be convinced of the need for the referendum. You have a reverence for life by virtue of your faith. To make it official ... shortly, Grace will lead you in a vote to record your cooperation in this matter. Time is important. The Central Zone has only a two year moratorium on exterminations. The collection of signatures here in the Western Zone should go fast, since you are a God-loving people. You value life. The citizens of the Central Zone have never heard of God. Still, they gathered the signatures methodically over time. We don't know what to expect in the other two sectors."

"How do you know all of this, Mrs. Bihari?" Boone asked with a firm, angry tone.

"For the safety of those in the Central Zone, I can't reveal that information," I answered and hoped that she would believe me and cease the questions that could unveil my true identity.

"Have you heard of Lady Christiana Applewait," Boone dug deeper.

"Who is she?" I asked, denying my own existence.

"She is a Legacy Citizen from the Central Zone who had started all of this sedition," she insisted angrily. "If you know her whereabouts, you are aiding a fugitive," she shouted.

Some who were present shouted, "Sit down." Others insisted, "Listen to Mrs. Bihari."

I coughed and actually could not speak for a moment. With most of my face covered, I saw a movement from the corner of my eye and assumed that Grace or Jason had come to my rescue. I was stunned when I saw who had been sensitive to my need. It was Raymar Goring.

"Masters," Raymar began and the entire fellowship of pastors let out a unified gasp. His knees visibly buckled and he grabbed the lectern. "Friends," he began again, "I am not worthy to come before this group . . ."

Whispers and uneasiness rose up among those present. Suddenly, a distinguished man with gray hair and beard stood up. "Are you not a Hollow Man?"

"I'm . . ." Raymar fumbled and stumbled with his words.

"Do you not have a brand of 'H' on your forehead, under your hair line?"

Raymar's face distorted in anguish. His mouth quivered as he appeared to be trying desperately to control himself. Then, he turned his face from the crowd and I saw that it was not anger he was trying to suppress. A tear slipped down his cheek. Kasamar started to stand up but Raymar put up his hand.

"Fear does cruel things sometimes," Grace spoke softly as she leaned into the podium, but conviction was in the tone of her voice.

"Yes," Raymar admitted as he slowly lifted the hair from his forehead. "I was branded as an infant. My entire life I believed I was not fully human, that I was an outcast, a man empty of all goodness and positive attributes, a Hollow One. When I was a very young man, I met the most amazing girl. She taught me to read and write and do my numbers. She taught me all I needed to know to be educated, and she filled me with love. Yes ... I was a Hollow Man. When she died, all of that love drained out of me, except for one day each month when love returned." He swallowed hard. "Recently, I met Simza Bihari," he turned and bowed slightly in my direction. "Simza means joy. Just having her eyes meet mine, and knowing she really sees me, has brought joy to my heart. When I was asked to help in this effort, I said, yes!"

"What can you do?" Boone asked with an indignant tone. "You should be dead. Now you claim to have come alive by a glance from a gypsy woman? Please, do not insult me."

Raymar's expression remained calm. His tone was convicting. "Ma'am, pardon me, but you insult yourself. I am alive, because the same people who considered me—and those like me—to be the walking dead, chose not to put us down. They are good people, a misinformed and ill-educated people concerning those in my class, but good in their souls. I will be honored to bring the Hollow People together and invite them to sign our petition."

"Sign the petition?" Several snorted in disbelief. One woman snickered, "They can neither read nor write. Will you have them make an 'X' on the paper?"

The crowd erupted in a combination of giggles and angry protests. I could see they had no tolerance for this man. I looked at Kasamar, but she was just smiling and remained calm. She seemed to be in prayer.

"But they do," Raymar protested. "They read because I taught them. In a cave in a high elevation, where moisture cannot damage the paper, we have a huge library of books I have acquired over many years. I have read every one of them."

"Did you steal them? Where did you get them?" People shouted from all corners of the auditorium.

Kasamar could not hold herself any longer. "Rachel Claudette gave him the books," she said as she stepped forward.

"Rachel Claudette? How does she know this Hollow Man?" some questioned.

Grace moved to the enhancer. "These are all very good questions. I am so glad you are asking them now, rather than sharing your doubts in small groups after the meeting."

I smiled to myself but said nothing out loud. *Where I come from, no one speaks up and certainly doesn't gossip.*

Grace leaned in closer to the podium. "We have invited Raymar to participate in our critical endeavor, because he is a good man, a man of integrity. Despised and rejected, he did not turn his grief on others. Instead, he educated everyone he knew to read and write. Yes, indeed, these folks can write their own name." Grace explained with firm conviction. "He has read many books. Have any of you enjoyed the novels of Robert Gross?"

Robert Gross? I hadn't heard of him. He must have been a novelist in the last one-hundred years. I knew I hadn't read his works. Since there is no exchange of culture between the zones, I couldn't have heard about him. But, most of those present had read the books. Many smiled and nodded. Some whispered among themselves. Kasamar smiled in agreement.

"My dear friends," Grace said, "I would like you to meet the tender and gifted writer, who only comes alive in the pages of his novels, Robert Gross—Raymar Goring." Grace opened her arms to the gentle shadow that had lived among them all along in the pages of the books they read.

Kasamar's face grew fluid and elastic as she tried to control the flood of emotions that threatened to drown her. "Daddy," she whispered.

The people were visibly stunned. They sank back in their seats and their shoulders drooped with emotion. The room grew completely silent.

Raymar leaned into the enhancer and opened his mouth, but nothing came out but the silence of his life. He cleared his throat and began again. "I know you will not call me friend. And, you won't see me when we pass on the streets. But, I want you to know that I have a little less hollowness when I see you laugh with your children or embrace a friend. All I ask of you is the opportunity to serve you, to serve all of us. You need the Hollow Man vote. I can get that for you."

The entire body of clergy rose to their feet. Applause and smiles and cheers burst forth. Some were slow to rise but quickly became infected with the enthusiasm. Raymar Goring was seen.

Chapter 24
Late Saturday Evening

10:00 p.m. - New Year's Eve 2112

Jason and I stayed up late. "Isn't it amazing to walk in the evening on the last day of the year and feel the warmth on your face? The climate of the Western Zone could grow on me," I said as I slipped my hand in his.

Some of our group were planning to stay up well into the night to celebrate the New Year—2113. We had had a long day so Grace Small invited us to stay with her and her husband. Our walk in the garden would be celebration enough. It would be a quiet together time, something we had not had in recent weeks. Although surrounded by others most of the time, it felt like it was just the two of us against the world. We were now alone in a crowded world.

"The backyard garden is beautiful," Jason agreed.

I ran my fingers over the graceful wrought iron poles of the accent lamps that lit the flower clusters and fountain. The iron felt soft and dimpled at the same time. "Just look at that fantastic rock wall around the entire back yard. It looks like it was built out of field stone." The irregularly shaped round rocks varied in tones of rose and beige and held together with mortar. "I feel safer in here than I have felt in days."

"I wish I could have protected you more," he whispered.

"That's your wonderful male strength pushing through," I giggled.

"I'm sorry if I have offended you," he apologized as he came around in front of me and took both of my hands in his. "I have learned you can take care of yourself."

"Offended me? No, Jason. I like your strength. Men are protectors and women are nurturers," I quickly added. "That was amazingly planned. It's not offensive. We were intended to work together, with equal strength in two areas that make a whole."

"What is so sad ... the people of the Central Zone have been drugged out of the very aspects that make them male and female," Jason reminded me.

"Well, I am very happy that you're a true male. I feel safe when I'm with you." I hugged him again.

He whispered, "And I love your leadership and your closeness to the heart of God before you knew his name. If you were President, I would love you and want you to be safe."

I paused and listened again to what I had dismissed as foolishness. We were alone in the garden. I knew we were. But, "I hear sometime ... movement ... over there." I pointed to the far, dark corner of the yard.

We listened together. "I hear it," he whispered so low I nearly didn't hear him. "Stand very still."

That was not possible. I took a step forward and folded myself into his warm arms. I strained to hear what had to be there ... but what?

My mind raced into all the dark corners of fear I had experienced over the last few weeks. Would we ever be safe again?

Then I saw them ... two shinning eyes stared at us from the bushes in the corner of the walled garden. Who was there? He must have known I saw him. We were locked—eye to eye. But, there was something wrong. The eyes were a frightening yellow. I thought of the evil beings in some of the old thriller books I had read to take my mind off my master's thesis. I frightened myself there in the lonely back room of the old library, but the books were too exciting to put down. There in the garden, my heart pounded as I gripped Jason even harder.

"I see it too," he whispered in my ear, so close I felt his warm breath on my cheek. "Stand very still. Maybe it will go away."

"What is it?" I couldn't see anything but the eyes.

Slowly, two rhythmic upper shoulder blades shifted and stalked gracefully, menacingly out of the darkness. His full mane blew gently as he moved, step by step closer to us. Suddenly, he threw his head back and roared in a deep tone of dominance. I squeezed my eyes closed and prayed for deliverance. The beautiful rock wall that bordered the entire garden also made it totally closed, sealing us in with the beast.

The warm breeze of the evening stirred the faint aroma of blossoms into the night air and mixed with the musky scent of the wild animal. Why did I smell flowers when I was clearly in immediate danger? Then I caught a strong whiff of petals again and let the aroma relax my body and sooth my mind. A warm wash of peace flowed over me.

In front of us, a lion lay down with his paws stretched out in front of him and roared again a fierce sound—loud and blood curdling. Then ... there was an explosion and the lion dropped his head on the ground. I gasped. Even the sound of my own frightened voice terrified me.

Suddenly the back door squeaked and I caught a glimpse of Grace just as she was lowering the rifle from her shoulder. "Sorry," she said as she walked out and inspected the cat.

"You all right?" Alfred called from the house as he came out into the garden. "What about you?" he asked Jason and me. "You two okay?" He looked down at the lion, spread out on the manicured back lawn. "Another one of those wild beasts the do-gooders set free."

"Is he dead?" I asked as I inched closer to the huge animal.

"No. I got him with a tranquillizer dart," Grace said.

"I called the wild game patrol as I grabbed the rifle," Grace stated matter-of-factly. "They'll be here in a few minutes."

"Wild game patrol?" I asked. My voice was still shaking from the experience of coming eye-to-eye with the beast king.

"The zone had to expand their animal control department to cover these wild animals that are still loose."

I walked nearer and bent toward the cat. "Can I touch him?"

"He'll be out for a while. Sure, if you want to," Alfred said.

I reached out my hand cautiously and touched his coarse mane. He felt differently than I thought he would. I expected him to feel like my soft little kitten at home and laughed to myself.

"And the lion will lie down with the lamb," Grace recited and walked back into the house.

Chapter 25
Sunday across the Western Zone

Sunday - January 1, 2113

At 7 a.m. the next morning, I woke up in one of Small's guest rooms. It was Sunday morning and the church service would start in two hours. I wondered if Jason was up yet. I got up and went into the adjoining bath, took off the night shirt Grace had loaned me and turned on the water in the wet area. The water felt soothing and awakening.

Grace had told us what to expect during the service. Since we didn't know if Chalky Boone and the animal that was with her were still in town, we all thought I had better go as Simza Bihari. The veil would provide a sort of mask. Jason would have to reprise his role as the good pastor.

In the long black costume, I left the room with the veil in my hand. As I walked down the steps, I liked the swirl of silk on my legs. There were stripes of satin ribbon running through it and it felt elegantly modest.

"You look beautiful as always," Jason whispered as we walked down the stairs together. He winked and put his arm around my waist as we entered the kitchen.

"Thank you, Reverend. Make sure your motives are pure," I laughed. Then I blushed when I saw Grace smile broadly.

"Don't mind me, you two. We can always use more love around here." She watched us for a moment then added, "Since my son Charlie died last year, there hasn't been nearly enough love on display."

"I see love every time you smile at fellow clergy and those around you," I assured her. "I see love when you interact with Alfred," I added. Grace smiled.

• • •

"We gather this day as we do every Sunday, to worship the Lord. Our sermon, however, will be different than most," Pastor Small began. "We will be linking all congregations in the Western Zone, a connection that has not been used in over fifty years, since the time of the Evangelical Awakening. This time, my friends, we are embarking on a great crusade. Our campaign will be to finally over-throw the despicable Length of Days law." She paused and addressed a man in the front row. "Sam."

Sam rose quickly and pushed a button that brought down an old-style giant screen used at sporting events and huge gatherings. It seemed appropriate in the arena turned church. I had seen pictures of Jumbotrons like this in the magazines I had found in the library. He gave her a hand-held-distance-unit and clicked it on.

Rev. Small pointed the HHD unit at the screen and a series of nine smaller screens appeared—three across and three down. "Good Sabbath to all the millions of you who are connected this morning." She tapped the HHD surface again and hundreds of smaller screens flashed in front of us, one after another in clusters of twelve. "It has been many years since this system has been used, and we thank the wise ones before us who kept it in working order. And now, we are using it for a great mission for humanity's sake, for the glory of God and our reverence for Life itself." Grace faced the screen and turned to acknowledge those in her own congregation. "The Length of Days law is still enforced in the Central Zone, and we believe it is in place in the Mid-Eastern and Eastern Zones as well."

"Pardon me," a voice came over the 'tron. Immediately, the screen filled with the image of a man of ancient far-eastern linage. "I do not mean to interrupt, but I must."

"No, Sir. That is why we are using this form of communication this morning, and not just sending out a message. Please continue and God bless you, my Brother."

"I am sorry, but I find it hard to believe that this evil law could still be enforced," he continued.

"I have some visitors here who may be able to detail our grave need." Grace motioned to me as I sat in the front row. "Friends, I would like you to meet Mrs. Simza Bihari."

I was worried that the woman named Boone and the man with her might be in the audience. Still, I believed that God had called me to this cause, and he would give me the words and protection. I had worn the veil so my appearance was covered.

"Good morning to all of you in every sector of this zone. I am here with praises for your love of one another, the grandparents whom you cherish, the infirmed, the young ... you value them all and hold life in reverence."

There was an uneasy stir as Raymar and Kasamar entered through the side door and took seats on the front row. The people seemed to recognize Raymar but how could they? Then I looked at the screen with Raymar's picture displayed in an image ten feet tall. The brand on his forehead was seen when his hair blew back slightly as he walked.

"I'm glad you were able to get here," I said to the father and his daughter. Then to the people assembled there I added, "Please welcome our dear friends from the C-I Board who have just arrived." I put my hands together to honor their presence.

The congregation relaxed, so I began again. "I have information from a Judge in the Central Zone, who attests to the validity of our position. I have a copy of the stay that Judge Brunner signed on December 25 that put a ban on exterminations for two years. In that length of time, we—you and I—will spread out across this country and get the signatures of all of our citizens. A signature on the petition means that you agree that a referendum should be placed on the voting ballot at the next election." I paused and let the daring plan catch up to them. "A Referendum is a citizens' bill that does not originate in congress and yet it becomes a law." Some of the people nodded and others stirred uncomfortably. Did these people understand the gravity of our situation?

I looked into the eyes of those gathered there and began again. "An underground group in the Central Zone has already secured enough signatures that the referendum will be placed on the ballot in that zone, so Judge Brunner has ordered the stay. We have two years, friends, to accomplish this sacred mission. We must secure the signatures of as many citizens in this whole country as possible."

"North California here," a man said and his image filled the screen. "I don't want to appear hateful, but ... why is that Hollow Man present?" Whispers spread around the room and the 'tron seemed to buzz with the chorus of it.

"Thank you for asking. I was just going to introduce the man, Raymar Goring." I stood back and motioned for Raymar to stand. "Thank you, Mr. Goring. Please be seated. Raymar Goring has a Hollow Man brand, I agree. Since we don't see the invisible ones among us, none of us knew that he is truly a self-educated man. And, not only has he read thousands of books himself, he has also taught his friends to read. And ... we need him. You know him as the gifted novelist, Robert Gross."

This time the crowd was louder than before. I was worried they might become out of control, but I had to stay focused. Did they understand what I had just said? Would the people reject him and turn on me as well? Would the Boone woman rise up with borrowed authority and discover my identity? I said nothing about the restless outburst. I merely raised my arms and lifted my eyes to the Lord. Stillness fell over the arena that surprised me and peace filled the room and filtered into my own heart.

I leaned in toward the enhancer. My voice was barely a whispered. "We need Raymar Goring. Believe me; we need him because he can get the Hollow Man signatures and … because there is no one with more drive, more dedication and more belief in himself … for one whom absolutely no one has ever believed in … than Raymar Goring." Raymar sat down with his back straight and his gaze fixed on the proceedings.

I continued my address and focused on the Jumbotron. "We are embarking on a great crusade that will decide if we, as a people with freedom as our heritage, will have the courage to stand up for freedom in our time. We need every one of you to sign the petition, copies of which were carried by currier to your senior clergy late last night, and contact everyone who is not in your sanctuary this morning, members, family, friends, and non-believers. Raymar will enlist a group of his friends to make sure every name is on a petition." I pointed to a stack of petition sheets that we had placed on a pedestal.

"This next part is up to those of you with the strength and determination of our founding patriots, to chart a new course. We need a team that is willing to cross forbidden borders with us, find volunteers in the Mid-Western and Eastern Zones who will blanket their sectors with petitions and get signatures from every living person." The people in the room, and those in the congregations seen on the 'tron, stirred with excitement. "I know that contact outside the area has been completely impossible, but the impossible is possible with God."

I lifted my hands and voice to draw on the Holy Spirit I felt in the room. "I truly believe that many of you have connections outside of the West that you have held close to your heart. I don't know how you have communicated with them and it doesn't matter. But, those connections are what you are going to need to make this work. Be brave." The people clapped with a newly ignited energy.

"Today is the start of a new year. We begin again! Be steadfast. Take courage. You have lived your whole lives for this moment. The time is now! This is the start of a fresh celebration of Life in our country and you are charged with the blessed task of making it happen!"

Except for the sound of tears, there was silence. From the Jumbotron came a sound, a song, from one person in a congregation hundreds of miles away and beamed into the arena like a whisper of the heart. "I have decided to follow Jesus. I have decided to follow Jesus. I have decided to follow Jesus, no turning back, no turning back."[2]

Like a growing, advancing army, the words started coming from each congregation as they joined in the hymn of commitment. "No turning back. No turning back."

**Chapter 26
The Arrival**

Monday Morning - January 2, 2113

The clatter and banging at the front door awakened Grace long before she had planned. In fact, after celebrating the new life the Referendum would bring with many of the pastors, their families and the visitors from far off who had been connected at the heart on the Jumbotron the day before, she had not planned to wake up at any particular time at all. She threw on a cover-up and hurried down the steps.

"What is it?" she barked as she jerked the door open.

"We are looking for citizens of the Central Zone who we believe have crossed the border," Chalky Boone snapped. Her accompanying thug took a step forward.

"Now you just stop right there," Grace ordered and held the door with her right hand and the door jamb with the other, so they would have to go through her to get into the house. "You're far from home Mister ... Ma'am. This is not the Central Zone. You cannot boot-kick your way around here. You got that?" She glared at the pair.

"I am sure you don't want to withhold information concerning a fugitive, Reverend," Boone barked.

"If you know anything, you better tell us." Daniel Washington's gravelly voice sounded like it had rocks in it.

"You don't talk much, do you?" Grace said as she maintained her firm stance. "You just like to let your muscle speak for you."

"That's why I'm valuable to the force," he smirked. "Lieutenant Boone asked you a question. You're here alone aren't you?" Washington grabbed Grace's arm and pulled her into the western winter morning.

"Officer!" The Lieutenant barked. "Stand down!"

"You get out of this zone! You have no authority here. You aren't permitted to cross the border either," Grace ordered.

"We have valid travel papers," Boone protested.

"Perhaps, I've never seen travel papers since no one can cross the border. I would have nothing to compare them to for authenticity."

"I'll ask you one more time. Are you hiding Christina Applewait?"

"No one is here but me and my husband."

She didn't lie. She wouldn't have. The travelers had stayed the night at Rachel Claudette's house. For the next week and a half, there would be long meetings every day with the C-I Board and all the volunteers that would be coming and going in preparation for the mission that lie ahead. Grace had told the truth. Christiana was not there.

Chapter 27
The Caravan

5:00 a.m. - Friday - January 13, 2113

"Maybe all of our efforts will finally tear down these borders. It would be a miracle if you and I could travel by car through this forest and stop as often as we would want." Jason took my hand and let me know we were together on this quest for life.

We were taking a longer, but safer route into the Mid-West Zone. Several of Rachel's friends on the C-I Board had arranged for us to travel north along US 101, the Redwood Highway. It picked up its name at the Golden Gate Bridge and ran for 350 miles along the northern part of California. Our bus caravan wound through the virgin, old-growth coastal redwood trees that the state had been wise enough to preserve. I sat back in the lead bus and watched the passing forest. I couldn't nap.

"Jason, just look at those trees. They are marvelous!"

Then, I felt an incline. "We're climbing," I said as we approached a steep stretch between San Luis Obispo and Atascadero called the Cuesta Grade. "Look at the mountains and the view into the valley below. They're breath-taking."

Everything outside of Capitol City amazed me. I wanted to see every bird, every plant ... all that spread out before us. My eyes drank in every sight.

As we descended from the higher altitude we came into the wide agricultural bottomlands of Salinas Valley. I remembered from my books in the library, this was the area known as America's Salad Bowl. The winters are mild in the area. I watched the sun glance off the rows of mounded dirt, evidence of the last crop of lettuce and other vegetables that had been in the field.

"I wonder what all of this looks like when green is everywhere and shoots push up through the soil?" I asked.

"It is amazing," Raymar offered from the seat behind us. "I've been in this area many times during harvest time."

"You worked in these fields, Raymar?" I asked.

"When someone would hire me."

"Was it hard to find work?" Jason wondered out loud.

"Like the old Romani, people think we are restless and can never stay in one place. We move because the authorities tell us to move on, after we have put in only a day or two of work," he explained. His eyes searched the fields beyond the bus windows, like he was looking for answers to questions that never made any sense to him.

"I'm sorry all that has happened to you, Raymar," I whispered.

"None of us can do anything about the past except learn from it. Maybe people will see our work for the lives of others with this petition campaign and learn to accept us." He watched out the window then added. "We're nearing our stop. Kasamar and I will get off and begin recruiting volunteers here in the northern part of the state."

I turned around and leaned over the back of the seat. "I'm privileged to have met you, Raymar Goring–or Robert Gross. Which do you prefer?"

"I am a child of God. My name isn't important. No one saw me when I was Raymar Goring. Then they loved me when I was Robert Gross, but they still didn't see me."

"I see you, Raymar. You are both, the man—Raymar and the novelist—Robert. I think people will learn to know you as Raymar Goring, the selfless, brave volunteer who, even though a ghost among men worked for the betterment of everyone. Robert Gross is the name you share your thoughts with. Now, we see you both."

Tears ran down his cheeks, and he brushed them away with the back of his hand. "You can see me?" he asked with a voice that cracked under the heavy weight of emotion.

When they stood up to leave, I hurried to my feet and hugged him and his lovely daughter. Jason shook their hands. The two got off in a little town in northern California and waved. I watched them through the back window and Raymar maintained eye contact with me for as long as he could see me. It was as if, once seen, he didn't want to break the connection.

We continued north where the highway again hugged the coast line. "Look, Honey," Jason nudged my shoulder.

I had tried to stay awake and not miss anything but everything had happened so fast. Even when we had time to rest, I didn't feel like I was refreshed. Each day I grew wearier. As we drew near the beautiful placid ocean, Jason awakened me.

"Oh, it is amazing!" I gasped. "We have nothing like this in Capitol City."

"We have nothing like this in the entire Central Zone," Jason laughed and patted my leg.

We traveled up the western coast throughout the night for sixteen hours and crossed into Canada to the north of Washington State. In Vancouver we turned east. Thanks to the logistics coordination of Herman Lincoln, we crossed the provinces of British Columbia, Calgary and Saskatchewan with no problem. We were all so tired. Luckily, the darkness of the night prohibited site-seeing.

"You are free to sleep now, my Lady," Jason smiled as he pulled a blanket up around my shoulder.

"I know you would stay awake with the force of sheer willpower if the sun were shining. We can thank the good Lord for the blessing of night."

"All right," I agreed as my eyelids grew heavy. "I surrender to the night."

Chapter 28
Border – Midwestern Zone

9 p.m. - January 15, 2113

"Winnipeg," Jason's spoke mechanically, apparently tired from sitting. It was 7 p.m.

We watched as the driver turned south along route twelve out of Winnipeg. "About two more hours," Gray Fox announced quietly for those not sleeping.

I know I drifted off again. I awakened about 9 p.m. when Gray Fox spoke firmly. "We're here."

We quickly got to our feet and made our way to the exit, tapping each volunteer on the shoulder as we passed to make sure they were awake and ready to get off. We stepped off the bus, out of sight of the border, and waited for a nod from Gray Fox to cross from Canada into Minnesota. It was the long way back to the United Zones, but the safest. Canada was still a free country and didn't care who traveled from Province to Province. I pulled my coat tightly around me to ward off the Canadian winter wind.

We were a large party for a stealth operation. One-hundred of us would approach the border. Like Moses leading the Israelites out of Egypt, it was hard to hide. Little Feather said hiding out in the open was our only recourse.

When we had all gathered, the signal came. We moved silently on foot from the buses through a snowy field. Gray Fox put his finger to his lips and withdrew farther into the shadows of the night. We were just inside the Canadian border, where, years before, the runway of the Piney/Pinecreek Border Airport was extended north of the U.S. Midwestern Zone and into Canada at the 49th parallel. With his hand raised, Gray Fox gave a signal for all of us to get down on the frozen ground. I looked at Jason for reassurance. When he smiled, I followed him down.

The freezing winter was thick beneath us. My toes quickly grew numb as I inched across the ground. We were flat on our stomachs on the runway of the old Border Airport, which a century ago had been one of only three Canada/US border airports. Now, with the whole country sealed off from the outside and from within, the airport lay abandoned. The runway, which had been made smooth with tire rubber from thousands of flights, had become overgrown with grass and weeds until the concrete was completely buried, like an artifact from a long forgotten civilization, waiting for an archeologist to begin an excavation.

The tall spikey ice-covered grasses camouflaged us there on our bellies. Like frozen stalagmites, the icy blades of grass and weeds poked and gouged at my chest and stomach. I hoped that my coat wouldn't tear and let the cold invade and penetrate to my bones.

The border closed decades ago, and it was dark—the ground and runway lights torn out and sold on the black market according to the C-I people. I reached out and searched for Jason's hand as panic began to well up within me. Although concealed in the dark, I was freezing cold and afraid of what else hid in the black night.

When my hand met Jason's, he held it tightly, soothing my anxious heart. Gray Fox gave another signal—he cracked one finger knuckle and the entire field of prone bodies inched forward another eighteen inches. The journey south to the border took a long time. My elbows and shoulders ached from the strain and the penetrating cold. I was ill prepared for the icy north. Rachel had given us other clothing: denim pants, turtle neck sweaters, jackets with hoods and gloves, but I was cold. My blood still ran with the promise of warmer weather.

I was surprised there appeared to be no guards patrolling the border. Had all the rumors about the danger at the borders been lies or were we too far away to see the detail in the night? Jason grabbed my hand again and nodded at something in front of us. We were within yards of our goal. Luckily, we had neared the border at an old checkpoint.

A laser with a highly amplified beam of radiation protected the boundary itself. They sent the laser beam by capturing it at frequent intervals and sending it along. A black and yellow trefoil sign, displayed on the side of the guard post, caught my breath. There were armed guards present inside the protection of the border house. As we neared, I could see them through the windows of the large building. The special glass allowed the officers to see out but it was only after we were close that we were able to see in.

When the guards seemed distracted by jabbing and joking inside, Gray Fox turned his back on us. At first, I was terrified. Was he saying we were on our own? Then Little Feather stood, turned ninety degrees and dropped again to the grass-covered runway. We were turning.

We inched along the flat open space and into a large wooded area. No one spoke a word. When Gray Fox gave the order to stand my body felt heavy and sluggish. I ached all over, except the places that remained numb.

Signaled to move, we followed into the woods in the footsteps of the one in front of us. If anyone were to follow, our group would appear to be smaller. We made sure no one strayed or got lost. When no light shone in any direction and darkness completely enveloped us, we knew we were deep enough into the trees. Gray Fox spoke.

"We have arrived at the northern boundary of the United Zones, or United States. The laser beam stretches from the west coast to the Atlantic Ocean. If you break the beam, two things will happen. You will die immediately, and you will alert the armed guards. If our information is correct, there will be three parallel beams. We will have to crawl under, or step over the deadly laser. If anyone believes they can't make it, don't try."

"Gray Fox," Jason began as he seemed to be digging a memory out of his past. "Before the enforcement of the Length of Days law, surgeons had used lasers to excise tumors from the human body. After several major operating accidents, they developed a way of protecting themselves if they were to receive a quick touch. They washed thoroughly. So, I'm thinking, if we roll in the ice until our bodies have warmed the snow, our clothes may be wet enough to protect us from the deadly energy. The huge consequence of soaking in the snow will be, of course, the possibility of slipping into hypothermia. It can happen very quickly. Once we are across, we will have to get inside, out of the night air immediately."

Gray Fox studied Jason very carefully then smiled. "You're the doc. How fast will the frozen death set in?"

"You'll have twenty to thirty minutes from the time you are soaked. That means the lead people cannot wait for the ones behind them. They will have to get to shelter immediately," Jason warned.

"We have to stay together," Little Feather protested.

"Then you will lose the front half of the group who stay behind to wait for the rest. That is for certain," Jason stated flatly.

Gray Fox paced for a moment. "Is there another way?"

"I don't know of any," Jason said.

"Little Feather, you lead the group straight to Musselman's barn. The rest of us will follow."

"We can do it," I reassured Little Feather. "How far is the barn?"

"It is just on the other side of the boundary, about a quarter mile," she answered.

"And, how long will it take to walk it, in this snow with the weight of our soaked heavy clothing?"

"About fifteen minutes, but remember, we will all be freezing wet and may enter a state of shock." Little Feather looked questioningly at Gray Fox.

"We must do it," Gray Fox pronounced, then turned to the group. "Friends, we are going to roll in the snow to get wet, a very dangerous thing to do in the frigid weather. But, the laser beams that could kill us will not be lethal through the layer of water. Wet your face or cover it with a scarf and soak that in the ice and snow. Once on the other side, you will have only about twenty minutes to get to the barn on the Musselman farm. We will go in waves so no one is waiting to move."

I looked at the wonderful volunteers who had trusted us this far. Now we were asking them to dance with the angel of death and question nothing. No one protested. Crouched in a cluster of trees very near the line, we waited our turn. We were all depending on Jason's knowledge and medical expertise.

"The first twenty-five of you need to step forward and roll in the snow. Try to get as wet as possible, as quickly as you can. Then you will run across the border and follow Little Feather to a farm with a large barn. Run because your life depends on it." Jason grabbed my waist and drew me to him in front of everyone. There were no public displays of affection in the Central Zone.

I felt the warmth of his breath as he whispered in my ear. "I love you Christy. You don't have to do this."

"And I love you too, Jason, but ... I do have to do this. Our people are being exterminated like insects that have infested the foundation."

"I know, Sweetheart. That's why I love you." He tipped my chin up and kissed me, while all the strangers and new friends looked on. "I want you to go in the first wave. You will be strong willed, a strong runner and an inspiration for others."

"All right." I knew he was right. If I had traveled from a different zone to lead a crusade for our people, I had better be willing to take the first step.

Gray Fox pointed across the border to a dark spot down the road. "There, in the darkest spot on the right, is a large old farm house and a gigantic barn. It is a milk farm so animals will be present and there will be hay. When you get there, crawl under the hay like a feather bed. Warm yourselves as quickly as possible."

I stood for a moment and stared at the ice crusted snow. Images of Mama and Daddy came into my mind. I wondered if I would ever see them again. Then the faces of Grand-mère and Grand-père flooded my thoughts. If I quit now, they would be dead in two years–guaranteed. They had already exceeded their Length of Days.

I could stall no longer. Taking a deep breath, I dropped to the ground, rolled and broke through the thin ice crust and felt the snow grow damp. The icy cold penetrated my jacket until I could begin to feel the pain of cold on my skin. I jumped up and ran for the border line and tried to crouch down into a ball. Three laser beams could stop us. Could I make myself low enough that only two of the beams would hit me?

I felt nothing as we darted across the border. Not knowing what to expect, I didn't hear or experience a zap or any of the other grave consequences my mind had imagined. Perhaps I thought lightening would surge through my body.

"Run!" I heard Jason in a loud whisper.

Dear Lord, give us speed, I prayed. Panic almost overtook me. *I will trust you, Lord.* I soon discovered, the laser wasn't the danger, the cure was. I ran as hard as I could and had less than twenty minutes to get to safety.

The clump of trees was just ahead but doubt began to take over my will to press on. *I'll never make it.* From behind I felt a gentle push as Little Feather nudged me in the direction of the old barn. She was out running me, and I knew what that meant. I wasn't going fast enough. Will I make it?

My legs felt heavy and stiff and the snow that clung to my boots froze my feet. I had been panting until my breath became so shallow each gulp of air was more painful than the last. I ran through the deep snow and now my lungs couldn't take in any more icy air. But the barn was still several yards ahead of me.

Please, Father, give me strength; give me endurance. You are a new friend, but I trust you. Then my thoughts became fuzzy and my vision blurred. It felt like my eyes had glazed over with ice. Then I couldn't think more. I had to stop and sleep. All I wanted to do was close my eyes. What could be the harm in that?

Suddenly, a hand reached out through the opening of a building that smelled wonderful, an aroma I had never experienced before. A large rotund man had grabbed my arm and was pulling me into the warmth and sweet perfume. I didn't care who he was. My legs went limp and every muscle in my body collapsed into the man's arms.

Voices all around me shouted. "Bring her in quickly," one said.

"Put her down over here," someone ordered. "I'll blanket her in the hay. Sophie, run to fetch a feather quilt," she barked with authority, but there was music in her voice. She sounded sure and confident.

The voices rolled and tumbled all around me like the waves of the sea I had seen for the first time at Rachel's house. It was so warm there in the sand by the ocean. Visions of the day Jason and I walked along the beach came into my mind. We had kicked and played in the sand while the frothy tide flowed across our toes. Was I dreaming or remembering? It felt like I was outside my body, experiencing the warm water but knowing it wasn't real. I couldn't hear the voices any more, only the sweet distant deep, rich hum of Jason's laughter and gentle teasing.

"Come on, Christy, I'll race you to that rock up ahead," he challenged.

"I don't want to run, Jason. Suddenly, I feel so tired. I can hardly lift my legs."

"You want to sit and rest for a while?"

"Yes, but I'm supposed to keep moving. It would be easier to lie down and sleep forever."

"Let's walk a little farther, Sweetheart," he said.

"Look, Jason, even in the sunshine there seems to be a bright light ahead. It's more beautiful than anything I have ever seen. It's warm in there. I know it is," I said in a dream, or something I didn't understand.

"Stay here, Christy. The tickle of the ocean around our ankles is wonderful. It's not time to go. The light is pretty, but it's not for you yet. Please, Honey, stay ... stay ... stay with me, Christy," he seemed to plead.

"Stay with me, Christy," Jason was yelling when I opened my eyes. At first everything was blurry but then I felt his dear face. "There you are," he said as he collapsed beside me. His body was shaking with chills.

"Doctor," the lady in my dreams said. But it was not a dream anymore. She was wrapping a thick downy comforter around Jason's shoulders. "You have to stay warm too you know."

"Jason, are you all right? Were you the last one? Did everyone make it across the line? Have we all arrived in the Midwestern Zone?" Questions flooded my mind.

"I'm fine, Honey. And the answer is yes to all of the rest."

"And now . . ." I paused and looked around, "where are we? I'm not familiar with this building. What is this place?" I asked.

"You're in my old barn, Ma'am. Built in 1897. It's been standing for more than two-hundred years. You know why?"

I had heard his voice before. The big man in the overalls and flannel shirt didn't wait for an answer. "It's 'cause this here farm has been in my family for longer than that, and we take care of our own things. Not like some of those other farmers who are afraid to touch anything that ain't theirs. Almost all of the family farms are gone now. All owned by the government, they are. You know how we kept ours?" Again he plowed on. "'Cause we kept low. We didn't brag or boast. We kept our mouths shut."

"Silence again," I sighed.

"What say?"

"We are in the Age of Silence, Mr. ..."

"Musselman, Ma'am, Edward Musselman. Glad to meet you. What did you say about silence?" The man slapped me on the side of my arm with the firm hand of someone who worked hard every day and enjoyed the work he did.

"We are in the Age of Silence, Mr. Musselman. But someone in the Central Zone was brave enough to break the silence and we're here to bring a voice to everyone," I explained.

"You must be Lady Christina Applewait. We've been waiting for you for days," he smiled a broad smile. "Maud," he called out, "come over here and meet Lady Applewait. 'Course no one around here has lady or gentleman as a moniker."

"Please, Edward ... May I call you Edward?"

"That's my name, ain't it?"

"It certainly is. We are a team of equals, Edward. My name is Christy," I said as I sat up, "and we have a very large task in front of us. We need equal voices and equal value to our work."

"That's what the government kept trying to tell us, equal everything. It ain't equal if it ain't free. It's the freedom that gives equal opportunity. We can all work for our best but there ain't no need to work if our laziness is our best."

"Can we quote you in the newspaper a friend owns?"

"Breaking the silence here, Ma'am, will cause me to lose my farm." Musselman shook his head and looked over at his wife.

"It isn't your name that has to be heard, Edward. It's your heart and your words. You don't need to mention your name to talk to the people. Like us all, you have a need to hold some treasures close to your heart. You have still spoken. Then, you decide if you can put your name on a petition. That will be a big step."

Chapter 29
Headquarters of the Blue Guard

Central Zone – January 16, 2113

"What do you mean, you lost them? Did you ever find them in the first place?" Stoner roared.

"Well, not exactly . . ." Lieutenant Boone stammered.

"Not exactly?" The Chief Inspector's voice was shrill. "Finding someone is a fact, not an opinion. You either did or you did not find them! Which is it?"

"I attended a meeting, a large gathering of clergy persons and a woman spoke who was very much like Lady Applewait."

"Clergy ... you mean religion? Why didn't you arrest every one of them? The ban on even the mention of God has been in force for a hundred years!" Stoner was in a rage. The memory of Applewait and her followers singing Christmas carols in front of President Alexander's home on Gifting Day eve was more than he could tolerate.

"Ward, I couldn't have arrested thousands of them by myself, even with that animal, Washington, along. He could have only growled and bitten so many people at a time."

"Lieutenant, why were you not able to identify her?" He paced back and forth, unable to sit and rest, unable to calm down.

"The woman I saw was wearing a Romani costume with a veil. She claimed to have laryngitis so I couldn't recognize her voice but it seemed odd that she would stand in front of thousands when she was barely able to speak."

"She couldn't speak at all and yet she came to the voice enhancer?" Ward barked in disbelief.

"Well, her voice was very hoarse and raspy ... you know ... laryngitis." Boone explained with impatience in her voice.

"All right, she spoke—sort of—then where is she? Where is this face-covered, squeaky voiced woman now? Did she disappear under her cape? Was she a magician as well as a gypsy woman? Did she evaporate into thin air?"

"Ward, she was a real person. She's just couldn't talk very clearly. She didn't go up in a puff of smoke. She was there and ... I really thought it was her."

"Okay, okay. Where is she right now?" Stoner demanded answers to his questions. "Boone, the question isn't that hard."

"I ... don't know! Washington and I attended the church meeting on Sunday morning. I have never seen that many people gathered together in one place. There was no crowd control in place. Citizens in the Central Zone cannot congregate in crowds. The woman was there in the same gypsy costume; she still wore a veil and her clothing covered her from her neck to her feet. They connected the church electronically with every congregation in the zone that morning. There were hundreds of links. I couldn't say how many. When they finished with the broadcast, thousands of people in the great auditorium we were in, stood and sang songs of praise with their hands waving around in the air. When I could finally see the front of the arena, the Romani woman was gone. No one, not one person, would tell me that they had seen her, that they knew her, and certainly not where she had gone."

The communication device that connected Boone and Ward Stoner went silent. Neither one said another word. Finally, she heard a deep sigh on the other end. "Come on home, Chalky. Your job is finished there—not completed—just done."

Chapter 30
A Gathering

Mid-Western Zone - Sunday Afternoon - January 22, 2113

"Ed Musselman, you come right up here," a woman in blue denim pants, heavy brown leather work shoes and a thick knit sweater said as she stood on a hay wagon. She amplified her voice with a hand held conical shaped object. It all looked very primitive to me and reminded me of pictures of singers in a long-ago time.

I took a deep breath. We were finally going to speak to the zone. The border had been a dangerous crossing and many of us had caught colds. I had developed bronchitis, and Jason feared it would go into pneumonia. We rested for nearly a week. Most slept in the barn on soft hay covered with donated comforters and quilts. Jason and I had stayed in Ed and Maud Musselman's home. Now, the hour had come.

"There he is," I said to Jason. When I looked around the barn at our group of one-hundred souls, I also counted at least another hundred strangers. "Look at all of these people. They're setting on hay stacks and some are dangling their feet over the side of the hay loft." I had to look closely. Some people blended into the surroundings of the barn. "Look, over at the horse stall. There are two young boys on the back of a chestnut mare."

"You sound like you've been here before," Jason joked. "Are you sure you weren't raised on a farm?"

"You know no farms exist in the Central Zone, just industry and business offices."

"Christy ... no farms exist in the Central Zone?"

"I just said that." Then I stopped. "Where have I been all my life? Why have I never noticed that we have no farms in our Zone? I have read books that painted vivid word pictures, farms from the dust bowl, the old south, the Amish farms, the farms and their families from the thirties and forties. I know what a farm looks like."

"I hadn't paid any attention either. History, neither regional nor zone, is taught anymore. I spend my time in my office, the hospital, and now, with you. We're in town all of the time. With no rapid transit out of the city and not many people have cars, very few people travel outside the city limits. The other thing is the drugs that are in the water. Everyone is so compliant, they don't question anything." Jason and I continued to talk between ourselves as we marveled at what we had overlooked all around us.

Edward jumped up on the wagon and waved at the people in his barn. "Okay, my friends, Maud has told you about the visitors to our zone. I know most of us haven't lived long enough to have seen a stranger in our midst. We rarely hear the word, "stranger." And that's what these folks are here to talk to you about."

Maud gestured in our direction and smiled broadly. I could tell we were welcome and perhaps they had heard of our mission already.

"Here in the Midwest, we farm and preserve, we bake and raise fiber for textiles. In the southern part of the zone, we have large mills and manufacture clothing and shoes. We export nearly all of that to the other three zones. We are the suppliers, not the users. Our ruling elites tell us, as farmers and factory workers, it is more virtuous to want little for ourselves. Those of our children who have wished for more, who have wanted a different life for themselves and their families, and have tried to escape across the border into another life, have been gunned down once their feet hit the foreign soil."

Murmurs arose among the people and nods of agreement. But, not all were in one accord.

"Ed, that's just not true. The other zones are just like us. They work the land and sweat in the factories just like we do," a man in denims and a plaid shirt argued.

"No, Art, that's wrong. Each zone is different but, in one way, they are all the same. They all live under the Length of Days law that applies to everyone. In the Midwestern Zone, as you near 70 years of age, your food rations diminish slowly. Do they not?"

An elderly woman's expression changed from interest to grief. Perhaps she had recently lost a spouse.

"Their excuse is," Ed continued, "you no longer work the land at your advanced age, so the greater number of calories you had been eating are not needed and would actually harm you. Each year, your rations grow smaller until you starve to death."

"No!" Some shouted from the back.

"What? It can't be. I don't believe that," a woman with a black, hand-woven headscarf snapped back in disbelief.

"You lie, Ed Musselman. You're lying and you know it!" A man waved his fist in the air and pounded the straw bale beside him.

"It's the Lord's gospel truth," Ed shouted into the megaphone. "You want to overturn that evil law?" he shouted. The crowd cheered. "Dr. O'Reilly, please step up here."

The crowd gawked and strained to see the new person in their midst. With no physicians in the middle zone, the people didn't understand his title. Ed raised his voice again. "The doctor is a person trained to cure people of what ails them. He finds medication for people to take, that will make them will again."

Everyone gasped and shifted where they sat. I wondered if there were any doctors in the southern part of the zone where industrial accidents could happen, and those injured would need the help of a physician.

Ed clapped his hands and encouraged others to follow suit. The people stood and became more excited with each cheer.

"I'm happy to be here," Jason greeted everyone. "And, I'm grateful you have all come out to listen. I sincerely hope you will support our mission. Mr. Musselman tells us that everyone in the Midwestern zone quits work when they reach the age of seventy. I understand, at that retirement age they cut your rations, supposedly for your own health. In the central zone, they exterminate people based on a precise scale of their value to the rest of the community. If they don't work at all, they will be put down by the time they are twenty-five." The people gasped and their expressions turned to fear and anger.

"For an elite," Jason continued, "they will use up their Length of Days at age seventy-five, regardless of how healthy and energetic they are." Those listening shook their heads in disbelief.

"We have just come from the Western Zone where they are organizing to support our cause. Even though the law requires some form of elimination at an age when people are still well and strong, just as it is in all zones, those in the West don't obey that law. With all of the advances in food, medicine and spiritual hope, those people live to the age of one hundred forty-five."

"One hundred forty-five?" Someone shouted and laughed among his friends. "Hey Doctor, you mean forty-five, right?"

"No, I meant what I said—one hundred forty-five years. And, you can add longevity to your years as well, with wholesome, healthy living. But first, let me introduce Christina Applewait."

A hush fell over the crowd as I came to the center of the wagon. Then a short lady with long greying hair asked, "Are you Lady Applewait, the seer?"

"I am Lady Christina Applewait. Lady by birth, not for anything I have done for others. I consider myself a *lady* only in my behavior." Everyone chuckled and shifted as they relaxed. "More important to that Lord and Lady nonsense, it is our cause that is a mission from God, not the messenger. There are no Lords and Ladies in the kingdom of God."

"Bless you, Christy," a woman called from the hay loft.

"Thank you. I am blessed ... and I have come to remind you that you are blessed, too."

"We have our work," a man up front said quietly, "but that is all."

"From what Ed and Maud have told me, you are a people with a strong vibrant past. Your ancestors owned the land you now work on," I reminded them.

"But, it's selfish to claim personal land ownership that others can't own," another woman protested.

"We are not elite like you, Christy," someone else spoke up with indignation in her voice.

"Yes, yes, you are. You are children of the King, the Lord God." Many whispered among themselves and snickered at the thought of being a royal anything.

"We have nothing of our own. What do you have?" a man snapped.

"It is not about what I have or may have in the future. It is about what you can claim if you will accept it. Ed told us of the second great Bolshevik Revolution. But, my friends, it was not the people who rose up and claimed what was rightfully theirs. It was the government who deceived the family-farm owners into believing that you could not farm on your own. In fact, they regulated the farm, textile and manufacturing industries until it was completely impossible to do business without government assistance. Then, while you relaxed in your effort to run your business, they stepped in and took them over ... every one of them."

The crowd gasped. Their faces distorted in anger. One burly man stood up in the back and began to pace. Then he turned toward me and shouted, "What happened? You mean our government stole everything our families worked for generations to build?"

"Yes, Sir," I stated flatly, "I mean exactly that. The government stole every single thing your family had. And, they continue to do that. They are now robbing you of your years of life. Years you could have spent with your loved ones."

"What are you talking about?" The big man asked, confused and angry.

"The Length of Days law, Sir. In the Central Zone, when people are injured or reach their allotted days, they are taken to the furnaces under Howard Mountain and are exterminated."

A woman near the middle of the group cried, "No, no."

"You here in the Midwestern Zone are quickly starved to death, once you are no longer able to farm the government land or work in their factories," I paused again as the people struggled to grasp the truths that were bombarding the lies they had been told.

Ed jumped to his feet. "My friends and neighbors, none of what these travelers have to say will make any difference at all ... if you don't believe them. I am telling you as your friend and neighbor, they bring the truth. The truth is hard to hear sometimes but don't say I didn't warn you," he shouted. "I did warn you. This illegal gathering of citizens, which could earn you a flogging, I remind you, we risked for one reason only, to being you the truth. It is up to you to believe the message these people bring from beyond our borders. If you don't accept their message today, you will be condemning your friends and family to certain death ... for treason." He turned to Jason, "Please, Jason, pick up and continue."

"We have come to get your help. We plan to overturn that terrible law," Jason announced with both hands raised. "I will now turn the megaphone back to Christy to give you the details."

I took the mouth piece and stood in the center of the wagon. At first, I felt myself holding my breath. Suddenly, a peace fell over me like a finely made prayer shawl. I knew I felt the presence of the Lord in our midst. The sun streamed through a high window and bathed the room in healing light. "Thank you for listening to us," I began. "I believe you know the truth of which we speak, deep inside. I have chosen to trust you with my life. Now, I need your help. I have brought along some papers, petitions for you to sign. If you believe the Length of Days law is evil and that we must put it down, you will sign the sheet and we will move on. At the top of each petition page is the wording of the citizens' bill. Enough signatures on these petitions will insure that a referendum is placed on the ballot at the election in two years."

With a petition held up in my hand, I pointed to each section as I spoke. "It's okay if you haven't heard of the term *referendum*. If the ruling class had their way, you still wouldn't have heard of it."

Again, I waited for understanding to catch up to their profound desire to take charge of their lives again. "A referendum is the same as a bill that congress writes to create a new law or to repeal a bad one. The Attorney General of each state prepares a title and summary of the chief purpose and points of the referendum. With our states further divided into zones, we don't have access to a state Attorney General. So, the government constructed a cover letter to accompany it. Dr. O'Reilly and I were able to procure a cover letter." I watched the people's faces as they turned to one another, trying to understand.

When the murmurs calmed, I continued. "A referendum is a law written by the people. It requires the signatures of a vast percentage of the citizens in order to get it placed on the ballot for all to vote on. We need your name on the line."

Again, I felt the information was racing past the people, like a giant snow ball that grows in size as it rolls down the hill. I paused and let the people catch up to our mission. "Besides being brave enough to sign the petition, we need people who are courageous enough to help carry copies of the petition to the entire Zone. A hundred people have followed us from the West to help you with this effort. Half of them will remain here to assist you. The other half will go into the Eastern Zone to help get signatures there."

"You can count on me," a young man called from the back of the barn.

"Me, too," the girl beside him echoed as she waved her hand over her head.

As others said, "You can add me in," I thought of Raymar Goring. Filled with new life only a few days, yet he had agreed to participate and head up a team to get the signatures of the Hollow people in the northwest.

"I will never be empty again," he had said.

"Are you comfortable doing this, Raymar?" I had asked him.

"I may not have talked to others or been in their world, but I have taught the other discarded ones every day." He had assured me with conviction.

I smiled again as I thought of him. He had gone from being a shadow in our world, to a valuable partner in our cause, in a matter of days. I handed Jason the megaphone. I heard him introduce Lomas Karl, one of the claimed children we had brought with us from the west.

"Thank you, Doctor," Lomas smiled as he stepped to the center. "I know I look young. I admit I'm only eighteen, but I have come to bear witness to what you have been told." He paused and looked around the group.

"You're doing fine, Lomas," I soothed. As I walked behind him, I patted his shoulder.

"In the Central Zone, families are permitted only two children. If a third infant is born, the parents have up to two years to decide which two of their three they're going to keep. After the parents decide on the two, the third child is given over to the state for extermination." Lomas lowered his eyes and stared at straw on the floor in front of him. He looked up again and met the eyes of all those gathered. "I am one of those discarded children. But a dear man was brave enough to start claiming the children just before I was born. I am one of the claimed."

Gasps rose up among many in the crowd. They seemed to take Lomas to their hearts. As tears rolled down the cheeks of many, they grieved with him for all he had lost.

"I want to tell you all, don't mourn for me. I'm the winner. In the Western Zone, they took me to Claimed-International, and within hours, a new family wanted me. In my claimed family, I have five brothers and sisters."

"Bless you," someone called from the side.

"I am blessed, Ma'am. You're right. And, I'm asking that you become a blessing to others. We must end this national disgrace, this abomination against God! We cannot let the Length of Days law stand. We must bring it down!" His rallying call filled the whole room. People stood and cheered.

Ed Musselman raised his hands and let out a whistle that rattled the windows in their frames. "Our travelers will be with us for another week and a half. We'll organize by township, with two leaders for each. Christiana will offer encouragement, strength and motivation. She and Jason will answer any questions we may have. Our goal is to have the structure in place for us to continue by the time they move on to the Eastern Zone. Are there any questions now?"

"Will we make the deadline?" a man shouted from the seat of the International Harvester tractor.

"I can say, 'I hope so,' I answered. "But, I'm sorry, my friends. That is not good enough. We absolutely must be successful and on time. There are deadlines put in place hundreds of years ago and a two year stay of executions. That is our reality. That is our goal," I sang out with certainty.

"We are together!" Ed Musselman shouted. "We will be counted!"

Chapter 31
Inspector Stoner's Office

A Few Days Later

Ward Stoner paced the short distance from his office door to the east window. He searched the parking area beyond the glass. The only strata cars were those that were there ten minutes ago. *Where are they?*

"Alvarez!" he shouted toward the door.

One of the new Blue Shirts stuck his head through the door. "Sir?"

"Have we heard from Lieutenant Boone? Anything?" Stoner leaned on his desk with his fists doubled.

"We received word that she and Washington had left the Western Zone hours ago. Perhaps she has gone home to get some sleep."

"Sleep?" Stoner roared like a pacing lion. "They will sleep when Applewait has been found!"

"But Sir—"

"Do not speak back to me, Officer!" Then in a whisper he added, "Don't you ever correct or challenge what I say."

Alvarez shrunk from the room as Stoner's glare drove him out. "I'll let you know when I hear something."

Stoner's eyes darted to the lot outside as a strata car pulled in. Then he hurried to the desk with a new thought, one he would have to execute quickly. His 281 Palm Device waited for his next message. With minutes to go before Boone would enter his office and reprimand him for investigating a Legacy Citizen, he flipped the 281 on. It glowed brightly; the logo hologram pulsed in front of him. "Call, Jonathon Fink … Fort Knox," he barked.

"Hi there, Ward," the image greeted. "I don't talk to you for years, now this is the second time in a matter of weeks." Fink's presence appeared in the form of a hologram in front of Stoner. "You're looking good."

"I'm calling you about that Applewait woman again." Stoner looked back out at the lot. Boone and Washington were just getting out of the car. He would have to make the connection short. His impatience mounted.

"Friend, I'm not permitted to speak one word about the members of the Council of Elders, or their families. Not any of the Legacy Citizens. I looked up that one piece of information for you, Ward," Jonathan protested. "That's it."

"You don't have to look up anything in your precious files about those uppity elites, Fink. I just need to find out the activities in general. You're in the Midwestern Zone. I just want to know if you have heard anything."

"About Lady Applewait?"

"About anything," Ward snapped impatiently. "Most of the time, these citizens have nothing out of the ordinary going on. They lead uneventful, do-nothing lives. I would die from stagnation if I lived as they do. Whatever you hear that is not as boring as watching the corn grow, would be something I'd like to hear about."

"Okay . . ." There was silence for a second. "There is something going on, but I don't have any idea what it is," Fink said. "There seems to be a new energy among the people. You know how these people are. They are all lazy. We let them live, at very little rent mind you, on the land they work and still they aren't satisfied."

"Have you heard any names ... Applewait or O'Reilly?"

"No. But someone said he heard of a meeting a few days ago. He didn't know any of the details, location or the names. No one is saying a word. You know, and they know, it is unlawful to congregate in groups."

"Maybe it's nothing," Stoner mumbled out loud.

"That's what I thought, Ward. But ... a report of a meeting is not nothing ... it's something."

"But, is she still in your Zone? The Applewait woman, Jonathan, is she still there?"

"I have no idea, but if I were to guess, I would say no, at least, I don't think so. I haven't heard about another big meeting."

Stoner's shoulders sank with anger and disappointment. "Well, thank you friend."

"Ward," Lieutenant Boone said softly at the door. The hologram shimmered in the room. "We're back."

"If you hear anything, let me know immediately," Ward said as he closed the 281.

"What was that all about?" Chalky questioned as she entered his office and removed her outer coat.

"Top secret," he snapped. "I'll tell you as soon as I can." He stared out the window again at the rapidly accumulating snow. "We're not done, Boone. I will find her if I have to chase her to the ocean's edge."

"You are the one who will drown if you interfere with the privacy of an Elite," she warned.

"Never mind that," he ordered. "Where have you been?"

"Where have I been? Ward, you sent Washington and me out of the zone. I have been to the incoming tide, just as you said, and she wasn't there."

"Not at all?" Ward shook his head in disbelief. "What about that woman in the Romani clothes? You probably had her then. Did she look like the Legacy brat?"

"If I did have her, like you said, there were far too many people present for me to get anyplace near her. She almost evaporated. The woman was guarded and then ... she was gone." Chalky stretched and yawned. "I'm going home to get some sleep."

"Make that a nap, Lieutenant. I've been asking questions, and I'm picking up on some movement. I tell you, it is something." He rubbed the back of his neck in frustration. "I have received word that the Mid-Western Zone has had a little ruffle in their waves of grain. Then everything all settled down again. There doesn't seem to be a disturbance now, but more movement than usual." He paced the floor, then grabbed Boone by both arms and got in her face. "So you saw that gypsy woman in the West. Then, there was a ripple of something in the Midwest. If the reason for that unrest was her ... she may be going to the Eastern Zone next. That is the only zone she hasn't been spotted in yet."

Boone pulled herself free from Stoner's grasp. "Ward, let it go."

"Let it go? These two fugitives have plotted to change a long established law. They have thumbed their noses at our President Alexander. And ... they have unlawfully left the zone and crossed several borders, in order to spread their treason."

"Ward—"

"Go home. Sleep a little ... pack ... and I'll pick you up in three hours. I'll drive. Washington will be in the back."

"Must we take Daniel? I don't trust him."

"He'll be our muscle."

"Why do we need added strength? Ward, you cannot lift a hand to a Legacy Citizen. We have gone over and over this."

"Don't lecture me like a child!" he bellowed. "I am the Chief of the Blue Guard! I can do anything I want to, when I want to, and for any reason I invent!" Stoner's face grew red with anger and belligerent revenge, a very dangerous combination.

Chalky closed her eyes and shook her head slowly. "No, I think you are right, Sir. There is nothing I can say that will change your mind."

Stoner looked out at his city as fresh snow began to float down. "It's cold out there, Boone. Dress warm."

Chapter 32
Eastern Zone—Border Crossing

6 a.m. - Thursday - February 2, 2113

"Put everything you're carrying on the table," a stout woman in low, lace-up shoes barked mechanically.

The border post was drab and poorly lit. Shadows lurked in places that need not have been shaded, except for the dull, monotonous drone of the job there. I wondered if it was the people who worked there or the room that was light-less. The whole room smelled of mold, like an old basement. But, we weren't underground. We were in a room with so few windows the dampness could get in but it couldn't escape.

This was the first border we crossed openly. *Openly* for the Eastern Zone. The Midwestern sector didn't even know we were in their territory. But, the border to the East was different. There was a border *understanding*—if you have the price of passage you can cross with no questions asked. The *understanding* was only in force at a few crossings. The bounty collected was shared on down a ransom line, that flowed deeply enough into the Eastern area, to make the crossings as safe as possible.

Jason made a slight gesture toward the woman as she opened and searched through my valise. I didn't have much. We had come with very little except what the Musselmans had pulled together for us. The crossing guard groped all the way to the bottom of the bag then forced it closed with the contents jumbled and crumpled. Next, she jerked Jason's carry pack to her without taking a step and rummaged through it in the same way.

Jason and I watched in silence as she dutifully searched every pocket and pouch. She did her work thoroughly, and I wondered what she would have done if she had actually found something. I also wondered what *something* would consist of. It was better that we gave her no information on our own. She didn't even look up when she asked, "Your crossing papers?"

Without saying a word, Jason handed the woman a small, bulging envelope. With it held very close to her chest, she barely opened it, peeked inside, ran her fingers over the contents and motioned for us to pass. Jason placed ten fingers on the cold surface of the metal desk, closed them and held up two fists full again. Twenty of us—twenty travelers passed while the woman pinched open the folder a little wider and counted her money. She didn't look at anyone. I doubt she even saw us at all. We were now the invisible ones, like Raymar Goring had been.

"I wonder if the border is an example of the technology in the east." Jason whispered when we were far beyond her hearing. "She had nothing. She just fumbled through everything. She couldn't even use the old x-ray technology."

"That's the way it appeared," I said, and wondered if things were as they seemed. "Maybe they have so few attempts at border crossing they don't need modern equipment to secure it."

"Let's hope. Ed and Maud were sure their information was correct. We would be able to cross here if we paid the guard." Jason never looked back. We kept walking toward the cars that waited for us in the fog beyond the passing guard post.

Great clouds hung low to the ground and drew a thin veil over all we saw. Suddenly I stopped. A vehicle, like a strata car, sleek with broad lettering down the side, Zone Patrol, went slowly past in the eerie fog. The windows were dark so I couldn't see anyone. A man who stood beside a long, black vehicle suddenly caught my eye and came across the road in our direction. The whole scene seemed odd.

The street was two lanes and the grass grew like fringe along the side of the pavement. The ice crystals that had gathered on top looked undisturbed and glistened in the light. Obviously, this was not a well-traveled spot. The man from the stretch car came closer, reached out and gave me a loosely directed hug.

"Sorry, My Lady, act like you know me and you were expecting me to greet you," he whispered while his face was near mine.

I smiled a faint smile. Then I turned and said, "Jason, you remember—"

"Harold, Harold Humphrey," the man said as he stuck out his hand in greeting. "You, Sir, will be called Jason Bogart and you, my dear, Christy Bacall. No one here knows the old cinema stars and if they do, perhaps they won't notice that Bogie and Bacall are together again."

Gray Fox and Little Feather came up from behind me and stopped at a brief distance. Harold stepped around Jason and me and offered his hand. "Gray Fox, I've heard about you. You have been in our zone before, silent and invisible, but the network knew of your presence." He offered his hand again, "Little Feather."

"You have an established network already in place, Harold?" Jason asked.

"Hurry, let's get into the stretch cars and then I'll explain it. The zone has seen cars like these before so we shouldn't be stopped."

"I'll get everyone inside," Little feather offered. Four, six-passenger long luxury cars waited at the side of the road. Little Feather helped five of us into each.

"You four will ride with me," Harold spoke to Jason, Little Feather, Gray Fox and me.

We all quickly got into the vehicles and Harold led the way down the road. I ran my fingers over the dark leather cushions and inhaled the earthy aroma of the entire interior. I smiled to myself. My usual mode of transportation was the Public Transit of Capitol City, not a luxury limousine. I allowed myself the brief privilege of sinking back into the comfortable seat.

Suddenly, I caught a glimpse of another strata car as it passed by. I felt ill. My hands started trembling and waves of nausea overtook my tired body. It felt like I had been stirred on the inside and the swirling had not yet subsided.

"Are you all right, Christy?" Jason put his arm around me.

"I saw a strata car and suddenly felt overwhelmed," I whispered out of some deep place inside.

"You're right," Gray Fox whispered, validating my experience. "I have seen several, but we are inside a rolling tank with tinted windows."

"I know this is all a shock, Christy," Harold sympathized. "But you are an answer to prayer."

"Answer to prayer?" I asked in surprise. "You know about our cause?"

Harold looked at me through the rear facing mirror. "We are under the Length of Days law, too. But, we also have more depravity here than anyone could ever imagine. Those who live in the city are the very wealthy and the moles live underground."

"The moles?" we all questioned Harold in unison. "What are you talking about?" I asked.

Suddenly, colored lights and a screeching siren cut through the morning fog. I grabbed Jason's hand and stiffened. I was frightened and tired. It would have been so much easier to handle all that had happened with rest.

"Put your head on Jason's shoulder like you're sleeping, Christy. Your face will be partially buried when the officer gets to the window," Little Feather suggested with the tone of experience in making her way through difficult situations.

"What's the party all about?" the uniformed man asked through the open window.

"Party?" Harold appeared genuinely confused. He was good at what he had learned to do in order to get around the city.

"This long parade of cars, Mister. What's this all about?" the officer snapped.

"I picked up some friends of Mr. and Mrs. Cornwall. They're having a reunion and week-long private festival," Harold said.

"Reunion of what?" the officer questioned.

"They do it every year and invite the same people. So, they call it a reunion. Other than that, it's none of my business."

The patrolman looked in the car at us in the back. I could feel him staring at me, but I remained silent and rested my head on Jason's shoulder. Flashing his light into the backseat he studied each of us carefully. "Is she okay?" he asked.

"Yes, just tired. We had started the party a little ahead of the others," Jason laughed. "I really need to get her to the house so she can rest."

"The house?" Again the office pried as he shined the light in Jason's face. "What do you mean, house? Are you trying to be funny, Mister?

"Mr. Bogart is joking. He means the Citadel of course. He is a man of understatement," Harold smiled as if making fun of the comment.

"It sounds like it. It is quite a *house.* Well, none of us keep the Cornwalls waiting and I won't be the first. Here, let me put a flag on your car as the lead vehicle in a procession." His attitude changed once he heard of our destination. He was all business, in the most efficient and pleasant manner. He waved us on and got back in his patrol car.

"I see him in my mirrors. He's going the other way," Harold said with relief.

"Are we actually going to ... the Citadel? The Cornwall Citadel?" I asked. We had heard nothing about the people in the Eastern Zone since all of the sectors are closed. But, I knew. Some of the reference books, available only to me and the Library Curator of old manuscripts, referred to an old New York family by the name of

Cornwall. And, I certainly knew what a citadel is. It's a castle on higher ground that protects those around them.

"Yes, we definitely know about your cause. We have two tasks in the Eastern Zone. The second will make the first possible." Harold drove a little further and then added, "The petitions are our main goal, but in order to accomplish that we will have to free the moles."

"The moles?" I questioned again.

"You won't believe it. I don't ... and I live here." Harold said no more. Again he watched me through the mirror. "Rest, My Lady. We have a long way to go."

I rested my head on Jason's shoulder. I couldn't actually sleep as thoughts of our mission raced through my mind: the Citadel, the moles and everything we had encountered. I smiled as I thought of the irony of it all. It had only been a few months ago, that all of my exciting experiences came through the pages of the books I read over and over. Now ... I was the adventurer and I still wondered how all of it could have happened. Only God could have called me to such a time as this.

Chapter 33
The Citadel

Late Afternoon

"I think she might have actually fallen asleep," I heard Jason say as I roused. The car was still moving. I knew I could have only napped a few minutes.

"She must have been really tired," Harold was saying as I looked out the window.

Something that sent flashes of light through the windshield at rapid intervals blocked the late afternoon sun. What was it? I squinted as my eyes adjusted to the bursts of brilliance. Buildings were everywhere. It was like driving through a box canyon surrounded by sheer cliff walls I read about. I couldn't see the tops of the buildings so I slumped down in the seat and peered above and out the window. Now, I know what my books meant by skyscrapers.

"We're here," Gray Wolf spoke softly from the back seat.

I strained to see the street sign at the next block. "Park Avenue at Fifty-Seventh Street," I gasped. The magic of New York City had been a reoccurring dream of mine since I found books filled with pictures of the city in the library. The brick and granite buildings rose up from the concrete like a field of enchanted pebbles that had split the pavement.

"The city mountains are almost as tall as ours, Gray Fox," Little Feather marveled.

"How will you guide us here, in a city you have never seen?" Jason questioned.

"Because we don't follow bricks and mortar. We follow people, and their scent is different than motor fuel."

"These are hydro-motors, Gray Fox," Harold said. "They have no sound and no odor."

"We'll see." Gray Fox answered with a doubtful grin. "But I can hear the whirl of the movements," he chuckled softly. Suddenly, he broke the silence again with a gasp. "Navajo," he whispered. "That sign is Navajo. It wasn't until the Great War in the middle of the nineteenth century that anyone wrote down the Navajo language. That sign said, 'Bilh-he-new Huc-Quo.' It says warning, come. Why was that there? Something is coming."

"I'll let Richard and Barbara Cornwall tell you. I'll say you are very important to the success of the second effort." Harold said no more.

The second effort? Then I remembered what he said—*we must free the moles.*

Harold pulled the car up to a huge iron gate. Beyond the fence was a circle driveway. It was dry even in the snowy weather. What appeared to be a large fountain, still flowing with fresh water from which red cardinals splashed and drank, stood in the middle.

"It's all heated Christy, the driveway pavement and fountain birdbath," Harold explained.

He pushed a button on the steering wheel and the wrought iron slowly parted with only the tiniest sound of scraping and squeaking. None of us talked. We drank in all the information the fortified estate in the middle of New York City had to offer. The high iron fence bordered the entire property, with surveillance devices mounted every twenty feet. The home was so large it reminded me of pictures I had seen of the mansions of the gilded era in one of the previous centuries. The Citadel reached up six stories above the street. The entrance area was large enough for all of the long-cars to park on the drive pad.

The doors to each of the vehicles seemed to open in slow motion as people hesitantly stepped out and craned their necks to see the very top of the house. Jason and I, Gray Fox and Little Feather stepped from the long-car.

"Where are we?" Salvador Pérez, a Westerner, asked as he got out of one of the other cars and filled his eyes with the massive structure.

"This is nothing like my vineyard in California," Frank Church agreed.

"Follow me quickly inside," Harold cautioned as he hurried everyone through the massive stained glass paneled doors.

Inside, the entry hall reached up three stories. A crystal chandelier hung from the tall ceiling by three golden cables. The floors were rose marble and shone in the entry light. The sounds of our shoes made a tapping noise on the stone.

"You are all safely here." A lovely woman in her mid-forties swept graciously down the staircase. She wore a teal dress that brushed around her ankles and moved like sea grass near the edge of the water. "I'm Barbara Cornwall." She extended her hand in my direction. "Lady Christiana Applewait? Welcome."

"Please, Mrs. Cornwall, call me Christy," I smiled and approached her to shake her hand. As she came nearer, I caught the scent of her perfume. It smelled amazing, but I wouldn't have known the name of the heavenly creation. Considered too erotic, there was no perfume manufactured or sold in the Central zone.

"Only if you call me Barbara," she said. Her smile lit up her face. "Come," she offered, "you probably haven't eaten in hours."

"We haven't eaten since early this morning, Mrs. Cornwall." Harold led the way into a dining room the size of which I had never experienced, not even in the books I read.

"Harold, I have told you many times, to call me Barbara. You are my friend first, my bodyguard second."

In the dining room she stood at the head of a wide banquet table and a man in a wheelchair was beside her along one end. "My friends, I would like to introduce you to my husband who is recovering from a fall from his polo pony last month."

With the mention of polo, I saw eyes roll. I knew, not everyone player polo. I didn't know that the other sectors would have followed such an elite sport ... and resented it.

Barbara saw the expressions of disapproval. There was not a hint of embarrassment or offense on her face. She smiled. "I will explain one time that things in this house are not as they seem. We have great wealth inherited from Richard's parents and my own. We seem to live the life of the idle, self-indulgent rich. I hope you will find that we are vastly different from our image. Please sit down. Enjoy your meal."

"Lady Applewait and Dr. O'Reilly, Gray Fox and Little Feather, please join Barbara and me at this end of the table," Richard Cornwall directed.

"I apologize for our cramped seating arrangement. Our table comfortably seats twenty, and with all of us, we have twenty-six. Thank you all for coming. Let us bow," Richard said as he gave thanks for the meal, for those around the table and the cause for which we worked and risked our lives.

Barbara turned as three servants came in and served warm drinks of coffee, tea or cocoa and the soup course. "I'm sorry, Maisie, we don't have enough places for you, Roger and Quinton to sit at the table."

"That's all right Barbara," Maisie said as she placed a soup bowl in front of our hostess.

"Well, that's wonderful that you understand. Please, if you want to make a picnic on the floor with your food, that would be fun," Mrs. Cornwall said with a bubbly smile.

I watched as the three finished serving, then brought in their soup in large cups, sat against the wall and ate. "Barbara," the one named Quinton began, "this is great. What did you use for that special spice I taste?"

"Quinton, that is my secret," she answered with a wink. Everyone was relaxed and comfortable. Although the three served our supper, there seemed to be no unequal relationship in the entire room.

"Barbara, you said that nothing here is as it seems. You preside over this table like a queen over her court, and yet you're a kind woman who seems to think of others before herself. You serve us this wonderful meal that you apparently had a major hand in," I said.

"She made the whole pot of soup," Maisie confirmed as she sipped from the hot cup.

"This is a mansion, styled in a gold, extravagant manner, and ... you do the cooking. I'm confused," I admitted.

"It's not hard," Barbara explained. "It's just out of the normal scene one would expect in a setting such as this."

Without gawking, I tried to survey the room and the entry hall we had first entered. "We don't even have houses like this one in the Central Zone," I said with amazement. "I feel like a school child on a field trip."

Our hostess chuckled and patted my hand. "My dear, you are an elite, not I, and yet you don't set yourself apart from others."

I pulled my linen napkin to my mouth. I was stunned. She didn't accuse me. She simply gave an example I would understand. "Touché," I surrendered.

"I like to cook ... so I cook. If you think we have fallen on hard times and must do the work around here, you have guessed wrong. Richard's parents, and my own, reared us to be selfish, arrogant, and uncaring. We actually lived the life of the above-grounders, the rich and self-absorbed. Then ... our daughter, Phoebe Joy, died and we needed ... something. We didn't know what."

"We walked and walked every day, trying to forget, trying to figure out—*why?* One afternoon we wandered into an old church on

Fifth Avenue. It had been a Catholic church but religion had vanished by then," Richard added.

"Religion had been banned in our zone, too. We know what you mean," Jason said.

"No, not here in the city. They didn't have to ban it. Money and prestige have replaced a belief in anything ... except *more*," Richard explained. "Their religion is the god of acquiring—gathering, not just enough—but more than all the others have."

"We went inside the church because we have always found peace in there. We used to wander in on some of our walks with Phoebe Joy. The beautiful stained glass windows sent shimmering color across the sanctuary, on the floor, the furnishings and the walls. That day, we walked in and found a prayer group," Barbara beamed.

"A Catholic group of believers was meeting there?" I asked. I had read a little about religious groups. I found them to be interesting yet quaint, deluded people from the naive past.

"No ... I mean yes ... we have no denominations, no Catholic, no Protestant, just Christians in prayer. We have been meeting with them ever since and it has changed our lives ... and our mission."

"Tell them about the moles that attend the group, Barbara," Roger suggested. "They are great. Not what we thought at all."

"You go to the prayer sessions, too?" I questioned.

Quinton tipped up his bowl and finished the last of his soup. "We all do now," he said.

"What do you mean by moles?" Gray Fox asked. "In Navajo, names have meaning. Mole means rodent. It also means the rodent lives underground. But, in this world's terms, it also means someone who is acting under cover. Which is it? I saw a Navajo symbol on this very building. Why?"

"To answer the last question ... the code markings ... there is a leader among the moles who knows the Navajo symbols. He said he is a descendent of one of the Code-talkers, a group of military men who devised a code for secret inscription based on their native language," Richard explained.

"It had never been written down, so the symbols were the first written language for the Navajos. You have one of my tribesmen on your side?" Gray Fox gasped. "He's a mole?"

"He is one of the underlings, the moles, who have lived below ground for more than sixty years. A few decades past the great crisis of the previous millennium, the elites convinced those dependent upon the state: with vouchers for food, medicine, schooling, clothing, public transportation—most all of their daily living supplies—that the surface was not safe. They told them bands of roving marauders slither about and kill just to remove a person's shoes," Richard shook his head in disgust. "During the first year, if an underling came up from below, someone was there ready to shoot them. After that, they accepted that the above-ground world was dangerous, even after the city dwellers lost interest and walked away."

I felt profoundly sad for the gullible people who believed such lies. "Why were they deceived?"

Barbara's face grew tight with grief. "All of the elite ones here on top, didn't want to see the common people anymore. They said they could smell them in their elegant stores and fancy shops. Some said they were like an infestation of common mold. Those with power told them, the only way they could be cared for properly and kept safe, was to move everyone underground. They started with the old subway system and converted it to underground lodging. Then they connected the basements of the stately buildings and skyscrapers, but sealed off the underground from any possible contact with the floors above—just business buildings, not residential."

"They haven't had any sunlight down there for all this time? Children are born into darkness and remain in the dark forever?" Jason asked. "Everyone knows that's wrong. With my medical background, I shake to the core. What is their life expectancy?"

Richard opened his mouth to speak and then paused, "Forty-five years." He shifted in his wheelchair and added. "They are convinced, if they come out of hiding, they will be killed. So they stay below."

"That is actually the truth behind Richard's injury," Harold offered, then looked at the Cornwall's who nodded slightly. "He was not actually hurt in a polo accident. That was his cover. They had to invent a story."

Barbara patted her husband on the hand and smiled. "Richard and I open the roof-top terrace to the underlings for a few hours every afternoon. With so many moles, young and old, it's hard to meet all their needs. The underlings make their way underground to the old manhole cover that opens into our basement. It had been sealed but we released the seal."

"Isn't it dangerous for them to have such easy access to your sub-level?" Jason asked.

"We have been able to trust every one of them," Roger joined in.

"Do they have to come up into your living space to get up to the roof?" I asked.

"No," Richard answered, then added, "But, that would have been okay, too. We were able to construct a special path for them. Not because we didn't want them in our home. Because they have lived in such dark, squalid conditions all of their lives we didn't think they would be able to take all of the color in our living quarters."

"From the basement," Barbara explained as she sipped her coffee and smiled at the faces around the table, "the people can take an express elevator to the roof where they take turns laying in the sun for fifteen minutes every day. Last month, the manhole cover slipped and started to fall on a woman. Richard grabbed for it and fell over backward and broke his hip."

I struggled to understand the vast hoax perpetrated on the masses. "In the Central Zone, the people are kept in a slightly drugged fog that makes them pliable and free from all emotions.

Here, it's different. Do they have their emotions down there? Are their riots and chaos in the underworld?"

"Actually, not very often. The severe vitamin D deficiency makes them cognitively dull even in fairly young people—twenties and thirties," Maisie explained. "We provided the brief time on the sun roof each day in the hope their bones will become stronger and they can fight off some diseases and think more clearly."

"You are not a servant girl, young lady," Jason laughed. "You're a smart young lady."

"I'm a surface mole," she smiled, "a former underling who was discovered during one of Barbara and Richard's trips below and brought to the surface."

"She is studying medicine right here in our home library," Barbara said and motioned with a wide sweep of her hand in the direction of the large library across the hall.

"A library right here in your own home," I marveled at the privilege of it. "So the moles are taught to read in the underworld?"

"No, all of that work will have to be done when they are emancipated."

"Well Barbara, that's not completely true," Maisie stumbled through her explanation. "Barbara taught me all I would have learned in the primary and elementary grades of school in the first six months after I arrived in the sunshine. With my tools for learning, reading and numbers, I have studied all the rest on my own and ... I have gone below and trained others to teach still more of them."

"Maisie, I didn't know that. That's wonderful," Barbara cheered. "Why didn't you tell us?"

"I didn't want to put either of you in danger. You would have gone back down, and then perhaps caught. Traffic between the under and upper worlds is forbidden except for the motormen who deliver the goods and supplies to the people below at the rail head," Maisie explained hesitantly.

"Well, I think what you have done is wonderful, Maisie," Richard said.

Barbara nodded in agreement, then she added, "We're trying to prepare all those below for the shock of learning that they have been deceived in the vilest manner. Their lives and the lives of their distant families sixty years back have been stolen from them."

"Are the moles of one race or similar beliefs or identified by some other grouping?" I wondered how this could have happened. Then I remembered our citizens who were also deceived, just in different evil ways, all for the purpose of control.

"None," Maisie said, "except wealth and position. They had no power. They were the receivers of society, like Richard said, those who received multiple benefits from the State. They were of every ethnicity. Now, living in such close quarters, they are a blend of many."

"They must be beautiful," I added, thinking of the gorgeous blending of cultures I had seen in our sector. Our beautiful friend Dahlia is of African, European and Native American heritage.

"They would be amazing if they were well," Maisie added.

Barbara continued. "The really hard part will be in preparing them for emancipation. We have no idea how they will accept the truth of their wasted lives. How will they believe that they will be safe on the surface if they have been told all of their lives that they will be executed if they come through the barrier between top and bottom?"

"What do you think, Maisie?" I asked the only one among us who had experienced the transition.

"You climbed out of the darkness. Were you afraid?" Jason asked.

"I could see small rays of light that streamed through the grates and manhole covers." She spoke softly as if she stood in a sanctuary of the deep. "I loved the steam grate over near the old Rockefeller Plaza, on Fifth Avenue outside of Saint Patrick's Cathedral. Although there were no services any longer, if I got there at just the right moment, I could hear music from the church. I didn't know who was in there or who was making the music, but it was beautiful. My soul knew there was more than the darkness. When I came up, the light was … I'm sorry, I don't know a word more powerful than breathtaking."

"So … you don't think they will be afraid?" I pressed a little further.

Maisie smiled with wisdom gained from experience. "They won't know until they climb those steps up out of the underworld, that they will be leaving fear behind—that they will be stepping into a world of freedom, freedom from fear. There are far worse things than fearing a violent death. Fearing you will live your whole life without ever being seen in the light is far worse."

"We watch Maisie bloom in the light every day." Barbara blew Maisie a little kiss. "Her unselfishness in teaching some of the others makes me say more confidently that they are the key."

"The key?" I asked.

"You are here to get signatures on a petition to over-turn the Length of Days law," Barbara observed. "Here in this huge city, we believe that the only people, who could get around unnoticed, are the moles. The above-grounders don't even think about them anymore. They'll never notice a few moles, traveling as a duo. So many moles live down there now they may come close to fulfilling your quota of necessary names. Richard and I can work on the elites."

"They will be very pale when they come above ground. How will you camouflage them?" Jason asked.

"Camouflage? Jason, women have been wearing skin covering for hundreds of years. Do you have any make-up, Barbara?" I asked with a chuckle.

"I have plenty and we can buy more. Men wear it sometimes too, so the male underlings will fit in quite well," she replied.

Little Feather had been listening, then asked, "If your goal is to have them all live above ground, where will they all stay when they come into the light?"

"The stores around the city are all on the first floor, occasionally a department store is scattered among them with multiple floors. Still, most of the levels above the ground used to be the apartments where the moles' parents or grandparents had lived. We don't know how many are down there. Since their Length of Days is very short, due to starvation, malnutrition, or Vitamin D deficiency and the diseases they cause, there may not be as many as there could have been if they lived in a healthy environment," Harold informed us.

The volunteers who came with us listened intently, with nods of agreement and displays of emotion.

"It may be possible, that a family could reclaim their ancestral home when they come up," I suggested. I pushed my empty dishes back, leaned my elbows on the table and folded my hands together. I wasn't disrespectful. I had finished eating and I was tired.

"That's true," Richard responded. "The records of apartment and condominium owners are still available in the county property tax records office, since the power-hungry elite never expected the underlings to be seen again."

"So it might be that my family could owe many years of back property tax?" Maisie asked.

"They would not dare!" Barbara growled. "They have enslaved nearly three generations of people," her voice rose with indignation. "And, they would try to charge them back taxes for being absent and unavailable for payment?"

"That won't happen, Sweetie. As an attorney, I'll make sure that it won't," Richard assured her. "I'll start to prepare the necessary counter-documents for any argument the political ruling class may try to impose on them," Richard encouraged. "I have my job to do, and I can work here in my office. Barbara and I would like to offer a suggestion for how all of you may proceed."

"Any ideas would be helpful." I was thankful for anything they had to offer. We were in a strange world with customs and beliefs that were evil and deadly to those who were not in control. And yet, the masses had gladly given up all that they had in order for others to take care of them. It all made me more tired than I was. I needed rest. My body demanded it.

Chapter 34
The Underlings

Monday - February 6, 2113

Barbara insisted that we rest all weekend. On Sunday, we attended a church service but, other than that, we didn't leave the Citadel. It simply wasn't safe. We sang songs around the piano in the gathering room, but most of the time we shared our stories and got to know one another. It felt like we had known the Cornwalls for years. On Monday morning, we gathered for breakfast.

"When everyone has finished eating," Barbara began, "I'll take you up on the roof to meet some of the moles. Then, if you feel ready … tomorrow, I'll go with you into the bowels of the city and see first-hand what you have to deal with."

"The underworld?" *Already?* I was afraid, but I couldn't let anyone know. For whatever God had seen in me that I had not seen in myself, he had called me to these people and the forgotten and discarded ones beneath their feet.

We had all finished our food and went into the entrance hall that stretched elegantly, high over our heads. I was amazed by the house and was learning that it sheltered many secrets.

"Christy and Jason please follow me," Barbara said as she led the way to a door beside the grand staircase. It opened into two areas, one was the door to a private elevator that provided access to the floors above; the other was steps that led to the basement. She flipped the lights on. "Richard can't do the steps with the wheelchair, so he'll join us on the roof. In the basement, there is another elevator shaft that is an express to the roof," she said. "When the house was renovated, many years ago, the access from the basement to the main floor was sealed off. It isn't possible for underlings to get onto any of the floors except the roof. Since the people we invite into the sun get to the top, straight from the basement, I thought we would take their route."

"You have never created a new opening in the shaft, so they can come into the residential floors?" Jason asked.

"No," she said with a sigh, "and it's not because we don't want them in our home. We have to be prepared. If authorities were ever to come in and search the house, they must not find an access from the tunnels below the house to the living spaces. The underlings must be protected from the above-grounders."

Everything about the above-ground people was new to me: their twisted vile philosophy, the grand homes and mansions all along the streets with devastation below, everything. Wherever I looked there was beauty, but it hid ugly lies. Now, I had to go into the basement, just steps away from the underlings dwelling place. I thought I was learning my way around my own country, and here, I stumbled down a rabbit hole where I couldn't believe anything. I hoped we hadn't been wrong in trusting the Cornwalls.

The steps were wide and made of concrete. I had never been in a basement before. I was surprised. I expected to see junk in every corner and rats running around. Even though it was black as pitch when we started down, once Barbara flipped on the lights everything I had feared was absent. Just a few boxes and storage crates were present and all of them were organized and tidy.

"This is a great space down here," I said. "If there were natural light down here, someone could call it home."

Barbara pointed to the walls. "The windows are covered in black cloth because that is a city-wide law. The authorities tell the underlings that there are coverings on all of the openings so the roving packs of human-animals cannot see them. But, the truth is, the good and proper people on the surface don't want the moles to see that the city is actually safe and clean and the sky is blue and the sun is shining." Barbara's tone was that of rehearsed disgust.

Suddenly, there was a screech and the sound of heavy metal scraping across concrete. The cover to the manhole slid to the side and a man climbed up the ladder and into the basement, followed by a woman who appeared to be with him, a boy and a girl, and several others.

"I am so glad you have come," Barbara smiled and embraced them, even though their clothes were tattered and dirty and their odor was putrid. "We have installed a shower up on top, in a warm wet room," she explained. "Since it is still winter, you will want to get wet quickly, dry off and change into clean clothes we have hung up for you. If you are quick, you can still turn your faces to the sun for another ten minutes."

The elevator was large enough to hold us all, those of us who were *fine and fancy,* the little family and various strays. It was tight inside the lift car. I gaged from their stench and buried my face in my hands which also provided a cover for my nose. When the doors opened on top, I burst out into the cold fresh air and breathed in as deeply as I could. Jason grabbed me around the waist as if to hug me, but placed his hands on my diaphragm to steady the spasms.

I watched as the others stepped onto the roof. They grabbed their eyes in obvious pain and held their hands there. It took several of their precious minutes on top to adjust their eyes to the brilliant winter light.

"Your glasses ..." Barbara coached, "the glasses I gave you, put them on quickly. Look at me, I'll put mine on." She forced the frames open and pushed them onto her face. "Quickly ... quickly."

I felt dazed and had to snap out of it. I dashed from one person to another and helped them to shade their eyes with the dark lenses.

Richard came up on the elevator and brought jackets and caps in his lap. "Up here, it's cold. The heat pipes under the city make the under-world pretty warm. Here," he spoke as he handed out jackets and blankets, "take these. You won't get as much sun as you will in the spring but we will build up to that as time goes on."

Barbara helped a child wrap a wool blanket around her. "I hope it's all right that we left the contingent of volunteers from the west downstairs." She spoke to me in a whisper. "I wanted you to get to know a few of the moles before we overwhelm the underlings with so many of you."

"That's probably a good idea," I agreed. I was one who was overwhelmed already. I could not begin to imagine what it would be like to live all my life underground. In the Central Zone, we live in the dark, but that's because we choose the dark over the light, not because there is no light at all.

"Is it too blinding for you?" I asked one young woman, about my age. She stood frozen to one spot as she held her hand over her face.

"Yes, the sky is brighter than I had ever imagined," she said through her fingers. "But, I want to open my eyes so much." She spread her fingers just a crack to let in the smallest stream of light possible. "I want to see it all ... even the bad parts."

"The earth is full of beauty," I told her as I helped her with her dark glasses. "See? Drink in the color of God's world."

"Lacy, Honey, there is so much to tell you ... all of you from below," Barbara put her arms around the young woman. "Now, enjoy the sun, shower and change your clothes, and then those of you here today will come below to the living area."

"In your house?" Lacy stammered. "But, we will all be shot or put in jail if we come out from the caverns." Her eyes welled up in tears and her expression grew tight with fear. She wrapped her arms around her body as the only protection she had for herself.

"It will be all right, Lacy. I'll prove it. This woman is Lady Applewait; she is a daughter of the ruling class. She won't let anything happen to you ... and neither will I," Richard assured her.

"The rulers?" Lacy recoiled from me and drew herself into the smallest ball of humanity that she could. "You are dangerous," she accused.

"I'm not dangerous to you, Lacy. Mrs. Cornwall is right. My grandfather is Sir Oliver Richly and my grandmother is Constance Richly. I ... I will protect you." I gathered her dirty hand in mine and patted the top. It was surprisingly soft. Her skin was thin to the touch. *How am I going to calm her, to reassure her? If I were her, I can't imagine I would trust anyone.*

I opened my heart to Lacy and tried to comfort her. "This is a lovely garden up here, above the city. Enjoy the blue sky. When you come down, perhaps the inside rooms will not seem as bright."

The garden on the roof, above the streets, was wonderful. There was a section of out-door chaise-lounge chairs where sunbathers could rest and drink in the sunlight. On the long edge of the balcony, along the surrounding wall, ran an unending dark brown bench with soft blue padded cushions. The Cornwalls had taken the seasonal cushions out of storage and placed them on the deck/roof minutes before the visitors arrived. An outdoor cooking area with grill, cabinets and bar with chairs was up against the interior wall, protected from the elements.

"Barbara, it is wonderful up here. How long have the cavern people been coming up?" I asked.

"We started in the fall. Then when it got cold, we didn't have the heart to close the basement entrance. The underlings are amazed by the sky and the light." Barbara's voice trailed off. "It breaks my heart that they had never experienced it all before."

Jason had been circulating among the people with the eye of a physician. "I have seen some with the beginning of rickets from the Vitamin D deficiency, and they are all pale with probable eye conditions, but when you think about how they have lived ... it is amazing how healthy they seem to be."

Barbara patted the youngest child as she squinted in the light. "The old subway train runs to the mouth of the caverns that branch off in several directions. It brings only a very small portion of meat, some vegetables and fruits that didn't sell in the stores. The underlings have to share with everyone down there. Diseases due to obesity are certainly not a problem for them. Richard and I would love to take candy and desserts to them, but we were afraid to."

"I'm glad you didn't. I'm not sure how their bodies would have reacted." Jason smiled and then put his hand on Richard's wheelchair. "Can I take you back down? You will only ache more if you get too cold."

"Let's all go back inside," he agreed. "Barbara will bring the rest of them down in a few minutes."

Jason and I walked over to the elevator and I turned for a moment. Lacy was already showered, dried and dressed. She stood facing the sun with her eyes closed and her chin up. She reminded me of a delicate flower in a spring garden that turns its petals to the life-giving sun. When the elevator car reached the roof, Jason, Richard and I went down to meet the other volunteers in the dining room.

We walked across the marble floor of the hall and onto the hard wood. Inside the dining room, the other volunteers were laughing and enjoying each other's company.

"We might as well stay in here," Richard suggested. "In a matter of minutes, Barbara will bring in a few underlings who have been enjoying the sun on the roof. Everyone, please remember to stay seated when they enter. I know it's the usual courtesy for men to rise when people enter, but this case is different. You will discover that many things are out of the usual. If you stand, the underlings will feel threatened."

As the house elevator doors opened, Barbara stepped off and invited the moles into her home. They were all very awkward. Their eyes darted back and forth, not only because they appeared to be taking in every sight, but because they seemed to be very hyper-vigilant, watching for any threat, real or imagined. A man, who appeared to have the thin bones of one with rickets that would cause him to struggle with walking, entered with distorted, bowed legs. The handicap that was the most visible among many of them was the shock and terror on their faces. Would they be able to hear or believe anything we had to say? Would they be able to adjust to a completely opposite view of life from the one they had lived under all of their lives? Would fear rob them of the ability to adjust quickly enough to seize this life-changing opportunity?

My impulse was to whisper, like one would sooth a frightened child. "Lacy, there you are." She was the only one whose name I knew, so I started with her. "You look so nice, Sweetheart," I assured her. "You have a little sunlight on you cheeks. Those clothes Barbara gave you are great."

I gently took her hand and led her further into the room. Surprisingly, her muscles had seemed to relax already from the shower and sun. She was compliant and easily led. "I would like you to meet some of my friends from far away, where the ocean is calmer than the one here."

"Ocean?" Lacy questioned.

"They have not seen anything above ground," Barbara reminded me.

"What about the view from the rooftop? Were you able to see anything up there?"

"With the dark glasses I could open my eyes for a few minutes. We have lights below, so we adjusted to some light—but not the bright sun. And, yes, My Lady, I did see a little of the view from up on top."

"Out beyond the buildings there is a wide patch of water that goes on and on," I tried to explain. "You couldn't see the other side, just water. That's the ocean."

"It was all so beautiful," Lacy said softly and smiled.

Well, there is another big ocean, miles and miles on the other side of our country. Many of the people here in this room are from that coast," I explained in a tone I hoped did not sound condescending.

"All of you ... come on in," Barbara invited the rest of them. "You can sit along the floor with the others." She pointed to floor space on the far side of the room. "Yes, there and there." Then she seemed to blush. "I'm sorry we don't have enough seating."

"I would like to give Lacy my chair, if I may," Little Feather offered as she slowed got up.

"Oh no," Lacy said. "I can't take your place."

"You aren't taking it, Lacy. I'm giving it to you. It is my privilege to offer you what I have." Slowly some of the other travelers got up from their seats and insisted that one from the underworld take it. They then took the floor space along the wall.

"Thank you all for having a generous spirit." Barbara smiled as she watched the moles hesitate then slide onto the velvet upholstered dining room chairs. They felt of the soft fabric. Their eyes lit up with some of the light they had just seen and were now experiencing in a different way. "Let's begin," Barbara announced. "Christiana, please sit at the table with our guests," she gestured toward an empty seat at the head of the table. "Most of you had met Lady Applewait and Dr. O'Reilly up on top."

The newly freed outcasts nodded and smiled. Some whispered between each other.

"Please, call us Christy and Jason," I urged. "We have a very important job that requires our equal ownership for it to succeed."

"Equal?" The man said who now sat on a real chair for the first time in his life. "Equal has never been used in our language. What does it mean?"

"It means—" I started to give a definition and then scrambled to think of words that were so simple they escaped explanation. "Equal means that I am no better than you, and you are no better than me."

"Oh ... yoke-sharers," he said as his face spread into a grin. "I'll carry the bucket on my shoulder if you'll carry the other one on your shoulder."

The underlings smiled and giggled.

"Exactly," I agreed, amazed by his ability to grasp a concept I had trouble putting into words.

"I don't want to offend any of you," Jason began cautiously, "but can those in the caverns below read and write?"

"Yes, nearly all of us, except the weakest ones. And even those can write their name and read short pieces. They get tired so fast it's hard for them to pay attention to anything for very long. They sleep a lot."

"But, could they learn?" I stumbled into the question without thinking about who might be hurt. "I'm sorry. What I guess I meant was, who taught them?"

"We have very little down there," a man of about thirty said with a set jaw and downcast eyes, "but we had loving parents who taught us to read and write. They would scratch in the dirt and sludge on the ground. Together, we would make up stories and Mum or Da would write them down on paper we found in the trash at the railhead, then we would read them back to them. Our history was learned through story-telling."

"And remember, Maisie has gone down to teach some of them and they would have taught others," Barbara reminded me.

"Yes, Maisie, I'm sorry. I did forget." Then I looked at the small group of moles and realized all they had done. "You have created your own society down there, haven't you?" I observed. "I don't know how to tell you, but the history of the world on top has been far different from what you had been told. What I mean is we are no longer the free society that you may have learned about."

"Yes Ma'am. We are not free," a woman said.

"That is true. But the reason for your living below all of these years ... was a lie. Not one word of what you were told was true." I felt so badly for them. They looked at me like I had switched my language into the native tongue of a distant world.

"What part of it was a lie?" Lacy asked. "We have all lived below because they said there are mutant human-animals that would stalk and kill us."

"None of that is true," I whispered. The underlings looked at me, then at Maisie, Jason and the rest of us with glazed eyes. I wondered if they would be able to absorb the deception they had lived.

Chapter 35
They Came in Search

We all heard some commotion in the entry hall. Richard Cornwall snapped his wheelchair around. I saw he was a man of strength, the protector of the house, and wheelchair or not, he would fulfill his duties. He slipped away from the rest of us and quickly made his way to the door. Just as he got there, the door flew opened. "Harold, what seems to be the problem?"

"Is this Mr. Cornwall?" A man at the door questioned and took a step inside the house.

"Stop there, Sir," Richard ordered. "This is my home, and you have not been invited in."

"Invited?" the man grumbled. "I am Chief Inspector Stoner of the Blue Guard," he announced brashly and took another step. "I have a right to enter wherever I decide."

"Not in the Eastern Zone, Chief Inspector. You have no reason to enter my home. We don't have our homes invaded—and certainly not here in the city. We are in charge of our own fate here. We enjoy certain privileges."

Stoner stood his ground but did not take another step. "Oh you do, do you?" he smirked. "It has been reported that several long cars pulled into your driveway and dropped off quite a few people. Congregating in one spot is illegal. We are on the trail of some who have crossed into your zone. They could have been in the party."

"We are coming in," a big burly man thundered.

"Hold your ground, Daniel," a woman ordered.

"You have no authority in this zone, Sir," Cornwall pronounced with clear determination.

"I have national papers, Mister. Now, move aside. In the Central Zone, we would *exterminate* you. We don't have men in rolling chairs ordering people around." Again Stoner edged his way forward.

"Well, we do. Your national papers only allow you to cross the border and observe. You cannot pursue anyone or interfere in citizens' lives. And, you certainly have no right to enter my home."

"Who I am in pursuit of ... Mr. Cornwall," the Inspector spit out, "is not a citizen of the Eastern Zone."

"But, he is ..." Richard spoke with measured tones, "he is a citizen of the United States ... before he is a resident of any zone."

"He who?" Stoner bellowed.

"He is the collective *he,* Inspector. *He* would refer to anyone who lives within the borders of the United States," Richard schooled him in American history.

"These are detached but United Zones—Mister. I do not recognize the United States," he yelled as his neck veins bulged.

"Sir," the woman spoke insistently to the inspector, "let's go. We can watch this house to see who comes and goes."

"Boone," Stoner seethed, "do not correct me," he shouted.

"I'm not, Sir. I'm suggesting another strategy."

"If you stay at least one block away, you have the right to observe any house in the city." Cornwall smiled with confidence. He didn't add that the underworld was vast catacombs deep beneath their shoes that connected all of the areas of the city.

"What do you want me to do, Boss?" Daniel asked; his face rock hard with anger. "The Blue Guard can go anywhere we want to."

"But, not here," Richard stated firmly.

Stoner stood back and looked down his nose at Cornwall. "You haven't won, Mister. Believe me, we will research our facts. If we find out that you are harboring illegal immigrants, you will be arrested."

"There is so much injustice in our land right now, Inspector, someone crossing a border within their own country, surely is not that important to you."

"She is not just *someone*." Stoner stormed out with Boone and Daniel Washington on his heels.

Richard sat silently in his chair and listened for the footsteps to fade on the front walk outside. Then he threw the dead bolt on the door. "Harold, be sure to keep the door lock set, even when we are home. It seems we have an overzealous police officer in our zone."

"Sure, Richard. Hopefully, he'll find who he's looking for and leave the zone."

"He has already found her. He just doesn't know it."

• • • • •

Richard wheeled himself back into the dining room where we all sat and waited in stunned silence. Lacy trembled beside me. Maisie had quietly come over and patted Lacy's shoulder and stroked her hair.

"Didn't Richard tell you that he wouldn't let anything happen to you?" Barbara began. "He didn't, did he? We will be as careful as we can be ... but it's true, there will be those who will try to stop us, all of us. I won't speak about the other zones, but the ruling elite in the Eastern Zone, want things to remain as they are."

"There isn't a lot of time for you to catch up to the truth," I started to explain. "For that, I am sorry." My words seemed completely unworthy of the situation. I had no idea how to tell these people that they had been enslaved underground all of their lives for no other reason than that the elites didn't want to see them in their world.

"We have come here from the Central Zone to get your help on overturning a law that you may not know anything about," Jason began.

"I'm Lincoln Jeffrey," the thirty-something underling spoke up as he straightened his back. "No, we haven't heard of any of your laws but—"

"We don't mean to insult you. There are things you haven't been told. That's what we need to explain. It is not my law. It's the law of the land. Some zones obey the law, others do not, or they adjust it to meet their needs," Jason said.

"The law is a despicably evil law, Lincoln," I explained. "In the short version, people are not permitted to live out their lives until they finally die of natural causes. A hundred years ago, the government worked out a formula that dictates how long a person can live, based upon how valuable they are to society." I looked around at the moles and I saw something, a connection in their expression. Some place within them, they understood.

"We didn't know about the law, but there's been a rumor for a long time, that people above ground live a whole lot longer than we do," Lincoln said.

I looked across the table at everyone who had gathered there. "We are here to get people's signatures on special papers called petitions, so we can vote to get rid of the law. We will need your help to call on other friends down below to try to get everyone's signature, and bring them to the Citadel, here at Richard and Barbara's house."

Suddenly their faces contorted in fear. "Will we come up through the basement? We can't come out in the open," Lacy gasped.

"There is something else, Lacy," Barbara began. "You don't have to live below ground. The town is safe. No bands of murderers roam the streets."

"That can't be true," the young woman barked in anger.

"Yes, it is true, Lacy," Lincoln agreed. "You know I've snuck into the church services in the big cathedral on Fifth Avenue." He turned to Jason and I. "I retell the sermon when I get below again. Isn't that true?" he asked as he addressed his friends. He wore sadness on his face like a shroud of tears.

The moles whispered around the table. Their voices became flat and despondent. Their tones grew grayer as they listened.

"Listen to Lincoln," Maisie pleaded. "You know him better than me. I was an underling too."

"That's a lie!" A man exploded as if his heart would burst if he remained silent any longer.

"No, it's the truth. Valery and Albert Zimmerman are my parents." She held her head high, as a dual citizen—one foot in the underworld and one foot on top.

"Maisie?" Lacy gasped. "You're my cousin. How is that possible? You went up into the world and everyone said you were killed."

"I wasn't killed. I'm here," she said as she laughed.

"After church," Lincoln began again, "I would go outside, onto the sidewalk after the service and watch the fine people going for a walk in the sunshine, laughing and loving their families all dressed up in fancy clothes." His eyes shone like he was seeing the fine parade of families passing by in their summer whites.

Some of the moles sat dazed by what they heard. Others gasped in stunned desperation, "What happened to us?"

Richard explained, "Those in the government with elected authority, some in entertainment with pseudo influence and many in business who had wealth—began to believe they were more important than those they hired. They believed they were entitled to live their lives away from the common people. They started to separate themselves from the people who worked for them by putting up high walls around their estates. They demanded abundant generosity from those whom they walled out, and lavish ownership for themselves. As time went on, they felt so guilty about their growing wealth they believed that people had to be taken care of with handouts of food, shelter, education, health care and, finally, nearly all of their daily needs."

"They made us all like their children," Lincoln realized.

I watched as their eyes welled up with tears, as grief over their lost lives began to pour out. Leaning my elbows on the table, I continued. "Then, they said, if the masses can't take care of themselves, why should we have to look at them every day?"

"Look at us?" Maisie asked, her voice filled with disgust.

They had to hear the truth. I continued. "They built high rise apartment buildings and gave the people a schedule of hours when they could be outside. They claimed it was the way to keep the population on the streets and in all of the stores at a manageable number."

"Manageable?" one said with a gasp. "We were managed–like the rat population?" His voice sounded strained and shrill.

"Then, one of the fancy people said, they shouldn't have to see any of you at all. That's when they started the big lie." Tears rolled down my cheeks as I tried to explain how selfish, evil people had robbed them of their lives.

"So ..." Lincoln tried to speak but his voice cracked, "there was no reason at all ... none ... for us to have been born, lived and died in the sewers, basements and subways of this city?"

"Absolutely no reason at all," I whispered. "It's like a political prison my grandmother told me about." Tears streamed down my face. "You all have been prisoners, too."

"You can all come out from the underworld," Barbara said. "Everyone can come into the light. For many of you, your ancestral home has been vacant since you or your loved ones left it. The dishes are in the cupboards, the books are on the shelves." Barbara said. "I have been in some of those homes."

"You mean we could walk right out your front door?" One of them asked as he fought tears and anguish. One woman laid her arms across the table and sobbed into the fold.

"Yes, you could. You can walk out of here and not come back." Richard stopped as the facts of their kidnapped lives soaked in. "You are all emancipated." He rolled his chair a few inches back from the table, as a gesture of freedom-giving.

"I feel like a slave being told they are free and can leave the plantation. But, I don't know where to go or how to get there." A middle aged woman's face, etched in pain and sorrow, twitched with emotion. She angrily brushed a matted curl from her brow.

"You have heard about slavery and the old plantation system of generations past?" I ask. I couldn't believe what I heard. "How would you know, with no one to teach you?"

"But, we do have teachers, Ma'am. Lincoln taught many. Our grandparents taught our parents, who taught us. Where there's a wish for knowledge, there's a teacher," the woman spoke with pride.

"And, as for places to live, we can help you find your home," Barbara offered.

Suddenly, anger welled up inside the woman with the curl on her forehead as she set her jaw and spoke in tense, chopped words. "What if I leave and never come back? What will you do then?"

"Nothing," Richard spoke softly, comfortingly.

The woman got up and started to walk out of the room, then turned. "You really aren't going to stop me?"

"Of course not," Barbara assured her. "Like we said, you have always been a free person ... but, none of you knew it."

"None of us?" She stopped. "My daughter is still down there. I can't go anywhere until I get her out. I have to get her out," she cried. "I have to get her out!"

"May I tell you the plan the Cornwalls, Jason and I talked about?" I asked. I was careful to make no statements but to ask her permission.

"All right? Do I have to sit back down?"

"You may do anything you want to do," I offered.

"Okay," she said hesitantly and moved against the wall without sitting.

"The volunteers from the Western Zone will go down with some of you to talk to the people and tell them that they're free. Jason and I will go, too. We will lead the people, your friends and family out, and up the steps through one of six subway exits so that we can help as many as need our assistance. I know there will be many, but Dr. O'Reilly believes we need to help the sick when they emerge," I added.

"There aren't as many as you would think, after all of these years," Lincoln reported angrily. Then he added with a sorrow-filled whisper, "They all die so young, so very young."

Lincoln's words stirred me so much it was hard to continue. "I am so sorry, Lincoln." Then I turned intently to all of them and added, "At the opening from the wretched bowels of the city, people will greet each one and ask them if they want to sign a petition to stop another evil that has been perpetrated on the people, the Length of Days law. It wickedly limits a person's number of years of life. Under that edict, people don't just die of disease or old age. When they reach a certain age, extermination is the law. We are trying to over-turn that abomination."

"Give me a pencil," the woman snapped to attention. "I'll sign that paper."

"Thank you for volunteering . . ." I waited for the woman to give me her name, so I could add her to my mental list of heroes.

"My name?" she asked with wide eyes. "You want my name?"

"Yes, Ma'am," I said gently.

All eyes turned to her as she shifted a darting glance from one of us to another. "My name? ... My name is Jennifer."

"What a beautiful name, Sweetheart," Barbara said and gently accepted the woman from below.

"Stewie?" one of the moles gasped. "I thought your name is Stewie."

Jennifer smiled sheepishly and nodded as she said, "They all like my stew."

"If I may, I'll call you Jennifer," I said. "The name is as pretty as you are." I couldn't help but notice the sparkle in her blue eyes, in spite of the conditions under which she had lived her whole life.

"Yes, please do." She smiled a smile that filled her face.

"The people collecting the signatures will not force anyone. They will not tell anyone that their signature is their ticket out of the darkness, or anything like that. They need no ticket. All they have to do is walk out. The people will just be asked if they want to sign it."

"Just like that?" she questioned. "We walk out on our own and no one will stop us or harm any of us. That sounds nice, but, how in the world will we be able to cope, in a world of light we have never known?"

"One day at a time," Barbara said.

"I don't' pretend to understand how you feel," I assured her. "I can tell you this—in the Central Zone, the water the people drink is laced with drugs that dull their emotions. They don't feel anger or anxiety, but they don't feel joy or love either. We have started to detoxify them. They have to learn how to relate to each other all over again, to know the feelings of attraction, to feel the love of their families. They have to walk that journey one step at a time, too."

The woman squared her shoulders and drew herself up to her full height. "Then I can do it, too. You can count on me. I have no idea how to do this, but I won't be helpless anymore. They can keep their free food and their free cast off, ill-fitting clothes. I will earn my own."

Chapter 36
A World Below

Tuesday - February 7, 2113

Very late in the morning of the next day, when the sun was nearing its peak above us, Jason, the Western Zone volunteers and I accompanied Barbara Cornwall, Lacy, Lincoln and some of the other underlings as we approached the opening to the belly of the city. It used to be a subway entrance. But, since the only transportation the wealthy enjoyed was their own personal flash-cars, limousines, or aerial lifts from rooftop to rooftop, the mouth of the River Styx was now nothing more than gum-blotched cement steps and a dangling bronze hand railing.

"It'll take a while for your eyes to adjust to the dim light," Lincoln explained as we descended into the unlit subterranean maze of tracks and tunnels. "Torches are placed on the walls at the entrance to the various areas. Then once you have gone deeper into the underground communities, you'll begin to see crude connections for electric lights. We still have to keep the light dim so we're not seen above-ground."

He sounded so educated, I was amazed. I said nothing. I had no words for this whole experience. It was so far from my own world on the top floor of the Indian River Apartments, I couldn't wrap my mind around the dank existence here. I was surprised I felt no disgust as we descended down further into the troll-like world below the streets of the beautiful city of parks and monuments. Lincoln was right. I saw the faint glow of light, but my eyes focused on the darkness all around me. I wondered if the underlings gazed more intently on the light than the dark. We inched our way through the below-world.

"Oh," Lacy moaned as she bent over.

"What happened?" Barbara asked and put her arm around Lacy's shoulder.

"I stepped on something and twisted my ankle."

Barbara looked apologetically at us. "I am so sorry. I'd better take Lacy back to the house and check her for any scratch or cuts. Infection can so easily get in. Their immune system is very low. She can rest her ankle for the afternoon."

"I'm glad you're going to take care of her immediately, Barbara," Jason said. "And, the rest of us—be very careful where you step. Inoculations for the diseases that may be down here, stopped a hundred year ago."

"Put your feet up, Lacy," I said as they left. "Thanks Barbara."

"Take care, Lacy," Lincoln said before he turned back to us and continued. "We'll be going above and sometimes below the sewers. Where they're below, we'll have to drop down through some manhole's to follow those trunks," Lincoln explained as he looked both ways into the dark recesses of the underworld. "Some of the large-trunk sewer lines were too large to change when the subway was built, so there had to be a large adjustment of the gradients of the subway in order for the line to pass them," he smiled with satisfaction. "I often spend time in the library and try to figure out what stands over our heads in the world above," he said. "At Canal Street and Broadway and at Duane Street and West Broadway here in Manhattan, the subways were built to go under the sewer. At Brook Avenue and 138th Street, in the Bronx, they actually raised the surface of the street by five feet so the subway could pass over the sewer."

"That's amazing that you found out about all of this, Lincoln. You're so valuable to us," Jason encouraged.

"Over the years, I've been through every inch of this maze down here," he said as we walked and climbed and maneuvered through it all.

"Are you going to make it, Christy?" Jason asked as we both looked at the obstacles in front of us.

"I have to," was all I could think of. And, it was true. I couldn't stop before I had even begun.

As my eyes adjusted, I found myself in a large tiled space with a train track running through it. People were everywhere: on steps that led to nowhere but another sealed opening; leaning against the walls; and even on the narrow walkway across on the other side of the tracks. Some children were playing a game drawn on the floor in which they tossed a pebble into a square and then proceeded to skip along, jumping over the square occupied by the small stone. I panicked a little until I heard the others climb through the opening behind us.

I had led a very sheltered life. Just a few months before, no one could even approach me because I was and am, a legacy citizen. I smirked at my own silly thoughts of privilege and position, while these people lived their lives buried under the ground.

"Oh, Jason, I'm so glad you're here." I felt like a child as I grabbed him and clung to his arm.

"I know, Honey. It's all so strange and different. But, remember, we have our depravity too ... under Howard Mountain." Jason assured me, "You are one of the strongest people I know. You can do this."

"Friends," Lincoln began addressing those who clustered near us as he closed an opening to the stale sewer on the other side. "I want you to meet some new friends. They're from the surface, but it's okay. You're safe."

The people huddled together while the children ran to some adults for reassurance. "The surface?" one of them questioned.

"Yes," Lincoln said quickly, "but they mean us no harm. Their message is the most important news you will ever hear."

Suddenly we heard loud voices and the sound of heavy boot thumps from a trunk line that intersected the one we had just come through. I held my breath. The faces of the underlings around us grew tight with fear and terror filled their eyes. The angry world above had found them.

"Where? Where are the man and woman? I don't know how they got down here but someone reported invaders in your midst." We heard a distant voice from the other track line. "Answer me!" the voice shouted.

I grabbed Jason's hand and drew it to my lips. My kiss was not gentle. It was urgent and full of the panic I felt deep inside.

The underlings around us clutched one another with fear etched on their faces. The older ones gently put their hands over the smaller ones' mouths to caution them to be silent.

We listened to the demands from the distant shouter. I recognized the voice. I knew who was down there. He had followed us to the gates of purgatory. I listen as another man spoke.

"What are you doing down here?" A different male voice bellowed from a short distance farther into the subway trunk. "You three, get out. We may be afraid to come to the surface, but I guarantee you, we'll protect our safety down here!"

"Mama?" one of the children whispered.

The woman made no sound. I wondered how she had caused the child to be silent. I couldn't see them, but I knew that staying in the shadows would be the only thing that would save us.

"I am Chief Inspector of the Blue Guard!" the man bellowed.

My breathing stopped. I was right. Stoner was here. My presence could bring harm to the people who had already suffered more than they even knew.

"Ward," a female voice urged, "let's go. The Lady wouldn't be down here."

"A woman said, those scum from below were meeting at the Cornwall house," the Chief demanded.

"We went there, Sir. Nothing was out of the ordinary. Besides, the citizens of this zone can be anywhere they want to be," she stated flatly.

"But, they choose to live in this wretched place. Can you imagine? They gave up the light for this sunless place," his voice was angry and erratic. "That is why we kill the feeble minded in our zone."

"Did you hear me?" the underworld protector hissed. "Get out of here!"

"All right, all right, we're going. But, if strangers are in the tunnels, you will let us know, won't you?" the growling inspector coaxed.

"Sure we will, right away," the voice agreed flatly. "I will escort you out of the lower reaches."

"That won't be necessary," Stoner barked.

The man stood firm. "Yes, Sir, it will be very necessary. No one, and I mean no one, comes down here on purpose."

We all remained motionless, silent. A small child squeezed his eyes shut, balled up his fists and held his breath. We froze in place, regardless of how uncomfortable our position had been. My back stung with pain as I tried to balance myself with one foot on the train tracks and one on the concrete pathway that ran beside and above it. We didn't move until we couldn't hear the footsteps and voices any more.

Lincoln spoke first. "That was Jefferson, my brother. He was the one who ordered them out of the tunnels. He'll join us here in a minute, as soon as he has thrown those three out. They were probably harmless, but we take no chances."

"They aren't harmless." I stated firmly.

"You recognized their voices?"

"Oh yes," Jason agreed. "We know them. They are very dangerous people. But, you are not their target."

"They aren't after you," I assured them. "They're after us, Jason and me. We will talk to your people, recruit those who can help and try to tie things up as quickly as possible." I looked at the faces of the little ones around me. I couldn't allow them to be hurt or even frightened. As I adjusted to the dim light, their sweet faces became clear. I didn't want my presence to bring harm to others.

"Okay, they're gone." Jefferson smiled as he backed into our area, not turning his back on Stoner and his crew.

"Lincoln . . ." I smiled as I put the two men together. "You have had history books down here, haven't you ... Lincoln and his brother, Jefferson."

"No books, but we have wonderful oral histories and keepers of the stories," Jefferson explained. Then he added, "Is Gray Fox here with you?"

"Yes, he and his wife are traveling with us. You know him?"

"Yes," he agreed.

Gray Fox and Little Feather emerged into the train passage once the ruckus had cleared out. His countenance was stoic and calm.

"I have a message for you." Jefferson offered a piece of folded paper to Gray Fox.

"How did it arrive?" the Navajo asked.

"It came across the Cornwalls' communication device. She wrote it down exactly as it was told to her."

Gray Fox took the paper and unfolded the sheet. "AL-NESHODI UL-SO ... Mission Accomplished," he translated, and then he smiled. "Rachel Claudette had worked with a tribesman of mine to get the message through in a language that could not be translated by others."

"So, the Western Zone has completed their petitions with an adequate number of signatures?" I questioned.

"Mission Accomplished," he pronounced again.

"They are finished with their canvass of citizens?" Lincoln asked. "Already?"

"The Western Zone has a vastly different demographic than the other zones," Jason explained. "There are a huge percentage of Spirit-filled people there. They signed petitions as they left worship services on the Sunday morning that we were there. Connected by the Jumbotrons, we reached a multitude of people in a matter of minutes. That left the collection of names by the Hollow People."

"Hollow? What does that mean?" Jefferson asked. "They're empty?"

"That's what has been said for many years. They don't circulate with the regular population. They can't work, participate in education or receive any benefits of citizenship, including the right to vote."

"Like us," Jefferson said bitterly.

"Yes, I suppose ... just like you," Jason agreed. "And, like the underlings, they are very much misunderstood. One of the Hollow Men, Raymar Goring and his daughter Kasamar reached out to the unseen people in their society and told them they were needed."

"They were needed?" a woman with pale skin and lifeless eyes repeated.

I watched the woman's face as something turned on inside of her. "And you are needed as well," I assured her. "Raymar told his people that they were vitally important to the cause of humanity and our reverence for life. We need signatures from as many of our citizens as possible to overturn the Length of Days law. A return to the old way will let people live as long as their body can," I added. "Life is so precious. You here in the under-world, live to be about forty-five years old. In the Central Zone, people live until they reach a pre-determined number of years. For my grandparents, because they are on the Council of Twelve, they reach the end of their Length of Days at age seventy-five."

"Ah," the woman gasped. "Age seventy-five?" She shook her head in disbelief. "How can that be? They would be old and decrepit by then."

Now that I had informed them, I wondered if they would even believe. "In the Western Zone, people live to be about one-hundred forty-five."

Her expression was not that of disbelief. It was of pain and sorry as she added, "Except for the Hollow Ones," she whispered. "They have no reason to live many years."

I knew she understood the tragedy of the Hollow Ones' lives because she had lived it in her own way. Her face fell in sorrow and her eyes rimmed with tears. "Except for the Hollow People, you are right. We will make sure they can live fully in society too and enjoy long years of life. You all can," I assured her, "with the elimination of the Length of Days law."

"Why would you do that?" someone asked.

"Because you all have a right to life, liberty and the chance to pursue your own happiness," I quoted. "You have a right to reclaim your ancestral homes, find jobs and seek your own joy in life ... above ground where the sun shines and the sky is a beautiful blue."

"I have seen the sky," a boy about twelve years old blurted out.

"Frankie, don't tell people that," a woman warned. Fear escaped her eyes as she clasped her hand to her mouth. "Hush, hush. It's very dangerous to speak out."

"But it's true," the boy said. He became excited as he revealed a secret he may have held for a long time. "I stand below the street grate when the sun is high in the sky and the colors are bright and beautiful. I can see that blue color you talked about. It's super," his young eyes shone with a heart that has seen the color of hope. "That's its name? Blue?" he asked. "But, I never knew that I would be able to walk into the world of light, the world of blue."

"It's so dark and dull here," his mother said as she put her arm on the boy's shoulder and gave him a hug. "We had forgotten the names of the colors, or how to explain the shades to our children. In the dark, we only see shades of black and gray. Blue is only blue when you can see it."

"Frankie," I said as I reached out and touched his shoulder, "yes. The color of the sky ... and your mother's eyes are blue."

Frankie reached up and touched his mother's cheek, as if he were trying to open her eyes even wider and inspect the new color of blue.

I wondered if the mother and son saw the tears in my own eyes. "Frankie, would you like to be one of the liberators ... one of the many who will tell others that they are free? We could use an important young man like you."

The boy's eyes filled with tears that made salty streaks on his dirty face. Finally, he was able to choke out a whisper. "Could I do that?"

I smiled and let the enthusiasm I felt inside, slip out into the open. "I'll bet you have been all over down here. I knew every alley, field of wild flowers, and pile of re-usable *good* trash in the neighborhood in which I grew up. You probably have inspected and investigated every nook and cranny in the underground. This is your world and you are comfortable down here. You know the tunnels, the subways, and the sewer line. I can just imagine you inching up manhole openings and darting down dark passages with no fear. Yes, you are needed."

"I am needed? Just like the Hollow Man?" he asked. "He had been all over everywhere, too, because they wouldn't let him stay anywhere very long."

"You would be just like that man. He is full of life now."

"Can we start today?" he asked. "I want to help. I want to be needed." He looked up and his eyes met his mother's. She nodded with pride and mouthed, "Thank you."

"We sure can," I agreed. Then, to all those gathered around, I explained, "Barbara and Richard Cornwall have placed trusted volunteers at several subway exits. They each have petitions and pens so we can get that law overturned. We hope everyone will sign one of them." As I looked around at all the eager faces, another thought came to mind. "Be sure you sign the petition only once. I appreciate any enthusiasm, but it will make the petition invalid if there are false signatures on them."

The people smiled and nodded. They understood the need for honesty, but their expressions revealed a thought that might not have been too far from some of their minds.

I wanted to laugh but thought they might not understand. "It will be important for everyone to come up from the underworld through the subway exits, not the manholes, so they can have an opportunity to put their signature on one of the documents. When they sign the petition, it will also give the Cornwall's a list of all those who had been enslaved on emancipation day. They have a committee ready to help the people relocate."

"I can take you all through the world of slime and darkness right now, if you're ready. Can we start now?" The boy reached for my hand and urged me along. I could feel the excitement through his fingers. They trembled with urgency.

"Frankie . . ." the woman cautioned. "Be patient. The lady will tell you when she's ready to begin contacting all our friends." She grabbed his hand but he pulled away from her, not in rebellion but in anticipation of the amazing task we had in front of us. I was surprised at how quickly a young child could pick up on the importance of our work. Then I laughed when I learned his motive.

"Please Mama, please!" Again his eyes filled with tears. "Don't try to stop me. This is my chance to be somebody."

His mother brushed his hair from his eyes and cupped his chin in her hand. "Always remember, Frankie," she soothed. "You have always been somebody, and you will always be somebody. Not somebody else, but the very best you that God has ever created."

"I know Mama," he said.

"All of you are somebodies," I said softly. "No one can be a better you, than you."

"You can go, Frankie, but I want to come along," his mother stood tall and strong. She squared her shoulders and inhaled deeply, filling her lungs with a new life. "I want to join in the enthusiasm. I want to feel like somebody, too."

"Follow me," Frankie squealed as he skittered off and led the way through the dark halls and tunnel-ways of his world, beneath the city, under the very feet of the ruling elite.

Chapter 37
Jewels

We had been groping our way through the underground passageways, basements, sewers, and subways of New York City. I was amazed how readily the people accepted the fact that they were a free people. Frankie and his mother joined another group and followed off in a different direction, a location where many children lived.

One man told us, "In this corner of the underlings' world we had always known that we were lied to. We went up-top to get the truth ourselves. Nothing happened to us. We didn't talk to people, and they didn't talk to us. It was safe." He stopped and sat down on an old up-turned barrel. He looked around at the old friends he had lived with and smiled. "But, our family lived all over down here, in various areas of the world below, and they had either not heard the truth or had refused to believe it. We stayed down here so they wouldn't be alone."

"That's a great sacrifice," Jason told him.

"It isn't a sacrifice when it's family," the man said.

"Will you come with us and find the rest of your people, Mr. - ?"

"Abraham Felding."

"I must tell you, Abraham," Jason warned, "we will be going deep into the darkest, vilest part of the caverns. It could be dangerous and full of disease."

"Then we must get them all out," Abraham said as he turned and started to walk into the dismal areas. "Some of my people are burrowed way back in there." Suddenly, he stopped and turned. His eyes were welled with tears and his jaw was tight with anger. "What in the world happened to our country? I have a couple of history books that I have read over and over. We were a people blessed by God. How could all of this have happened? Were people that dumb?" He started to pace back and forth in the narrow passage we were on. "They had no right to be that stupid!"

What could I say? He was right. I tried to comfort him but he pulled away so I tried information, a path into him that he had taken on his own in the past. "During the great upheaval of the previous century, some leaders became frightened. Not that the country was endanger of losing its treasured spot in the heart of God, but they feared they would lose power, they would lose control," I answered him with truth. "That is what I understand from my study."

"All of this," he stammered in disbelief mixed with grief, his eyes wild with anger, "all of this horrible existence is because a few of the ruling elite didn't want to lose their power?"

I wanted to tell him that everything had been lost in a great war. Or, a natural disaster had turned society upside down and they took extreme measures to save the little that remained. That would have been kinder. A huge lie would have made more sense than the truth. But, that's not what had happened. It had all slipped away years before Raymar and Kasamar and others who were called Hollow, or Underlings who had been called Moles, had their lives stolen from them by the imposition of a label. It was all so unbelievable.

The entire population of the Midwest, including the major cities like Chicago and Indianapolis, had allowed a Socialist government to seize everything people made with their own hard work. They then shared it with no one, but allowed only the ruling body to own it. Sure, new land cooperatives had permitted the farmers, shop owners and industrialist to eke out a miserable living by working for them, the government ... deceptively called, The People. But the people were no longer "we the people."

Here in the Eastern Zone, those who were unimportant people with no power and wealth were duped into hiding, into not being seen any more as they lived out desperate lives under the fancy feet of the ruling class. But, I couldn't lie to them again. I looked at the man squarely in the eyes and said, "Yes, that is exactly what happened."

"What a stupid, lazy-thinking bunch of people they were," Abraham said, shaking his head in disgust. With his arms folded tightly around his body he paused and rocked on his heels. Then, he quickly announced, "We must be totally silent as we pass through this next sector. It is the entry for the Engineer," he explained.

"Who is the Engineer?"

"Shh, he is at the head of the stairs," he whispered. "I hear him and it sounds like others are with him."

"Why?" I whispered. "Who is he?"

"The Engineer comes down the dangerous steps and waits for a pretty girl or a strong man to go by. He asks them if they want to work above-ground. He will protect them, he says, and he'll make sure they never have to go outside again once they're in a new job. They'll be completely taken care of in exchange for food and shelter and a comfortable bed." He watched with widened eyes in the direction of the stairs.

"Slavery, Abraham that is the same as slavery. What color are the people?" I could not believe the lies upon lies told to these sweet people.

"Color? You mean the color of their skin? They're any color. What difference does that make? What matters to the Engineer is if they are pleasing to the eye. Skin color has nothing to do with it. But, it can't be slavery," he shook his head in disbelief. "I've read in the history book about slavery and these people are not sold. They are glad to go to the surface." Abraham pressed his body against the wall in the darkest part of the entrance.

"But they can't leave their employer," Jason concluded.

Abraham nodded. His eyes searched the floor, lines of pain visible on his face. Then he stopped and listened intently.

"I told you not to follow me," they heard the Engineer say.

"We are looking for Lady Applewait and Dr. O'Reilly," the man barked.

I almost gasped out loud. Inspector Stoner had continued to follow us into the underworld, the world of mortal pain. Would we ever be free of him? I clutched Jason's hand as we hid in the dark shade of gray below.

"You are looking in the sewer, Mister!" the Engineer laughed as he shrugged and threw out his arms in a demonstration of disbelief. "Just look around you! Where are you? You're looking down here for a fine lady and a physician—in the filthy underbelly of the earth? Now that's what I call intelligent!"

"How dare you mock your superior!" Stoner yelled as the veins in his neck bulged.

"You aren't my superior ... in anything ... Sir," the engineer spit out through clinched teeth and glaring eyes. "I'm not the one looking for gold and fine silk in a filthy crypt."

"Ward, what are we doing down here? She isn't here, not in these tunnels and ghastly places," Stoner's female companion pleaded.

"Boone, you ... so we should just go back home? And leave Miss Uppity to cross borders unlawfully and whatever else she is involved in."

"Yes, Sir, that is what I'm thinking," the female answered.

"Home? Lieutenant what is wrong with you? You have known me for how long now? Have you ever seen me retreat from a case just because it's difficult?" He didn't wait for an answer. "Well, forget it. I will never sound retreat on this mission."

"Nothing is wrong with me, Ward," Boone said with her head held high. "Just think about it. Look around you," she looked at the underlings who clung to the walls and bottom steps. She lowered her voice to a whisper. "Do those faces look like the kind of people Lady Applewait would call *friend*? You aren't thinking clearly, Ward. Think about your pension if nothing else."

I could see the woman from deep within the shadows as she pleaded with the Chief Inspector. She may have been the woman who interrupted the church services in the Western Zone, I couldn't tell. But, I knew I recognized her voice as the woman who came with Stoner to the Citadel. She sounded reasonable but she was arguing with an irrational man. Then, I quickly drew my head farther back when a third Blue Shirt stepped around the lieutenant and began to inch further down toward the subway platform.

"Washington!" Stoner barked. "Get back here. We've seen all there is to be seen down here," he looked around at the squalid, lifeless conditions. "Unless you like derelicts and packs of dirty kids running around."

Little ones had come into the station platform when the above-grounders came down the steps and had stayed to watch the commotion. Now, they scattered like stray kittens when Stoner roared. I couldn't blame them. I was frightened, too. They had slipped into the area in silence and now they had slid out just as quietly. Instantly they were gone.

"No, I won't believe that our friends are walking into captivity on their own," Abraham argued after he watched the Engineer close the opening to the above world. "They just want to earn a little money and get out of this ... place."

"But, once they are above ground, they can't go anywhere, can they? Abraham, that isn't freedom to work. That's bondage," I insisted.

"I can't think about that," he whispered and then said little more as we pushed on through the debris and the garbage. In the recesses of the tunnels, there was less light and less of everything else.

"I'm sorry," he apologized. "It's going to get even darker. But, we're lucky that the moon is full tonight. But, remember, with a bright moon, people above will take walks in the night air. Be quiet. Be unseen. We will get some light through the grates above."

"It reminds me of a prayer I read. *God Bless America*." I said out loud but actually, it was a thought that slipped out.

Suddenly, Abraham began to hum a few notes of the melody to the great old song. I recognized it. "Music had been banned in the Central Zone, but a few of us had gathered in our building to sing," I said as I thought out loud. It was my way of stemming the fear that gripped me.

"That one does sound familiar. I can't remember the words," Jason added. Although he was right beside me, his voice sounded as distant as mine. Perhaps we were dissociating ourselves from the horror of everything around us.

As we passed under an open grate, moonbeams danced through the flat bars above and cast streams of light along our path. Then I heard Abraham softly hum again as we made our way through the dim paths.

"Through the night, with a light from above[1] . . ." he sang to himself, like a hymn of faith and encouragement.

The words came back to me like the waves of the sea, one line folded in on top of the other. I clung to the song like Abraham did. Then Jason joined us in our melody of hope and praise in this most unlikely blessing of a home.

We moved on through the darkness and talked to the people who hid there. "The petition will let you live out the lives God has given you." We told them of their right to freedom and happiness.

"What room is this?" I gasped and gaged on the stench of it.

"This is where the gatekeeper to the garbage room stays. See the large, metal door over there? That leads out to the river where barges line up at the dock. The gateman opens the hatch when trash needs to be disposed of, and dumps it into an even larger room. At some point, the entire contents of the room on the other side is loaded onto a barge and hauled to a dump site. The gatekeeper must stand guard to make sure no rats escape into the underworld."

"This is the disposal for everyone down here?" Jason asked with his hand across his mouth and nose. "How big is the space beyond the wall?"

"I don't really know," Abraham admitted. "There actually isn't as much garbage as you would think. These people have so little, they use everything they get or find. There is not much thrown away." Then he spotted a woman near the door and stopped. "It's all right Jewels. They mean you no harm."

The woman was crouched on her haunches against the wall near the floor. A staff with a crook on the end of it was in her hand and stood erect on the concrete. She froze when we came near her, her eyes wild with fear.

"Jewels?" I cautiously approached the thin, young woman who huddled near the door. "Hi." I reached out my hand to touch her dirty hair but ... I was surprised, it didn't seem repulsive. My heart went out to the young woman who would have been beautiful on the surface. Down here, she had dark sunken eyes, a vacant stare and pallor complexion.

At first she pulled away from my touch. Her eyes darted from side to side, as hyper-vigilant as anyone I had ever seen.

I stooped and crouched in the filth around her. "Jewels, please look at me."

Her eyes flashed back and forth, then they met mine and she stopped with a gasp. It was like she finally recognized the presence of another person. Someone had stepped into her world and saw her there. "Jewels, you keep watch very good. You have a very important job to do."

"We're thankful you're here," Abraham joined in the conversation, welcoming Jewels back into the family of the living.

"I do?" She looked puzzled. "An important job?"

"You keep everyone down here safe from rats and the diseases they carry," Jason encouraged her. "You do a great job. Any rat that comes your way, you push away with your staff." He waved his hand in front of her eyes. She was able to lock on and track his movements as her eyes followed his hand.

"Jewels, these people have a very important message for you," Abraham said. "Everyone down here are receiving the message and passing it along to their family and friends. By morning, everyone will know," he said with pride. "We're doing something wonderful, Jewels. We're setting everyone free."

"Free?" Jewels stumbled over the word, like she had never heard it spoken.

"All of you down here can leave. You can go to the world above. You can go anywhere you want to go." I watched her expression and reached out my hand to her.

"No!" she shuddered. Suddenly, she pulled back from me like someone burned. She coiled herself into a ball and rocked her body back and forth.

"Jewels," Abraham coaxed, "we're all leaving. We're going home."

"Home?" she whispered, "I am home." She looked around her filthy squalor with lifeless eyes. "When you all leave ... will I be here alone?"

"No, Sweetheart," I urged her. "You are coming with us ... to the surface."

"We will all die," she breathed out with a weak sigh. "We will all die."

"Jewels, you've been told a lie!" Excitedly, Abraham paced back and forth. "We have all been lied to. You can live with your family in the other home your parents' parents grew up in ... up top. Come on Jewels."

"No, Abraham. No. I have no parents ... no one."

"Yes, you do," he stopped his anxious roaming. "Why would you say that?"

"No, I don't. I should know. They are all gone. They died." Her voice trailed off and fell on the floor at her feet.

"Baby, I just talked to your brother, Sonny, a few hours ago. He made me promise to bring you out of this hell hole."

"Sonny? Sonny is alive? But ... how?"

"May I ask you a few questions, Jewels?" Jason asked gently.

She nodded her head. The dirty blond curls bounced on top.

"When did you last see any of your family?"

"I don't know. Before I was told I had to do this job."

"Who told you that?"

"The Engineer," she looked back and forth from Abraham to me.

"So you haven't seen your family in all this time?"

"I haven't seen anybody. No one comes down here." Tears rolled down her face and dripped in the dirt below. "They say it smells so bad they can't breathe. I don't notice it any more. I stopped breathing a long time ago."

"Then, who told you that your family had died?" Jason asked.

"No one. But . . ." Her speech broke down into great sobs of grief. "They would have come for me if they were still alive. It's been months and months." Her face distorted with anguish and the filth of the place.

"They couldn't come for you, Jewels. No one is allowed to be down this far in the tunnels." Abraham pronounced each word distinctly, as if a better enunciation would bring understanding to a confused and grieving girl.

I took a step toward her. At first she started to raise her staff, but then lowered it slowly. Finally, she didn't pull away. I put my arm around her shoulder in spite of her terrible odor. "Jewels, people are waiting for you at the entrance to the world of color and music and hope. They will ask you if you want to sign a petition. We are getting signatures from everyone we can, so the law that limits the number of years a person can live can be overturned. Sweetheart, you don't have to worry about that. We have volunteers from the body of believers on Fifth Avenue collecting signatures from exit sites all over the city. You will have a chance to sign sometime in the next week or so, if you choose to." I waited while Jewels absorbed what I was telling her.

"We will try to have your family at the very opening to the underworld from which you will emerge. Your loved ones are far more important than the petition right now." I wanted her to know she was of more value than anything else we were trying to do.

"You said everyone will be signing the petition?" She looked me in the eye and seemed to grow a little stronger as she spoke. "Every single living person?"

"Yes, they are."

"Then, I will sign it too," she stated decidedly. "People have a right to live, don't they? And, people have a right to be called a living person."

"Yes, they do," I smiled. "Now, let me help you off the floor," I offered as I stood and held out my hand. She reached up and let me help her to stand, slowly, but with new strength. Together, we walked back through the tunnel, past abandoned cooking pots and snuffed out fires, and up the steps the Engineer used to lure those who longed for light and an escape from the darkness. But, this time, the underlings were setting themselves free, not into the back of a truck that would deliver them through the back door of a residence or business. They walked boldly up the forbidden steps and into the light the moon cast on everything around them.

Chapter 38
Free

This was a walk I had lived for. Although I had been in the Eastern Zone for a short time, the exodus seemed like emancipation for me as well.

We came out from the underground at the far end of Manhattan Island. Abraham put his arm around Jewel's shoulder, but even safe in his grasp, she held the heavy staff firmly in her hand.

It was night, but the moon illuminated the darkness of the hour. The street lights shimmered on the backdrop of the night-time sky. There had been a little rain while we were down below. The air was clear and clean, the freshness like unmatchable cologne. My lungs ached as I sucked in the miracle of life ... the breath of God.

My eyes searched the crowd for any sight of Stoner or his small group of Blue Guard. "Are they here?"

"I don't see them, or any city police either," Jason assured me as we continued to scan as far as we could see. "There are many official exits, with sign-up tables for the underlings at each. Maybe they are at the main one, the Engineer's Entrance. Stoner probably thinks we want a large audience as we emerge, and we would get it at the main opening."

Harold Humphrey waited for us beside a small group of volunteers. They had gathered around a portable table they had set up for the underlings to sign the petition when they emerged. Small, wireless heaters warmed the feet of those who sat at the tables and those who came near to sign the papers. Nearly every soul who came up those steps from the dungeons beneath clustered around the table to sign the paper that would increase their lives by one-hundred years. Jewels and Abraham walked as boldly as they could, on the feeble legs of malnutrition. They leaned their grimy hands on the table and drew their names on the petition slowly, as an artist would draw a masterpiece. They also put their name and the names of as many relatives as they could remember on the register that would eventually reunited them with their family and relocate them to their ancestral home.

"Jewels?" a voice from behind called out softly.

Jewels gasped when she turned and embraced her brother at the liberation table. "Sonny, oh Sonny," she sobbed.

"Jewels?" a woman who looked years older than the stated age on the papers she had signed, touched the young woman's shoulder timidly.

Jewels turned and stared at the woman who had touched her, the warmth of the contact still remained as she touched the spot with her hand. "Mommy? Is it you, Mommy?" she wept and fell into the arms of the mother she had not seen in over six months. A man and the young man, Sonny, embraced them both. I watched with my eyes and my heart. A family reunited, rescued from beyond the River Styx.

I didn't want to intrude on their reunion, but I had to make sure each of them knew what was next. I approached them carefully. "A volunteer will take you all to the processing center where you will be linked up with all extended family who could claim your home of origin. Go slowly, be generous and kind, and know that God loves you all."

When I turned again, there was a young woman, immaculately groomed in a soft blue shaysilk dress, with real pearls sewn at the oval neckline, like in a Vogue Magazines of old. I could see snatches of the lovely garment beneath her evening coat when it flapped as she moved along. The dress fell to mid-calf, just above matching pumps with chunky heals like in the movies from the 1940's I had found in the library.

She curled her lip as she looked around at the people, the table and the volunteers. "What are these inferior ghosts doing on the top?"

"Ghosts?" I questioned in disbelief. Had she heard of the underlings? Did she know of their plight?

"Of course, ghosts," she snapped back as she tossed her long, golden hair over her shoulder. She put her hands on her hips and strutted closer. "Ghosts are unreal beings. They are in your presence but they aren't really there, are they?" she explained with a smirk on her face and her jaw thrust out.

What a brilliant explanation, I thought to myself but didn't want to give her the satisfaction of responding to her. She couldn't have been more than nineteen or twenty, and I wondered what she was doing out in the evening alone. We couldn't have done that in the Central Zone.

She continued to stand in front of me, leaning her whole body in my direction in an aggressive stance. She let out a long string of obscenities and stomped her foot on the ground. "Well, my daddy will see about this! I should be able to walk all the way home without seeing anyone or anything that would offend my eyes," she whined in a spoiled baby voice.

"So, if you see someone on the street, in your path, it would offend you?"

"If they don't look like me, of course it would," her hands flapped in a feeble gesture of tired frustration. "Get those ghosts off my street," she demanded and walked on.

"They aren't apparitions, Miss," Jason called after her. "They are real people."

"They are not!" she yelled. "They are no-bodies. Their carcasses belong in the other place, the garbage dump of the under-world," she shouted back. "No one should offend me. I have rights."

Jason and I stood motionless in disbelief. "She has a right to not be offended? And ... she gets to decide what offends her," I shook my head. "Oh Jason . . ." my head was swimming with questions that had no answers and grief that had no justifiable cause.

"We'd better move on quickly." Harold nodded in the direction of the block south of us. "That man, Stoner, and the others are here looking for you two. They moved on to the Engineer's entrance. Some of the freed people have seen you. They may say something in their excitement."

"But, not many of them heard our names," Jason reminded him.

"It only takes one," I sighed.

We moved back against the buildings where the street lights would not be as bright. How many shadows had I found over recent months that I didn't even know were there? My heart pounded and I was getting tired. It felt like I was racing inside. Would life ever be normal again? And, was the life I had left behind in Capitol City really normal? Normal for whom? For me ... Lady Christina Applewait? Normal for these forgotten of the world, the underlings and the Hollow Ones ... what was their normal? Lives of slavery, of being outcasts or scapegoats ... sent out from the city to bear the sins of the *nice* people.

"I'm parked up here, in the next block," Harold took my elbow and guided us toward a block to the north. "We'll have to be careful. That man, Stoner has been up and down Manhattan, from the Battery to Harlem."

We inched along through the growing crowd of the newly freed, with our eyes fixed on the long car ahead of us. Then, we spotted them. Stoner and the woman he called Boone were going from one freed refugee to another. They held a 281 Palm Device and a hologram likeness of me shimmered on the sidewalk beside them. One of the women I had talked to earlier looked over at me as I hid in the darkness, and shook her head, "No." Then she walked around the hologram as she moved on down the sidewalk following the others. Her movement caused Stoner and his minions to shift position as well, which took Jason and me out of their line of sight.

With Stoner positioned with his back to us, we quickly darted across the wide sidewalk and got into one of the black long cars with the heavily tinted windows. Harold got in and slowly pulled into traffic without looking back, so as not to draw attention to us. He drove us back to the Citadel. Maisie greeted us at the door.

"It's all a miracle," she chattered as she led us into the large living room. "My family was liberated an hour ago. The Cornwalls invited them all to stay here with us until they research their claim to the family home. They're upstairs showering and resting." She continued to babble with excitement as she led us into the parlor. "Barbara will join you in a moment and then I'll hurry back upstairs to be with them again."

"You go along Maisie," I offered. "You have waited for your family for a very long time."

Barbara rushed to embrace us the minute she entered the sitting room. "You are all back and safe. I know the underworld has two extremes. It is very violent in some parts and quite safe in most of the other areas. I'm glad you found the safest areas."

"I don't think that trash hole is safe for anyone," Jason shook his head in disgust. "They don't live very long because death is waiting everywhere." Then he asked, "How is Lacy's ankle?"

"She's resting it. The skin wasn't broken so I don't expect any infection."

"Oh, thank goodness," I said.

Richard wheeled his chair into the room, applied the brake, braced himself on the arm rests, pulled himself out of the chair and reached out in friendship to Jason and me. "You are our Moses, Christy. We had been gathering volunteers to provide the safety net for the liberated underlings. It has taken a long time, and we didn't know how they would receive us. If we brought them above ground with no shelter for them, that would have been a cruel consequence of trusting us to free them. They not only had to trust us, they had to feel worthy of freedom in order to muster the courage to leave the only existence they have known. You were the one for whom we waited to provide the catalyst for the emancipation effort. You provided another cause, a noble reason for them to come above ground."

"Thank you, Richard," I said. "The real praise goes to those brave souls who are stepping into the fresh air for the first time in their lives."

Suddenly there was the sound of hurried footsteps in the outer hall. The racket startled me. Too much had happened. The Inspector had intruded on our lives so many times before, I expected him around every corner.

"Christy, it is so good to see you," Martin Spires burst into the room with outstretched arms, followed by Rebecca.

"My dear," Rebecca said as she embraced me. "Barbara told us what you have been doing. How can we help?"

"How did you get here?" I was shocked. "How did you get out of the valley without being seen?"

"We are all a network, Christy," Barbara explained. "Sean has been sending his newspaper across the border into all of the zones for a long time. Gray Fox has buried code into the page heading. It looks like an abstract picture but the code is silently waiting for another code talker to translate it."

Martin smiled. "In the last paper, we received word from Barbara to come to the city to help re-locate the ones from below."

Barbara reached for a tray that Quinton had brought in. "It has been a very long day. You all need to get some sleep, and cocoa is just the right prescription to help you." She poured the hot chocolate brew into fine china cups. "Maisie took some up to her family as well."

I laughed a little as she handed the cup to me. "I'm sorry, I was just thinking. The underlings have had absolutely nothing. They lived like cave people in the ancient past. Tonight, they will sip cocoa from translucent, white china cups and sleep on silk sheets. Wow ... none of this could have happened, if you and Richard had not prepared a way for them."

"Tomorrow morning, Raymar, Kasamar and Rachel Claudette will be here from the Western Zone," she brushed away the compliment and dwelt on the service of so many others. "Also, Ed and Maud Musselman will arrive about the same time. We will review the work thus far. We'll make sure the planning for gathering all the signatures for the petition is perfect. The work must be able to continue when you two go back to the Central Zone." Barbara paused and drank the warm sweet brew from her cup.

When she put her cup down, she added, "And, we must begin to plan strategies for getting out the vote when it does get on the ballot."

My heart pounded with excitement. Was it all possible? Was the evil law going to be overturned? We had traveled far and we were tired. We had even dug people out of their burial in the earth, to bring them into the light ... not so they could add their signatures to the petition ... but because they belonged with the living. Maybe it was all possible.

"Yes, Christy, it is possible," Martin laughed. "Don't ask me how, but I believe I know what you are thinking. Maybe it's because it's all so miraculous, I have also wondered about our success." He thought for a moment and added, "But, that is wrong. We couldn't have come this far if the hand of God had not helped us. It will happen, Christy. We will get the signatures needed."

Chapter 39
The Gathering

Wednesday Morning - February 8, 2113

"I will come in!" the voice of Chief Inspector Stoner growled at the open front door of the Citadel.

"No, Sir," Harold stood his ground. "As I told you before, you have no authority here. You will not come in. Now, go back to your fancy strata car and be on your way."

"This officer has authority," he snapped his fingers and shoved a New York policeman into the open space at the door.

"Good Morning, Officer Cardoso. It's a beautiful day today." Harold greeted the neighborhood officer while standing his ground in the expansive doorway.

"Hi, Harold. This Central Zone Blue Guard Commander seems to think that travelers from his zone are here. He aims to take them back and charge them with crossing the border illegally."

"That, and plotting to over-throw the government," Stoner seethed.

"Yes, the Inspector was here the other day." Harold added no more to his statement. The least said the better.

Cardoso turned to Stoner, his jaw tight and his eyes fixed on the man who tried to push himself into a world in which he had no power. "You bothered the Citadel before this? And, now you're back with the same demands?"

"Sir, you hold your tongue. I out rank you by many promotions." Stoner's teeth gritted in anger.

"Not in the Eastern Zone you don't," Cardoso insisted.

The yelling at the door filtered into the dining room where we had all gathered to plan the next phase. I was setting near the end of the table, and I could see the three that Harold appeared to be blocking. I froze. It was Inspector Stoner of the Blue Guard ... again. He had pursued us all over Capitol City, and now he had disturbed the Citadel again. He seemed to pop up behind every building and sewer line.

"From the activity in the house, I would say you have guests," Stoner bellowed as he craned his neck to try to see farther into the house. I slowly turned in my chair so my back would be toward the door.

"Actually, we have a lot of people in the house today—"

"Many people ... they're the ones I'm talking about. Boone, go in there and see if Lady Applewait and Dr. O'Reilly are here."

"You will not," Harold blurted out before the woman could take a step toward the door. "The Eastern Zone has had moles, underlings living in the subways and basements, passing through one area to another along the sewer and subway system lines. It has been a tragedy beyond words to express." Harold spoke with compassion and determination. "These people have just been emancipated from a lifetime of isolation and slavery. A few of them are staying here at the Citadel. They have been through a lot. They will *not* be disturbed." I liked Harold's forceful handling of Stoner and his crew. I turned a little to peak at the reaction.

"Under the city?" Boone asked with astonishment on her face. "We had started down an old subway entrance. You mean they have been living in the sewers? How long have they been down there?"

Harold whispered and nodded toward the stairs that led to the refugees in the rooms above. "Most of them were born in the underworld. Since their life expectancy is only forty-five years, they would have died down there as well. Their parents have all suffered a miserable existence in the underworld and have died without ever seeing the light again."

"Oh, how awful," Boone muttered.

"Don't take pity on them, Lieutenant. They probably are paying for crimes they have committed," the inspector sniffed with superiority.

"They are not," Harold stated firmly. "They were tricked out of their entire lives with lies and deceit by evil people who cared for no one but themselves. The lie that was perpetrated on their ancestors is still in place."

Boone looked over in my direction as she scanned the whole area and the rooms she could see from the door. When she caught my eye, she didn't turn away. She said nothing. She didn't smile. She just gazed at me with what seemed to be warmth in her eyes. "These people have been through enough, Inspector. We had better leave and let them try to pull their lives together." Boone put her arm gently on Stoner's shoulder and steered him in the direction that turned him away from the room in which we all waited in silence. "It sounds like these people have been hard at work, freeing a group of people they didn't even know. I call that pretty wonderful. Let's get back to Capitol City and look for the Lady and her doctor there."

"Maybe we can figure out what road they took out of the zone and put up a road block," Stoner agreed, although his voice sounded like his heart wasn't in retreat. "When they come back, we can grab them at the border."

As they walked out the door, Boone turned and smiled at me. She nodded a gesture that seemed to me like mutual respect, and left the house.

• • •

One by one, the chairs in the dining room filled with people we had met since we walked through Howard Mountain, key people in the other zones. Rachel Claudette, the Musselmans, Barbara and Richard, Raymar Goring and Kasamar, Gray Fox and Little Feather, and Jason and I, all sat around the table and summed up the progress we had made in a very short period of time. The other volunteers went from room to room upstairs and tried to answer questions and meet the refugees' needs.

Rachel handed me a large package. "I brought your beautiful cloak with me from the west."

"Thank you, Rachel," I said and was so glad to get it back.

The beautifully polished table shone, and the exquisite seventeenth century floor-standing clock in the corner, pulsed—ticking like a metronome keeps the beat of a song. No one said anything about the authorities who stalked us. That was a frightening reality none of us had an answer for.

"Never forget," Richard began, "you are not breaking the law by gathering the signatures. That doesn't mean that those who want things to remain as they have been won't look for ways to try to stop us. So far, the only law you have broken is crossing the boundary lines between zones."

"What you are saying is we have become wanted criminals because we have traveled around our own country." It all seemed so ridiculous to me.

"Those pompous, self-righteous, power-hungry, ruling elites thought the people would be more manageable if they were confined to smaller sectors. It doesn't make any sense. Each of the states used to have a unique quality all their own," Rachel added. "Now, most of that diversity is gone."

"But, we can get it back," I jumped in. "We have seen such unique characteristics of each of the zones in the short time we've been here. And, since people don't travel more than a few miles from their homes in order to preserve fuel, those distinctions could still be present. They weren't free to go anywhere. If anything, hopefully, the sweetness of the uniqueness may still be there."

"So, you're saying that we can get the Length of Days law over turned and put our country back together, too?" Ed Musselman asked. "I've been waitin' for this moment all of my life."

"The Citizens' Referendum will be on the ballot at the next election and ... we hope to run my grandfather, Sir Oliver Richly, for President of the re-United States. I know he can bring our country together again."

Everyone around the table stirred with hope and enthusiasm. Maud announced with energy, "We in the Mid-Western Zone have enlisted a huge body of farm people to help. They have friends or family all over the zone, from rural farm life, to the cities of Chicago, Indianapolis and Cincinnati." Her excitement spilled around the table. "Another great aspect of mid-western living is the connectedness they have maintained with those family and friends." She sparkled as she continued. "They had recently started or continued an old practice of family round-robin letters. They use them to make contact with each other on a monthly basis. Drivers of milk tankers, grain semi-trucks and anything else that continues to move on the highways carry the letters. Family is as important to them as their country. You should see the excitement in the families we have already contacted."

"Perfect," Barbara said as she smiled. "The army of volunteers will grow. The wonderful people in the Mid-west listened to all of the fancy speeches about sharing everything one has with those less fortunate. They forgot that you can only give away all you have once. Then there is no money left to help yourself or anyone else." Everyone around the table either nodded or spoke words of agreement.

Maud added, "In the present system, no one can strive to be the very best that they can, because, the best that they can be is no more than the least among them can become. Now, the government has all the power, all the wealth, and all the future. Those in control, the elite, never gave away anything. The people in the Mid-western Zone are more than ready to get their lives back."

"Wonderful," I agreed with relief. "How did you manage to keep the dreams of the past alive?" I asked as I thought of the stilted emotions of those in the Central Zone. They had no memories of yesterday, let alone images of their family's history, the story of their lives. They were flat in the present, and walked a path with no destination or starting point.

"We kept hope alive, 'cause we're country," Ed explained. "There are few of us. Large groups of urban people could not corrupt our stories. Those in the cities don't even think about us out in the country. We were left alone with our traditions, our family histories and our beliefs."

"I'm sure that's right," I said. "I wish more of our large country had been left untouched."

"That is wonderful, Ed. I'm wondering how the Western Zone has fared?" Richard inquired.

"There was a huge percentage of people in worship services that morning Christy and Jason were there," Rachel smiled. "With Grace Small's help, we were able to contact all of the worshiping groups in the entire zone with the use of the Jumbotron. Raymar Goring organized the Hollow People. He is here with us today, to map out the next step in reclaiming our blessed country."

"The moles have been freed from their slavery that was forced on them by the ones who hold the purse. Nearly all of the molls signed the petition as they left their vile underling squalor," Quinton said.

"But how will you convince those who have it all, that some others have nothing?" I questioned as I thought again of the monumental task ahead.

"Not all of the influence peddlers, ruling class and elite business owners have hearts of glass. There has been an Age of Silence here in the East as well. Most have been afraid to speak truth to lies and deceit, even the most despicable, vile injustice perpetrated upon a group of people." Barbara eyes filled with tears. "The underlings thought they couldn't make their own happiness on their own. The more they depended on others, the more they lost respect, until they were stored away in tunnels like useless old paintings no one wanted to look at any longer. But, many who were above ground thought that was wrong. There was no way to speak out in the past. If we did, the label of dirty underling-lover followed us. We can get their help to gather signatures."

"But, they didn't appear helpless below," Jason said. "It looked like they had carved out small communities, unique villages, down below."

"Isn't it ironic? Once separated from the ones who provided for their every need, they began to take care of themselves and each other. They became creative as they found ways to make things out of stuff considered trash to others and sent to the caverns below. But, they couldn't leave that dark life, buried beneath the feet of others." Barbara added.

"We have decided to dress them in fine clothes," Richard laughed. "Barbara will teach them to apply make-up to their pale, sunless complexion, and introduce them to New York Society as royalty from abroad."

"The above-grounders will believe it because they will want it to be true. Nobility in their midst will make them feel even more important than they already think they are. If Baron Oakridge tells them that signing the petition will give them knight-like valor, they will arm-wrestle with one another to be the first to hold the pen."

"Is that honest?" I asked. "I'm not judging. I mean will the signatures be valid based on a lie?"

"Everything they tell the people about the petition: the over-turning of the law by a citizen's referendum, the facts of the paper itself, will be as true as true can be. The only fabrication will be the name and position of the one who asks them to sign it," Richard explained.

Barbara quickly added, "The name and position of the underlings have already been taken from them. Their existence blotted out of current history, even census records. If it weren't for the old property tax records, their names would never be found."

We sat in silence for a moment as the full tragedy of the underlings' lives penetrated all the way to our heart. In the quiet of the room, I felt a sudden breeze from the entry hall. The doorbell had not sounded, but I looked to the area to see what might have caused the gust of wind. The woman, Boone stood silently in the entrance and quietly closed the door. My heart pounded.

"Christy, what's wrong?" Jason asked when he saw my expression freeze.

"Jason, I—"

"I am so very sorry, My Lady. I would not have dreamed of entering a private home uninvited a few months ago. But, I was there. I was there on Christmas Day evening when the whole city sang for the first time and you and the others brought the signed petitions to President Alexander's home. And ... I saw it, Christy, I saw your drawing." She paused for a moment as her eyes filled with tears.

"You are Boone?" I asked.

"Yes, Ma'am, Lieutenant Chalky Boone." She shifted her balance as the snow dripped from her shoes and made a small puddle on the marble floor. She glanced down and gasped, then stooped to wipe it with a cloth she pulled from her pocket.

"Lieutenant," Harold placed his hand under her elbow and helped her to her feet. "Please, I will be happy to take care of that for you."

"Thank you, I—"

"How did you get past the alarm at the gate?" Richard was impatient but controlled his emotions.

"The Litchfield Master Lock Company springs every lock of any kind with a tonal frequency that sets up a vibration." She pulled it from her pocket and embarrassingly revealed it in her outspread hand. "My Lady, please, give me a few minutes, I beg you. I mean you no harm. I would have told the Inspector and that creature, Washington when we were all here a few minutes ago if I did."

"Where are they, the two men?" Raymar questioned. "I know a dangerous man when I see one and those two are both dangerous."

"They are at a nearby restaurant. I excused myself for a few minutes. Please, let me speak."

"They will come looking for you." Fear rose up inside me. "When they find you, they will find all of us as well."

"I'll leave. I just wanted to tell you that Ward Stoner is not the man you have been seeing. Before his wife died, he was kind and even funny at times. But now, you have become the focus of his anger and resentment. I have seen nothing but good in you and what you are doing. I'm sorry I judged you differently when you were in the Western Zone. Then, I saw all that you did today to help others. I'll stay close to Stoner and try to divert him away from you," she explained as she backed out of the room. "I've got to go so I don't lead him back here to you."

"Thank you, Lieutenant," Barbara said as she rose to escort Boone to the door.

"Please stay seated, Ma'am," Boone motioned with her hand and quickly slipped out the door.

"Regardless of Stoner or Boone or whoever, we must continue to help the newly freed underlings find their families and their homes," I said. "I would like to help get it started. I know we can take a few days more to do that. I would not miss the beginning of a new life for so many."

Chapter 40
A Plan

Friday - February 10, 2113

"Christy?" Jason called up the staircase.

"In here," I said from the sitting room. I had found a comfortable chair near Barbara Cornwall's floor to ceiling library shelves of books. I placed the leather bound book that smelled as good as it was beautiful, on the table beside me.

"Can you imagine having a personal library of this size in your own home?" he marveled.

"My few shelves wouldn't hold a full box of books and these cases are ... well, they're wonderful!" I scanned the books that filled two sides of the room and ran like a river of words across the top of the doorway.

"Honey ..." he paused, came to me and rubbed my shoulders. "You don't have to go if you don't want to, but ..." He stopped caressing me and seemed to be at a loss for words. There was heaviness in the room I didn't understand.

"But ... what, Jason? You're worrying me."

"Richard has invited me to the opera this evening."

"The opera?" I stammered. "People are upstairs who have only been free from their prison of fear and slavery for a few days ... and you are going to the opera?" I couldn't believe it. This was not the

Jason I had come to know. "It's sort of like the French Revolution, 'Let them eat cake.' How can you be so disconnected from their suffering?" I stood up but felt trapped. I didn't know if I should run away from him, beat on him as hard as I could with all the confusion and sudden anger I felt, or fall into his arms for the honest attempt at putting his mind on pleasant things for a few hours.

"No, Baby, it's not like that." He touched my arm but I pulled away. He didn't try to hold on, but his voice held all the love we had been feeling and I stopped.

"Then, why?"

"Richard said that Alister **Bedlam would be in his box tonight.**" He nearly whispered as if a gentle tone would make a kinder man of Bedlam.

"Bedlam?" I gasped. "He's a monster."

"That's why I have to see him. We know the things he has done and I ... I have to see the Devil face-to-face." Jason's fists clenched and has jaws grew taunt with anger. "I want to know who our enemy is. I want to be able to recognize him if he comes near you."

"Oh, Jason," I sobbed with dry, exhausted tears.

"I know you're tired, Honey. I don't expect you to go. It'll be all right."

"No, Jason. Can Richard get another ticket?" I felt more worn down and worn out than I could ever remember. My arms were too heavy to lift, but I had to go. "Is Barbara going?"

"Yes, they have a plan."

"A plan? For the opera?"

"No, a plan for the elite and it will start at the opera." Jason held me in his arms, and I felt warm again.

We stood for a moment in our togetherness. "A plan for the elite? I don't' know what that means."

"There is absolutely no reason for the elite to help the underlings and the underlings are going to help get out the signatures for the petitions."

"They have the same reason to put an end to the law as all of us. I thought the Eastern Zone upheld the Length of Days Laws. They and their loved ones are terminated at a prescribed age, too." It made no sense to me.

"Yes," Jason said, "Richard told us that the law is enforced in the Eastern Zone, but not in the city. The wealthy can buy extra-year credits."

"Credits? You mean they can purchase addition life-years for themselves? Under what law?"

"The law of the affluent, Christy. Here, in the city, it's all about who you are and what you have. At least in the Central Zone, everyone is under the same law, as corrupt as it is."

"If they can escape all of the consequence of the laws they create, they would have no reason to help anyone else. How can we stop that?"

"Richard has a plan to expose Alister Bedlam." Jason raked his hand through his hair with nervous anger.

"Expose him for what? Do they know what lies beneath Howard Mountain?"

"I don't know ... maybe." Jason looked out to the hallway, around the room and beyond the English Tudor glass panes of the windows. Then he whispered, "Richard said that a huge, secret network of world-wide, cross-hatched connections filter, launder, and hide all of the money that comes in across the whole country for life-credits. And ... it is all paid to Alister Bedlam."

"I don't know if I can look at him, but I will go to the opera. That is, if Barbara has something I can wear." I thought about what Jason had just said and I wondered. "How can Bedlam hide all of that and how could Richard have found out?" I still couldn't wrestle it all around in my head.

"Richard ... is Bedlam's son-in-law, Christie. Barbara's father is Alister Bedlam." Jason stood in front of me, his eyes danced with a mixture of so many emotions I didn't know whether to shrink in fear or shout with joy.

"Barbara? Our Barbara ... here?"

"Yes, Christy, our Barbara."

"Does she know about the *plan*? Is she part of it?" I thought about my own parents and my dear father. Would I be able to turn on him?

"Honey," Jason caressed my arm. He surely knew I was thinking about my family. My love for them was the catalyst for all of this, everything. "Barbara came up with the *plan.* She hasn't seen her dad in over ten years because of his corrupt ways, his corrupted soul. But, her mother stayed with him so she could get to the bottom of what she had suspected for years. Barbara and her mother have collected the final nails for his cross."

"He's no martyr. He is the vilest of crucifiers." I wrung my hands in frustration and anger. "How can one man have so much power?"

"He holds life in his hands, Christy," Barbara said as she came into the library.

"But how?" I asked as Barbara walked over to the fireplace mantel. "One cannot have power over another unless that other relinquishes their own."

Barbara pulled back a large portrait above the broad oak beam to reveal a heavy, old-time wall safe. She spun the dial right, then left, back and forth, then pop, it was open. She reached in and withdrew a tan envelope. "Mother gave this to me weeks ago, before she went into hiding."

"Hiding?"

"From him ... but, she won't be able to hide for very long. He won't even know she's gone for months. In their home he lives on the first floor and she lives on the second. He uses the back entrance and she uses the front."

"Why hasn't she left? Is whatever she was looking for, worth it?" I put my hand in Jason's and connected to my anchor.

"She was afraid to leave. The only way I got out of there was to marry my Richard. He's from a wealthy old family with quiet money and elegant power. While Father is the wealthiest man in the world, he is feared not revered." She sat on the edge of the sofa and tapped the unopened envelope in her hand. "When Mama took the document, she fled from the house, came here and gave me the envelope, slipped through the passage in our basement and has been staying above the underlings. No one would look for her there. But, once we start our campaign of discrediting ... him, he will start searching for her. We won't have a lot of time."

"And the underlings are above ground now. Where is she?"

"I'm afraid to say it out loud." She scratched at her hands and then dropped them in her lap.

"You can trust us, Barbara. If we can't trust one another, we'll all hang." We sat in silence for a moment.

"You've been in the basement. Under the stair steps, behind a set of shelves that used to hold canning jars, there's a door that leads to another staircase. Those steps open only into the kitchen near the old chimney and do not have access to any other floor until you get to the attic. We fixed up a comfortable suite of rooms for Mother up there. She just can't have a light on after dark."

"Your family has sacrificed so much. I hope it all works out." I smiled and looked at my watch.

"What time is it," she asked, then checked her own time piece. "Oh my, I'll have to hurry. You too Jason if we're going to get there in time for the curtain."

"Would it be alright if I went too?" I asked.

"I'm sorry, Barbara," Jason jumped in. "I assumed she would be too tired to go."

"Oh, My Dear, I would love for you to come. We have plenty of room in the box." She checked her watch again. "Now we're really going to have to hurry. I'll ask Maisie to hang the dress Rev. Small sent with Rachel in the closet in your room, along with some shoes. Gotta run," she rattled out as she jumped to her feet, replaced the document in the safe, the shooed us out of the library and up the steps to get ready.

Maisie brought in the dress and shoes while I was freshening up. As I dressed, an energy I hadn't known I could call on rose up within me. I had no idea what was in the envelope Barbara had, but if she believed it could move that evil man off his throne, then it would be so. I prayed that God would reveal the horror that our whole country had been living under, each in our own zone, each in our own way.

Chapter 41
A Song for the Devil

7:00 p.m.

I felt like a Lady of old as I stepped out of the Cornwall's long car and my fancy shoes hit the sidewalk. I wasn't sure how we would make this work. How could we see Alister Bedlam without him seeing us when we were with his daughter and son-in-law?

"We'll take the stairs to the upper floor. Our box is on the left facing the stage. The Bedlam box is directly across from ours. He will be there with whatever concubine is current in his life."

"Barbara, won't he see us? He probably watches you, his only daughter." I insisted a little nervously.

"I know I have never seen him before. I don't know how he could recognize me," Jason added.

"We are both legacy citizens, Jason. He probably knows every one of us." I shuddered at the thought that someone could recognize me while I had no idea what he looks like.

"Christy, people aren't even allowed to approach you on the street," Jason reassured me. "Theoretically, no one is in the ethereal world of the Council of Twelve and the Legacy Citizens. To my knowledge, no pictures of you ... of us exist. It is forbidden to even try to find our addresses, except perhaps our office and work," Jason said as he put his arm around my waist and drew me closer.

"Besides," Barbara reminded me, "since you are dressed in the Romani mourning clothes of Simza Bihari, one of your alter personalities, the veil will shield you when we walk in and take our seats. You can unbutton the veil and set it back once you are in the shadow of the box." Then she tuned to Jason and added, "You look passable as a vicar."

We stopped outside the door to the box. "Four chairs are in the front row of the box," Richard explained, "and another four behind them. My parents are coming tonight as well as my sister, Valery and her husband, Oscar. With your permission, I have placed you two in the row behind us along with Valery and Oscar. My parents will sit in the remaining two chairs beside Barbara and me. I mean no disrespect, My Lady. My parents are against seating you two in the rear, but I thought you would be less visible in the back row."

"Disrespectful? Richard, I hope I'm not an arrogant princess. I think you're brilliant." I felt a weight life from my shoulders. I could see everything from the shadows—see but not be seen.

"Thanks, Richard. I was concerned I might not be able to protect Christy in this great theatre," Jason said.

"Protect me?" I felt my chest fill with a feeling I hadn't experienced before. Detoxed for less than three months, many emotions were still new to me. Since we had been outside of the zone for those months, we were fairly sure the other zones didn't drug their citizens. The drugs were probably out of my system by now but I was still taking the small white detox pills. That may have accounted for my anger and apprehension at times. I quickly added, "I know I have been pampered all of my life, but I'm learning fast to take care of myself."

"You sure are," Jason agreed. "You amaze me."

"Maybe that observation is not just the small white tablets," Richard added, winked and pulled the door open to the fabulous private boxes of the first tear of the five level surrounding balconies.

I had hoped that we could enter the box with little notice. I had forgotten how much attention those who sit in pretentious elite seats can draw in a huge gathering. We had been traveling around the country incognito for months, in simple clothing, except for Simza Bihari, silently crossing the borders in the dark of night with no attention paid to our passing at all. As we entered the theater box, the entire gathering rose to their feet as if royalty had entered.

"These people here in the city need their pseudo-aristocrats in order to make their own pretense more real," Barbara whispered. "They lead make-believe lives of self-importance and must have a few people to act as those they worship in order to find meaning in their own lives. The closer they are to their demigods, the more important they believe they are." She turned and waved to the crowd.

"My dear," Mrs. Cornwall, Richard's mother, offered, "put the opera glasses to your eyes and you can look around the entire auditorium. They will provide another layer of anonymity. Even if Bedlam has seen pictures of you two he will not recognize you behind your costume and veil or glasses."

We took our seats and I checked my time piece. The curtain would go up in five minutes. I leaned forward and whispered in Barbara's ear. "You said you were going to launch your program to gain Bedlam's cooperation this evening? How?"

Barbara put her hand to her mouth to cover her words as she spoke. "Basically ... he will never cooperate. He would lose power if he relinquished an inch, at least in his mind." She paused and nodded slightly in the direction of the opposite side of the auditorium.

A man with graying dark hair strutted into the opposite box, followed by a glitzy woman in flowing gown and dangling diamonds. He flipped his opera cape lined in red satin from his shoulders with a fanfare and flourish. When he took his seat, the woman fluttered like a swan into the one beside him.

I watched him through my small binoculars and suddenly felt suffocated by fear. The face of the man was so full of evil I trembled. Hate and anger had carved deep lines around his mouth and drew it down into a tight scowl. But, there was an attractiveness that was frightening. The aura of the magnificent power he emitted could suck one into his vile cunning.

"Are you familiar with the opera, *Diablo*?" Richard asked with a friendly smile, behind which he hid the cunning plan.

"It's much newer than the traditional ones, maybe seventy-five years," I said. "Not that I have ever heard it sung before. They banned singing in the Central Zone a hundred years ago. But, I've read about it. A banned book turned up in the general stacks of the library. They were going to destroy it and they gave it to me to dispose of it."

Barbara handed back a manuscript bound in colorful leather binding. "Here is the libretto. The words are in Spanish. You can follow along if you want to. I want you to pay particular attention to Act II scene four, not to the stage as much as the opposing box. I want you to enjoy his full expression as we get near the end of that scene. Bedlam knows this opera. He will recognize that some lines have been changed."

"Will everyone know they're different?"

"Most of those here are familiar with the opera, but I don't know if they will hear the change in lyrics." Highly animated, she seemed to relish the thought of his first hearing. "He is so self-centered he will assume that everyone will know the meaning of the changed words. He'll think that the entire city will know the secrets of all he has done. I certainly don't think he'll miss it. He liked to play the music at his home and sing to the top of his lungs—if one would be so mistaken as to call it singing.

"What has he done?" I asked as the lights dimmed and the opening curtains revealed a village in South America. I sat back. This was no time to talk. It was time to fill my heart with song and hope.

I reveled in the beauty of the Latin melodies, the flashing dances, the exotic charm of the people depicted on the stage. I followed the libretto in snatches, but mostly, I let the music flow through my pores like the parched earth drinks up a spring rain. There was an intermission at the end of Act One but we all stayed in the box.

"Mother was able to finally get into Bedlam's safe a few weeks ago." Barbara laid out the introductory phase of the plan. "The man loves to hold on to trophies of his many sins."

"We know," Jason said with grit in his voice. "We have seen some of his handiwork."

"Tell me about scene four. What has changed?" I needed to know. I wanted to be able to see Bedlam's reaction and I might miss it, if I reacted in shock as did he.

"Act One has been about the Alvarez family in Columbia. They are part of one of the leading South American families. All admire Don Alvarez, but he controls his family with an iron fist. His son, Javier, has fallen in love with Angelica, a peasant girl. He is against the union. His actions to discredit her and imprison her family are evil. The whole community loves Javier so they're on his side. They begin calling the father Diablo, the Devil. Some have jokingly labeled Javier, Pequeno Diablo, Little Devil because he has turned on his father. So—" The lights dimmed and the auditorium grew silent. Barbara faced the stage as the footlights glowed and the coloratura soprano began her aria.

Act Two, Scene One flowed melodically into Scenes Two and Three. The story built as Angelica's sensuous love wooed Javier and tried to coax him out of his personal hell, as a son of the king of evil.

"You are my love, Alister. You do not have to follow evil," she sang in Spanish.

My eyes snapped from the stage to the dark box across the wide expanse of unaware people. Like someone struck by a stray bullet intended for his heart, Bedlam's posture immediately changed. He covered his eyes with his hands and I wondered if he was suddenly ill. Then, he stole a glance past his trembling hands as if searching for those who had made the connection and were staring at him. I looked through my opera glasses as well, still directed on the stage but with enough peripheral vision to see that no one else seemed to catch the change. Bedlam's reaction was as Barbara had predicted. He looked like a guilty man caught in his own evil, like one so self-centered he would believe that all eyes were on him.

Bedlam continued to search the auditorium, the general seating and the reserved boxes. All eyes appeared to be on the growing climax to the opera on the stage.

The baritone stretched out his stance, stage left, stage right and began his grand pleading in low tones that built to a crescendo, then to an angry request. "Diablo is what they call you and Diablo you are. Release me from my prison of lies or I will release the Alister menagerie for all to see," he sang. The singer aimed his gaze into the Bedlam box.

Again, Bedlam seemed to shrink inside himself. His shoulders slumped and his posture recoiled into the plush opera chair. Amazingly, no eyes but ours watched the emotional melt-down of the powerful man. The audience seemed interested only in the story on the stage before them. They were unaware of the drama inside his mind.

Just as the last scene was nearing its finale, I saw the door to Bedlam's box open. A man stepped through and handed him a note over his shoulder. He unfolded it and gasped loudly enough the audience was finally aware something was going on. They stirred and whispered as Bedlam gathered up his cape and his woman and exited the box. The curtain closed.

Chapter 42
Assault on the Citadel

11:00 p.m.

We sat in silence as the long car pulled into the stream of traffic and headed back to the Citadel. A light, chilling rain peppered the windows. We had left as soon as we felt that Bedlam and his friend would have cleared out of the large marble lobby. I felt giddy with excitement. The evil one had finally received a direct hit without body-armor. The rain seemed to baptize us with a holy mission, rather than soak us with droplets.

I couldn't hold my question any longer. "What was in the note?"

"Yes, Richard, was that part of the plan?" Jason asked. "What caused him to bolt out of there before the final curtain?"

"I wondered when you two would ask about it," he laughed. "The small note read, 'Like distant grandfathers, like Grandpa, like Father, like son. Don't block the petitions to change the Length of Days law.' Bedlam knew what that meant. What was at the bottom of the note sealed his fate."

Barbara spoke with whispered disgust. "He didn't even hesitate to figure out its meaning. He knew immediately. The note was bordered with 23-66-62-31-51."

"And he knew what that meant?" On the first telling, it made no sense to me.

"Oh, he knew," she stated decidedly.

We watched the buildings pass by for a few blocks then Jason asked, "Okay ... we can't ride in effervescent silence. We have to know. I know that note would have meant more to him than to anyone else or you wouldn't have revealed it out in the open. What did that note say to him?"

"Bedlam likes, no he is compelled, to collect trophies from his evil actions," Barbara explained. "So did his father, his father's father and back two more generations. Evil must have flowed in their veins like acid. Every one of them was corrupt of heart and soul. Back in the thirties, my distant grandfather was the head of one of the largest mafia families here in the East."

"The mafia?"

"You have heard of the la cosa nostra?" Barbara gasped. "How is that possible? They have been underground, completely invisible, for well over a hundred years. Some said they began to engage in legal businesses, but that's just silly. They never changed. How have you heard about them?"

"The back stacks of my library," I said flatly.

Richard lowered his voice. "Every kill, every bribe, every profit from human trafficking was written in ledgers and journals. Photographers who worked full time for the mob photographed it all. Can you imagine the evil arrogance of it all? They had no real need for that information. It's not like they would be audited so they had to keep copies," Richard added. "They didn't need proof."

"They kept it all so they could revisit the crimes; re-experience the thrill of the kill. They were evil men." Jason explained then looked at Barbara. "I am so sorry, Barbara."

"No place near how sorry I am to be a part of his family." She stopped and watched the traffic light beckon the cars to proceed. "Christy, he had a huge, walk-in vault, full of shelves with all that data orderly placed in files and ... a statue or something of a chubby man in a three piece suit, sealed behind glass." She grabbed her mouth as if she felt ill.

"We have seen similar trophies in his secret museum in the Central Zone." Jason and I said in unison.

"Oh precious Lord, deliver us from this evil one," Barbara whispered.

"Diablo is his name," Richard stated with finality and reached for his wife's hand.

"Now . . ." she stopped and directed her words to the driver, "Harold, hurry to the Citadel. I'm worried about Mother. He will know she is the one who gave out the information."

"Yes, Barbara, I'm hurrying. I can run the blue flag up the standard. We can go as fast as necessary," Harold offered.

"No, if we were watched, our urgency could give away our knowledge," she answered nervously.

"We're almost there," Harold announced.

"I have to tell you," Barbara cautioned, "no one knows about the attic apartment but those of us in this car. I cannot express enough how afraid I am ... for Mother."

"They wouldn't have to enter the house. They could bomb it or burn the whole place down," I thought out-loud, and then wished I hadn't spoken the words she probably already knew.

"No Christy," she said as we turned into the driveway of the Citadel, "the whole place is a giant bunker and totally fireproof. We had prepared for Bedlam's appearance when we renovated it."

This time, we didn't get out at the front door. Harold pulled the bullet-proof vehicle around the building where he punched in a numerical code on a panel inside the car. When the door opened, he drove down into a parking structure that went under the building. The door slammed shut as soon as a sensor detected the back bumper.

"Let's hurry. I expect Bedlam to arrive in a matter of moments." Barbara opened the door before the wheels stopped moving. "I need to ask you two to disappear upstairs for the reminder of the evening. I hope that's alright with you."

"Of course, Barbara," I agreed. "Would you want us to go up and visit your mother?"

"There isn't enough time for me to warn her you'll be coming, but that would have been nice."

As we stepped from the car, a flashing red light above the elevator door blinked feverishly. "Oh no, someone is at the front door already."

"What do you want us to do?" I felt a little panicked and didn't like the feeling.

"I have to get upstairs. If you go up on the lift with me, we will open onto the main floor. You won't be able to get to the grand staircase or continue up on the elevator, since both are in the entry hall." She glanced right and left then caught Richard's eye with a look of indecision.

"We have to go up. Walk over there behind the steps," he began as they got onto the house elevator. "Do you remember what we said about the hidden express elevator?"

"Yes, yes," I agreed as my eyes flashed to the corner.

He stopped the elevator with his hand and added, "Behind the shower on the roof is a door to another staircase. You can walk down from the roof to the attic."

"I guess you will visit Mother after all," Barbara whispered.

Jason and I hurried to the darkness under the steps. We had to hurry since we didn't want there to be any noise from the basement if Bedlam made it into the house. "There it is," Jason gestured with a silent mouthing of the words.

I nodded. With trembling hands, I opened the door to the lift. "Hurry," I whispered but was surprised at how loud my voice sounded. "I don't want Bedlam to hear the sound of the second elevator. Maybe we will get past the first floor before Harold opens the front door. The express is faster." I grabbed Jason's hand and we stepped on.

"I'm here Baby," he said and held my hand.

The elevator swept us up to the roof, out of the reach of anyone below. We would find the stairway door with only the moon to light our way and walk down to the attic and Mrs. Bedlam's apartment.

• • •

"Mrs. Bedlam?" I called carefully through the slightly open door.

"Come on in, Christy," she called, her voice low.

We walked into the large comfortable apartment. From the doorway, I could see a small kitchenette appointed in sleek glass-fronted cupboards and glistening appliances. The furniture in the sitting room was mid-century overstuffed chairs and sofa, upholstered in a spring flowered fabric. I could see a bedroom through an opened door. "This is lovely, Mrs. Bedlam." I felt immediately at home.

"Please, call me Ms. Sondra. I detest the name—Bedlam."

"Yes, certainly Ms. Sondra," I replied, confused. "Do you know this guy's name too?" I pointed to Jason.

"Dr. Jason O'Reilly—yes, my dear, we haven't met, but I know you all. This is a very busy house," she added as she waved her hand with a broad sweep, and gestured to the wall of video screens. She giggled a little and added, "What a cast of characters we have here."

"Wow," I gasped as I saw Raymar Goring in the hallway of the second floor on one of the screens. He moved swiftly, slipped down two rooms and knocked on Kasamar's door. "What is all of this?"

"This is my present home, Christy, here in the tower of this beautiful house. Barbara and Richard installed these screens many years ago. She has known what her father is for some time now, so they prepared a watch room. See over here, those are live shots of the city. There is Fifth Avenue and beautiful Central Park. They just tapped into the surveillance cameras that network the city." She pointed to the screens on the far right.

"And these?" I didn't recognize the images on several screens.

"Those are locations outside of the city," Jason observed as he studied them. He pointed at three. "That is the art district in Albany," he smiled and moved on. 'Look Christy, that's a horse farm in Virginia." He turned to Ms. Sondra. "I have read about amazing country places like that, but I didn't know they still exist. Christy, look at the horses!"

"I have seen no animals, except my small cat, and Martin and Rebecca's dog, Buddy. The Central Zone has no animals. The authorities claimed they polluted the air." I loved the beauty of the rolling hills. "And, this one? Where is this?" I pointed at the third image. There was something familiar about it.

"That is a rotation between Philadelphia and Boston and the scenes around the two cities, the historical sites we Americans hold dear," Ms. Sondra answered and smiled. "The Liberty Bell, Betsy Ross's house, the Old North Church."

"Those aren't just pictures. It's in present time. People are walking around." It was all so amazing.

"Everyone is tracked and monitored." She picked up a pointer the size of an old fashion fountain pen. No one writes much anymore, so few pens are actually around. "This is a PID, a point and isolation devise. I can enlarge anyone on any screen and listen to their conversations."

"The screens would emit light that could be seen from outside," Jason observed. "I thought there could be no light up here after dark." Then he stopped. "Oh, I see you have black-out shades on the windows."

"I just press a button and they go up and down." She smiled sheepishly. "I have the screens on all the time. I like to listen to some of the conversations. It feels like I'm part of the community, when I'm not."

"It's scary to think about that, but it is wonderful for you, Ms. Sondra." I surveyed each of the screens and then stopped. There was a camera in the main hallway down stairs, where a new drama was unfolding.

"He's here," Sondra whispered. She used the PID and immediately we were able to hear the frightening words.

"Who do you think you are, Missy?" Bedlam roared as he charged through the front door.

"One of the many differences between you and me is—I do know who I am," Barbara asserted with a calm voice and a spine of steel.

Bedlam pushed himself over the threshold and into the opulent entry. "Is she here?"

"Who?" Barbara questioned.

"Your mother, my wife," he demanded. "You know who I'm talking about."

"My mother," she spit out, careful not to refer to Ms. Sondra as his wife, "is probably at home. We were at the opera, Sir," she announced defiantly. "Richard and I know you were nowhere near my mother's Park Avenue residence." Barbara's chin was firmly set.

"Who I go to the opera with is none of your business," he shouted.

"What are you doing here?" Richard questioned with a tone of superior force.

"You had better tell me where she is or I will call out my personal muscle and over-turn every inch of this town until she's found."

"Your *muscle*?" she mused. "My, my, your sophisticated charm in slipping, Daddy Dear."

He glared at Barbara with a steely gaze. "You ain't seen nothin' yet, Girlie."

"Again, what are you doing here, in our home?" Richard insisted.

"There was a note . . ." Bedlam stopped.

The video images on the screens in the attic were clear and sharp. I could see Bedlam's fists clench inside his exotic leather gloves.

"What note?" Barbara jumped into the battle of power and words, as if Bedlam had to prove to her there actually was a note.

"It doesn't matter 'what note.' A man passed a small piece of paper over my shoulder just as the opera ended. Some numbers were neatly typed on it that only your mother and I know."

"Have you forgotten her name, Old Man," Barbara sneered. "Her name is Sondra."

"I know her name," he bellowed. Then his expression and his voice changed. Vulnerability showed in the creases on his face. "The numbers are a very important code. If ... Sondra didn't write that note, then someone else knows the code." His shoulders slumped and his energy wilted with his sunken body. "Barbara, this is serious." He paused and his voice changed to pleading. "I have to find her."

"You lost her long before this dark night," she fired back with quiet furry. "But ... we might be able to help you ... if you help us."

The muscles in Bedlam's face contorted as his manner switched from pleading, to that of a cornered mountain lion. "What's all this about, Barbara? Did you know about the note?"

"I did not touch any note," she stated honestly. She had not touched it. "As for Mother, if she wants to talk to you, I will help you find her ... on one condition."

"Here it comes, Babe. The old Bedlam squeeze," he sneered. "Your great-grandfather and each grandfather Mafia Don who followed built their empire of power and money by blackmail or intimidation ... and now, Miss Goodness-and-light is following in their footsteps. What do you want?"

"Mafia?" I gasped as we watched the screens in the attic apartment above the drama below. I hoped to spare Barbara's mother that humiliation. "Ms. Sondra, did you know?"

"No ... well, not Mafia. I don't know what that is. But ... after the many years I had lived with that man, I certainly knew that evil was at the core of his being. He shared the little bit of love he could dredge up from the depths of his soul with one flashy woman after another. We got none. I kept Barbara away from him as much as possible." Her tired eyes turned again to the screen. "And, now she knows."

"She already knew," I said, feeling the weight of all Sondra's losses in love and family. We turned back to the video transmission.

"You may be surprised, Don Corleone," Barbara enunciated with bullet precision, "but, I have read some of the old gangster books, and now," she squared her shoulders and aimed her eyes like daggers, "I know who you truly are. I will tell you this; I am nothing like you."

He shrunk from the accusations in her eyes and focused his gaze on the marble tiles of the floor. "If you are holding information over my head in order to get me to do what you want me to do ... then you are exactly like me."

"I know nothing of your precious note. I am only offering you my assistance in communicating with my mother. But, there is an urgent matter we are dealing with and I am sure, if I help you, you will want to help us."

"Help you do what?" He growled the sound of someone not used to having the power shift from his own hands and slip into another's.

"While we search throughout the city for where Mother has taken refuge from your abuse, we will accomplish another goal. We'll also gather names for a petition, so a referendum can be voted on to over-turn the Length of Days law." Barbara was firm and confident. I could see her stand so tall she seemed to stretch her spine to its full stature.

"Length of Days law? What do you care about how long people in other zones are permitted to live?" His brows furrowed as he tried to understand someone, unlike himself, who had character. "Besides, I would buy as many years for you as you would want."

"Thank you, Daddy Dear, but I wasn't thinking about myself. I was thinking of all those people who cannot buy years for longer lives. And ... remember the underlings? They have to have their lives restored. Richard and I will be very busy assisting them. We need for you to put your blessing on these petitions. Of course, you won't block the effort in any way. The elites of the city have nothing to gain by giving freedom to the moles or letting people live full lives. They won't want to see those beneath them walking the same sidewalks where they stroll to show off their fine clothes and jewelry. You will use your influence and power to convince the above-grounders of the merits of our cause so we can get this job done as soon as possible. It will come up for a vote at the next election."

"Why will the wealthy ruling class want to have the moles in their world?" he asked again and shook his head, evidence that kindness made no sense to him.

Barbara crossed her arms in front of her and flipped her hair impatiently. "When the underlings are safely restored to their homes and rebuild old family businesses, there will be more people for the elites to sell their goods and services to. The bankers will have more depositors and the clothing manufactures will have more people who need clothing—I think even you can understand the wisdom of a prosperous middle-class."

"I will do all of that so ... you will help me find your mother? That doesn't sound like a fair trade to me." Bedlam's eyes narrowed into reptilian slits.

"A balanced barter is in the eye of the beholder. You know that. You want to talk to Mother about something. I can't promise you anything. She may not want to talk to you. But, you will have to decide if that conversation with Mother is equal to what I am asking of you." She rubbed her folded arms and planted her feet firmly on the floor. "Well, is my request worth your assistance?"

"How do you expect me to convince the elites of anything?" he stammered.

"You're a bright man. I'm sure you'll think of something," Barbara insisted while Bedlam shifted from one foot to the other.

Upstairs, Ms. Sondra smiled as she watched the screen. "Look at him squirm. I can't think of a time when someone has gained the upper hand on Alister Bedlam. He doesn't know what to make of it," she chuckled with satisfaction. "Oh how he does not want to admit that he will be getting more out of the bargain than the millions of people it will affect."

"What are those numbers, Ms. Sondra?" Jason asked. We had both wondered but no one had offered the information. Should we ask?

"They are the numbers to his safe—his huge walk-in safe that holds all his family's secrets. He displays them like trophies. Can you believe it?"

"We can believe it, Ms. Sondra," Jason agreed.

"We have seen his atrocities. We have touched his trophy cases," I said and thought of Howard Mountain and all of the evil Bedlam had caused. "It must have been a miserable life living with him."

"Trust me, My Lady; there is enough evidence in that safe, of his family's vile acts of violence, to convince anyone. There's murder, manipulation, corruption, bribery, racketeering, malfeasance, money laundering, human trafficking—Christy, it goes on and on. But the pain and grief of his life and the work of his, and his family's hands, is too much to speak about."

"Will he help us, Ms. Sondra?" I asked, hopefully.

"Watch him leave. He has his orders and, like a school boy in knickers, he will follow them in every detail. He'll do anything to make sure people show him respect. He has so little respect for himself he must get it from others." She watched the screen as the front door closed.

"Doesn't he know that people are only putting on a show? Has he no idea what they say about him behind his back?" Jason and I had the same thought, the same unbelievable question.

"He has masqueraded as a benevolent man of honor for so many years, he's come to believe it himself," Ms. Sondra whispered in silent acceptance. "Now, it's his daughter who has pulled back the mask." She shook her head as we learned more of the futility of their marriage. "Oh, he'll cooperate. What hides behind the false face he wears is too grotesque for even him to look at."

Chapter 43
Bedlam's Humility

Saturday Morning - February 11, 2113

In the morning the Citadel was alive with people. The underlings who had taken refuge in the Cornwall's home shared several of the rooms on the upper floors. Rebecca and Martin were on the second floor, down the hall, across from Ed and Maud Musselman. Raymar Goring and his daughter were in each of the small rooms toward the end of the hall.

I listened as I stepped out into the hall. The video screen in every room was broadcasting the same message. Even the hum from the lower level had a cadence that matched the voice in the rest of the house. Every screen displayed a special announcement.

I pounded on Jason's door as I hurried toward the stairs. "Hurry, Jason. Are you hearing this?"

I listened as I ventured down the steps with several others. Jason was right behind me. Like water seeking its lowest level, we all moved into the flow that ended in the library. We found Barbara and Richard listening intently to the television, with a pot of coffee and white sculpted cups. We smiled and nodded at each other, received our steaming cups and sat quickly on the edge of our chairs.

"Good morning everyone," Barbara welcomed.

Everyone nodded and smiled in response. Several sat on the floor, while I chose the beige wing-back chair. Martin and Rebecca were on the sofa; Ed and Maud stood by the fireplace. Jason came in and sat on the arm of my chair. Maisie offered flavored cream and sugar for our coffee. We nodded a thank you but no one spoke. We sat in polite silence with our eyes fixed on the screen. The intensity of the live activities testified to the importance of the upcoming announcement.

Harold checked the front door for security and joined us in front of the screen.

"Everything okay, Harold?" Richard asked.

"Yes," Harold commanded with fierce determination. "I was just double-checking. Those three may be in the vehicle parked down the street. At least they are keeping the required distance. They don't know that the Eastern Zone brought back the old frontier laws from centuries ago. I can shoot them if they try to come in. They had already violated the sanctity of the home. They have no idea it is the house of the daughter of Alister Bedlam." To Jason he explained, "The Citadel has twenty-four hour private police on duty as well as surveillance cameras, connected with the police station."

I wondered if we were really safe. Questions bombarded my mind as I sat back in my seat, shaken but relieved. Jason put his arm around me and caressed my shoulder. There seemed to be no time for me to catch my breath. It was all happening so fast.

"We interrupt the regular service programing and yield to our distinguished guest, Alister Bedlam," the professional talking figure stated. "Mr. Bedlam," the monotonous drone continued, "thank you for being here."

"Thank you for having me," Bedlam smirked with puffed up self-importance.

Bedlam smiled and stiffened his neck in an arrogant pose. "My fellow New Yorkers, I am sure most of you will rejoice with me when I tell you that people, who had been lost to our city many, many years ago, have returned. Thousands of our citizens have been living beneath our city in the tunnels, sewers, subways and basements for more years than some of them know."

If there had been an audience, there would have been a mix of disbelief, discomfort and rebellion at the news that no one wanted to hear. If they were interested in them at all, the underlings would have still lived in their own apartments and homes. I closed my eyes and felt a uniform gasp from all over the city.

"These people will be restored to their former residences and businesses. There is a committee to facilitate their relocation, and I have guaranteed them I will pick up some of the bill. I'll buy the food for their pantries, the clothing for their closets, and pay their utility bills ahead for one full year." He paused, smiled some more and looked around as if he were being cheered, but no one else was there.

"There is another grand and glorious effort I am sponsoring. The rescued people will need to earn some money until they have their businesses up and running again. I will pay them a generous wage to complete a huge project, not just here in the city but in the entire Eastern Zone. I have discovered that the old Length of Days law, which established a prescribed number of years for each person's life, still stands in some sectors. I am hiring these poor, misfortunate and mistreated people to organize the various communities and get every single citizen's name on a petition to over-turn that despicable law. Please, welcome these people into your home and," he paused and pointed his finger right into the face of each person viewing the broadcast, "and, every one of you ... sign that petition."

"Thank you, Mr. Bedlam," the public voice said. "I believe we will hear this message repeated many times throughout the day?"

Bedlam stepped forward again. "Yes, I am underwriting the entire get-out-the-signature effort. This announcement will run every hour on the hour until every citizen has signed the petition."

Then the screen switched to a pre-recorded program of a woman who was showing the proper way to wash your hands. "Remember," she said, "for those of you who have been underground all of your lives, you may not have had the opportunity to wash properly. In order for you to stay healthy and for the safety of the people with whom you will come into contact, proper washing will prevent the spread of germs that cause illnesses we, above-grounders, have not had in decades."

"I wonder what Bedlam has to say about all of those germ carriers?" Jason asked.

Suddenly, Bedlam stepped back into the picture. "My friends," he cunningly coerced, "don't be afraid of the underlings. They are carrying no diseases. I will be having a full team of physicians check them thoroughly." He smiled at the speaker with a stern eye, "Now, Miss Garrison, I can personally vouch for the health of these newly discovered citizens." He looked at the camera and back at Garrison, "I am sure you will prepare the people for the canvassers who will come. You will repeat my message of welcome and ... take note ... I did say ... you will personally pass on my message ... the citizens are not to fear my new employees. Do we understand?"

Garrison stared with glassy eyes, "Yes, Sir. I will be happy to reassure the people on your behalf."

The eleven of us sat in the library for several minutes before anyone spoke. "Well, he did it," Barbara smiled wryly. "He managed to force the people to sign the petition or they will have their programs interrupted every hour-on-the-hour. And ... he managed to come out as the people's savior in the process."

"The mission has begun," Rebecca Spires whispered. "I find it all absolutely amazing."

"We'll stay and help organize the underlings. They'll need a lot of encouragement," Ed stated.

Raymar and Kasamar sat on the floor near the window. "I've been an outcast most of my life. I think I can help with the moles, too," Raymar added.

Kasamar smiled, "You will be great at it, Dad. Barbara, I can help you if you need me."

"That would be perfect," she said.

"Jason and I will go back to Capitol City, through the opening in the mountain, Martin." I thought about the trip back and the border we would have to cross. "We brought nothing with us. You all have provided generously for all our needs. I want to thank you so much. We must leave within the hour," I stated. "You are right Rebecca. It has begun."

Chapter 44
Trapped

Saturday Afternoon

The afternoon sun was low over the spikey outline of skyscrapers. The canyons below grew dim in places where the shadows met the pavement. It was time to go. Jason and I were to meet Harold at the front door. Barbara waited in the hall to say goodbye with my cloak draped over her arm. It was the end of phase two of our mission.

"Well, Christy, the petitions from the Central Zone were delivered on Christmas Day eve, and now the process to obtain the names from the other zones has been put into place," she paused. "We're ready and well-staffed with volunteers. I can guarantee you we will have the petitions turned in on time. We'll vote on the referendum at the next election ... as well as for a president for our newly unified country."

"Praise the Lord," I sighed as the words spilled from my heart.

"I can't believe you have been here for these few days and I already feel close to you, Christy," she said as she placed the wrap on my shoulders. "I know a lot of people in this city, too many to count, but I think I know you best and I've known you for the shortest amount of time."

"I know. I've found many friends since this whole thing began. At home, it is forbidden to even approach a Legacy Citizen." I thought of everyone I had met on our journey to the other zones. "I

295

have begun to realize how much I have needed friends. I plan to keep the new friends I made on this adventure."

Jason and I, ready for the weather, stepped out into the clear air of the late afternoon. Harold held the door as we got in and settled in the back of the long car. Martin and Rebecca sat in the facing seats, Little Feather was beside me and Gray Fox sat up front with Harold. We all looked both ways for evidence of Stoner's presence. We saw nothing by that hour on a Saturday as he pulled into traffic.

"I can take you all the way to the border," he offered. "Richard has arranged to have you picked up and taken back to the Valley of the Keepers."

"Thank you, Harold. It'll be good to see my family on the other side of the mountain, but I'll certainly miss the freedom you have in the other zones." I watched Harold through the rear view mirror. He fixed his eyes on something in the street behind us. "What is it?" Jason and I both turned and looked back.

"I don't know, Christy," Harold said with measured speech. "Richard told me to zigzag through the streets. I have been, and that car behind us has matched every turn," he said as he careened around the corner, the last turn more sharply zipped than the other.

I checked the side of the car as it followed us around the bend. "That's no strata car. There's no signage on it at all."

"I've heard of the strata cars of the Central Zone," Harold said. "We have few official cars on the streets here. Since the middle and lower classes were still under-ground and the upper class put on great pretenses about being honest, the streets are safe. Our police cars are actually quite old. We've had them for thirty-five years. The motor, tires and running gear are up-dated every quarter." He looked again. "That isn't one of those, but then Stoner is not here under the auspices of the police authority. That looks like a hired coach."

"I don't like this," Jason said. "Harold, is there anything you can do? If that's Stoner, he'll follow us all the way to the border and arrest us there."

"These long avenues run for miles, like open racetracks. He's so close behind us, we won't be able to outrun him but we might be able to out maneuver him. He doesn't know his way around the city." He checked again in the rear view mirror. "Hold on."

Jason grabbed my hand as we shot around the corner at the next light. There was an assistance strap by each door to help one get out of the car. We both grabbed onto the one nearest to us.

"Sorry, but I think it's better that we shake this guy. The traffic isn't too bad at this time of the day—just enough to hide in but not too much to become trapped," Harold said as he snapped around the next corner to the left just as the light changed. We breezed through on red. For a flash in time, we were out of sight of the car behind us.

"Barbara," Harold said into his communication device. "We're enjoying this ride times two."

"Wonderful," those in the car heard her shoot back.

Harold raised two fingers and pointed behind him with his thumb. Easily, he meant there were two cars traveling together.

"That sounds nice. She's a lucky lady tonight," she sounded back in a code I didn't understand.

Harold checked the mirror again, zipped to the left on another red light and pulled to the curb. "Jump out here at the Lucky Lion Pub, hurry down the subway stairs and turn to the right. Barbara will have someone meet you to take you both back to the Citadel."

We asked no questions, leaped from the car and dashed down the snow covered steps. I grabbed the railing after slipping a little on the way down, but I had to get to the bottom before our stalker caught up to us. I looked back to see Gray Fox pick up a handful of snow and toss the crystals across the treads to cover our steps. We disappeared into the eerie darkness of the rusted tracks and dripping, melted snow from the occasional grate above. As we moved deeper into the bowels of the city it became darker with each step.

"I don't like this, Jason," I said as I grew apprehensive in the dark silence below.

"Harold said they were sending someone to guide us out. Let's keep moving. I have no idea how many blocks we had traveled before we got out of the car."

"We made several turns. We're not as far as it seems," Gray Fox said.

"Down here, in the dark, everything seems distorted," Little Feather added.

"We were down here yesterday. It seems so different now ... dirtier, scarier." I knew we had to press on but my eyes couldn't adjust to any more darkness. We were rapidly walking into blackness, without enough light to cast a shadow.

"Hold my hand, Becca," Martin offered. "Maybe together we can see something."

"You need new glasses, Martin. You can't see in broad daylight," she reminded him.

"Eek," I screamed as a large rat ran across my boots. "Ugh," I gagged. "Oh Jason, I don't know if I can do this." I stopped in the middle of nowhere. I couldn't touch the walls. They dripped with ooze I couldn't see. I grabbed Jason's arm and buried my head in his chest.

"Christy, we have to move on. I believe Harold. The Cornwalls are sending someone to bring us back to the Citadel," Jason assured me.

"But, how do we get back home if we're trapped in the city?"

"I don't know, but there is a way," he assured me.

"This is a large city. We can contact some of our Native American friends if we need to," Gray Fox added.

Suddenly, an animal of some kind jumped out from a left running passage and pierced the blackness. It leaped on Jason's back and pushed him a few feet down the darkened passage to where a beam of light streamed in from a man hole above. Jason turned and whipped himself in every direction until the thing flew against the wall and fell to the floor. In the dim light, I could see it was a small man, who jumped to his feet and grabbed me with his forearm around my neck. The stench of him was nearly unbearable.

Jason turned sharply and was ready to lunge when he saw the six inch blade in his filthy hand. "Now, calm down," he said softly to the underling. "We mean you no harm."

"Where are they?" the man whispered, his voice trembled with fear.

"Who?" Jason asked.

"Are you trying to find your family ... your friends?" I asked hoarsely, the man's arm still pressed against my throat.

"Mama?" he gasped.

"She's on top," I tried to reassure him. Although I didn't know him or who his family was. Clearly, it seemed no one else was still below.

"No!" he screamed. "She wouldn't. She would be killed or jailed up there." He drew his arm more tightly around my throat. "Where is she?"

Another figure appeared in the tunnel, hunched and menacing. He stared at the mole with empty eyes and the evil that exuded was more than I could look at. Who was the hulk of a man who leaped into the breach and jerked me from the mole's grasp as the underling weakened with the new one's gaze?

"Raymar," Jason cautioned. "Hold him but don't hurt him."

"Raymar?" I gasped as I whipped around to see these two utterly abandoned souls. The mole's eyes were empty and the void went all the way to his soul.

"He won't hurt you," I said to the underling. "He is here to protect us, to guide us out of this forlorn world." I touched the man's shoulder and felt an electric tingle of love pour forth. "They are above. We released all of them from this prison of slavery yesterday.

Where were you?" I could feel the man relax his muscles under my fingertips.

"I snuck up to the park and hid beneath one of the bridges. The air up there is so clear. When I came back late last night, everyone was gone. I couldn't find anyone." The man put his dirty hands to his face and sobbed the grief of the frightened and abandoned.

"They are on the surface, I tell you. Go up the steps at the next subway entrance and find the nearest church. That's a building with a cross on top," I told him and made the shape of the cross with my hands.

He looked at us and back at Raymar. His body grew limp as he stepped back, with fear still written on his face.

"It's all right," I said as I watched the man's eyes still fixed on Raymar, like a hungry lion maintains eye contact with its prey. "He won't hurt you. He was just protecting me." He backed away, then turned and ran off into the darkness.

My hand on Raymar's shoulder, I could feel his tension and fear. "You are good, Raymar," I soothed. "You came just in time to save us."

Tears rolled down his cheeks and he wiped them away with the back of his hand. "I felt so hollow again," he wept.

"You were feeling anger," Jason said.

"You're afraid the bad feelings will take over your life and leave you with that empty feeling again," I told him. I wondered if I should have said more. I looked at Jason for a sign and he nodded.

"You aren't hollow and never have been. Abandoned to a life of isolation, your spirit grieved for the loss of contact with others. When you came to help us, you lapsed into survival mode again but, Raymar, you weren't fighting for your survival ... but mine."

Chapter 45
A Surprise Rescue

Raymar led us back through the tunnel to the opening below the basement of the Citadel. "See how close we were?" he said. "You were only three blocks away and Richard said to turn left and go straight."

"Why did he send you since you're not from the East?" Jason asked.

"No one but the underlings had been below and they were afraid to go back down. I volunteered," he explained.

"That's wonderful," I said with amazement and patted his shoulder again. "You're not a hollow man. You're our hero."

Raymar pushed the manhole cover with his shoulder. With it open we scrambled up the metal ladder to the basement of the Coldwalls' home. Barbara was just hurrying down the steps from the main floor when we emerged.

"Come, the Blue Guard has been diverted to the Battery, down on the south end of the island."

"How did that happen? The police wouldn't help them, that was evident," Jason said as he helped me hurry to the stairs.

"I called Bedlam. I told him to leak a message to Stoner and his group that someone had seen you in the Wall Street area. He was so sure you both are wealthy, it would be logical that you would have gone to Wall Street, even on Saturday." She laughed as she thought of Stoner. "I've only known you a few days, and I already know you wouldn't be interested in the Stock Exchange."

We emerged through the basement door into the grand entry hall. "Hurry," Richard cautioned as he wheeled his chair to the elevator door.

"I'll say good-bye here," Raymar said as he offered his outstretched hand. "And, I want to thank you both. You will get the Length of Days law overthrown, I know you will. But, you've also saved thousands of lives, the underlings ... and mine. You are a blessing to us all." He came over to me and touched my shoulder.

With opened arms I said my farewell. "Raymar Goring, you have come back from the living-dead on your own. You let love fill all the hollow places. It is an honor to know you. I'll look forward to reading the novel you make out of all of this. "

"Do you think anyone would believe it?" he laughed. It was so good to see his eyes light up and joy enter his soul.

Richard rolled over to the elevator. "Bedlam has ordered his old-school Osprey to fly you back to the Valley," he said as he maneuvered his chair onto the lift and waited to press the button. I waved to Raymar as the door closed. Richard and Barbara rode up to the roof-top garden with the six of us.

"Fly us?" I asked. "Where will they land the airplane?"

"Not too many airplanes are made anymore," Richard explained. "Since people are confined to small geographic locations for control, air craft aren't needed as much now. You will be flying in a refurbished Osprey. It has **vertical takeoff and landing, and the long-range, high-speed cruise capability of a** regular airplane."

When the doors opened on top, the roof garden was vastly different. A great wind from the Osprey blades had been blowing, forcing the plants and some of the smaller pieces of furniture up against the wall.

"So that's the Osprey," I marveled. Stunned by how fast life was flying, I turned to say goodbye. "Jason . . ." I reached out for him and grabbed his arm.

"I know," Jason whispered in my ear. "We can't slow down life, Christy. Right now, we'll have to run as fast as we can go, but it won't always be that way. I promise."

I held onto my hat as I hugged Barbara and Richard then boarded the flying machine. "Hurry," a woman inside the aircraft called. "We want to be out of the city before your Blue Guard officer gets back to this part of town. If he doesn't see us take off, he won't know you have left. You'll be a little ahead of him for a while."

"He isn't my Blue Guard officer," I insisted as I sat back and closed my eyes. I reached for Jason's hand, brought it to my lips and fell asleep on his shoulder.

Chapter 46
Return to the Valley of Hope, the Valley of the Keepers

6 p.m. - Saturday Evening - February 11, 2113

The Valley of Hope appeared like a magical hamlet as the Osprey flew over the ridge cap. From above, the valley below looked like piles of jagged boulders awash with crawling green moss. But, I knew better. Hidden below a projected image of rock covered mountains was a hidden treasure.

"Look, Jason, it's just as you told us, Martin." I had watched the ground from the aircraft window when we were high up and as we came closer to landing.

"It does look different from up here," Gray Fox added. "Look, Little Feather, I'm not sure our braves could have tracked us here."

"It is amazing," Jason agreed. "Martin, you said they release a harmless gas into the area above the valley and project the one-way image onto the backdrop the gas produces. Like a one-way mirror, it's transparent from the valley side and it looks like the projected picture from above. In this case, piles of rocks."

"There is an approaching aircraft about five miles out but still below the ridge line. Are you expecting company?" The pilot questioned.

"What about a radio signal?" Jason asked.

"We've had that off the whole way. There are so few big birds in the sky these days there isn't any real chance of running into anyone up here."

"So we really don't know if we were followed," I asked as I looked back to the vacant sky we had left behind.

"I can turn it on for a minute, if you want me to. We won't be broadcasting ... so . . ."

"I can't stand not knowing," I admitted with a gasp. "Will they hear us too?"

"If they do hear us, it will only be on for a second. The open channel will hear any sound around us, and if we point the receiver in the direction from which we came, we should hear if something is there," the pilot said as she reached over, hesitated a second and then flipped the switch.

Schhh, schhh, the rushing wind broadcast its monotonous drone over the receiver. "Ha_e yo_ _icked up an_ thin_?" the radio squawked. *Schhh, schhh* "Try it _gain," an order barked.

I froze. I knew that voice. The sound blasted a scar on my mind in the spot where fear is stored. "Stoner," I mouthed to Jason, careful not to make a sound.

The pilot threw the radio switch in a flash. We all sat in silence for a few seconds. Finally I asked, "Can they see us? Do they know we're here?"

"They can't hear us ... but if they break that ridge before we duck under the veil of invisibility ... yes, they will certainly see us," the pilot said as she sat up straighter. Her eyes darted from one gauge to another.

My thoughts raced, and I couldn't control the tangents my mind raced down. I grabbed Jason's hand and willed myself to breathe. Would there be a problem for us to fly through the veil of gas? Will it be bumpy? Could the gas affect the engine?

Suddenly, the Osprey fell rapidly a few hundred feet as the pilot forced the craft into a dead drop. Just as quickly, the descent slowed and the flutter to the ground gradually lowered all souls on board safely to the valley floor. Just as the wheels touched the ground, the pilot flipped the switch to silence the engine. We sat frozen. No one unbuckled their safety belt. No one spoke. We waited. Rebecca mouthed words to Martin, "We're home."

In a confused mix of freedom and captivity, I looked out beyond the window onto the sweet valley we had left months ago. Large patches of soil had been push up through the moist earth on what must have been several really warm February days. But, it was not Spring. Crocus did not dot the valley. There was a patch-work quilt pattern of old snow and bare winter grass. The sun bounced off the puddles left after a winter rain, and sent ripples of sunshine on the surface. I wondered how I could even see the beauty while I feared for my life. Then I realized—God had given me the grandeur around me to calm my fear within.

The sound of an aircraft overhead shattered the silence within the Osprey. Instinctively, we crouched in position and gazed into the sky, as if ducking would conceal our hiding place. A silver metallic, roaring monster bird-of-prey flew directly overhead. The craft swooped above us, like a flying dinosaur in a science fiction novel. It roared with a scream of death across the expanse of the heavenly space above. Then, the noise faded into the distance.

Air escaped in one unison exhale. Jason smiled and grabbed me in a great bear hug. "They're gone."

Still, we crouched low in the craft and waited for a sense of security to return. Finally, Martin whispered, "Let's go."

We slipped silently from our hiding place and inched across the lawn a little below the Spires' place. There the terrain was flat and large enough to hold our flying angel under whose wings we were sheltered.

"Buddy," Martin laughed as the dog bounced down the road in leaps and bounds. There was no stopping him. "Hi there, boy," Martin said as he scratched behind the dog's ears. The animal dropped to the ground, rolled over and presented his tummy for proper scratching. "Come along," Martin said as he stepped over the dog and motioned for him to follow.

People emerged from their homes at the hour when children had started settling in for the night in their pajamas and selecting their bedtime stories. There, in the middle of the square sat a grounded flying machine the likes of which no one had seen before.

"Hey, Mr. Spires," red haired Gabriel gasped with widened eyes, "what ya got there?"

"Well, Gab, this here is a fancy flying machine, just as you probably saw," he winked and rumpled the boy's hair.

"A flying machine? Wow, can you take me for a ride in it? That would be streaky!" he shouted with excitement as he tried to inch toward the Osprey.

"Well, now, I just can't do that, Son. It was dangerous for us to land here in the first place, but we made it. We'd better not put God to the test to try it again."

"Test God? What ya mean?" Gabriel wrinkled up his nose.

"When a person does something they know good-and-well they shouldn't do ... and then ask God to protect them ... that's putting God to the test. We shouldn't do that. It's like sayin', 'I dare ya God to protect me.' They might as well add that they're smarter than God."

"I know I'm not," the boy admitted.

"I can testify to that, Young Man," Mara said as she came up behind them. "I saw your last test score." She laughed as she put her hand on his shoulder. "Come on now, I'll walk you back to your house." She smiled at all of us. "I am so glad you are all safely home."

"Bye," Gab waved, actually more at the Osprey than at Martin.

"Martin," Rebecca called after her husband as she, Little Feather, Gray Fox, Jason and I walked ahead toward their house. "Come along. I'll fix some coffee. Then, Christy, we'll have a bite in town before you and Jason rest before heading back—"

"Home," I whispered before she could finish her sentence. I really wondered if I would ever feel at home again.

Chapter 47
Through the Mountain of Tears

Eventide

"We have quite a job ahead of us," I thought out loud as we sat on Rebecca's front porch and waited for the night to gather around us a little more. Silas had not yet returned. I wasn't really worried. But, I did wonder. I wondered about so many things. Mostly, would our country ever wake up in time to save even a remnant of what we had before, long before ... before the silence?

"Smell the winter rain?" Jason inhaled deeply as he closed his eyes and sucked in the aroma of the earth around us. "It came down over an hour ago, but the sweetness remains."

"Why is everything more enjoyable on this side of the mountain?" I asked. "I could just sit here and relax for hours." Then the memories of home rushed back in, and I answered my own question. "The drugs."

"The coded messages Silas has gotten through Sean's newspaper are very hopeful," Rebecca said as she rocked in the ladder-back porch rocker.

"We've been gone for two months," I said. "I feel guilty that I hadn't kept up with what has been happening at home."

"How could you, Honey?" Jason reassured me. "There is no communication between the sectors."

311

"Rebecca has stayed in touch," I sighed.

"My Dear," she explained, "I didn't catch up to you two until a few days ago in New York. I've talked with Silas a few times as he was able to sneak, unseen, through the mountain opening. Since we were gone, he left a note for me on the kitchen table and that's what I wanted to share with you."

"Thanks, Becca." She did manage to make me feel better when I didn't feel sorry for myself. "Did Silas' note tell you anything about what's going on over there?"

Rebecca pulled the piece of paper from her pocket just as Martin joined us on the porch.

"I see you got the note," he said as he sat down.

"Did you read it?" she asked her husband.

"No, I didn't have time. I checked on the animals in the barn. Dixie is about to drop her calf."

"She's awfully early isn't she?" Rebecca questioned.

"Seems she likes the idea of more freedom too," he laughed.

"How wonderful, Martin," I thought out loud. "A new beginning all over the country and a new calf to celebrate new life for everyone." My thoughts clung to the promise of new life and the wobbly calf that would soon come into our strangely divided country. Life was still going on as planned.

"Rebecca," she began reading the letter, "I had to come through to tell you what's going on over here. Tell, Lady Christy, if you are with her, that her grandmother had been very ill this winter—"

"Oh, no," I gasped and sat up straight in the chair.

"Wait Christy, there's more," she cautioned, "... very ill this winter ... but is doing much better. The Blue Guard Chief told Sir Richly that they captured My Lady in New York and shot her during the arrest. Her grandmother collapsed under the grief of it."

"He what?" I gasped as I pounded the arm rest of the porch chair. "The liar!"

"Christy," Jason soothed, "you know Stoner can't be trusted with anything. He probably thought the news would make you drop your guard."

"Where that man is concerned, my guard will always be up!" I said as I ground my teeth. "Did Silas say more?" I hoped for a better outcome than I had heard so far.

Rebecca continued. "Rumor has it that Lady Richly was so upset by the news, her health took a downward turn. But, I was able to get word to her that you were okay. Tell Christiana and Jason that they must be doubly cautious when they get back. The people's emotions are really uneven due to detoxification. Some have gotten hyper-excited about putting Christiana's name up for President at the next election. That could be dangerous for her."

My eyes jerked to attention. "I told them I'm not old enough to run."

"But Honey," Jason patted my knee, "your supporters don't sound reasonable right now. You cannot apply logic to an illogical argument."

"You're right. I know you're right but Jason ... it's Grand-mère ... and it's this election ... that will continue to keep us running. Now ... maybe some are unaware they are putting our lives in danger."

"I know, Baby. I understand." He took my hand and squeezed it for reassurance. "Is there more Rebecca?"

"The word is that Alister Bedlam has put a bounty on Christy's head. Maybe they should stay on the valley side of the mountain. Sincerely, Silas ... p.s. I will check if you are back at 9 p.m. on February 11."

"A bounty?" Jason bellowed as he charged out of his comfortable chair.

"What does he mean by a bounty?" I gasped.

"It means anyone can catch you and turn you in to authorities," Gray Fox barked as he rocked harder and faster.

"On what charge?" I asked. "I know Jason and I crossed borders, but Stoner doesn't have proof that we did, and Bedlam doesn't either."

"Bedlam's power has been threatened. He has no one to blame but the visitors at the Citadel, and he has decided to blame you since Stoner is after you anyway," Martin figured.

"I have to get back home," I insisted.

"Then make sure you aren't caught before you reach your apartment," Martin insisted. "He can't say you're missing if you're there in front of him when he arrives. It'll be dangerous. Watch yourselves."

"I'll go in and get your hat. You've already changed into your own clothes. Although, Christy, you look so much thinner than you were."

"I know my clothes are really loose." Then I thought, "But, maybe that's good. I can say I've been sick and have been regaining my strength. Now that the Length of Days law has been suspended until after the election, I won't even have points placed in my life file."

"I'll go get my things, Honey. It's nearly nine," Jason said, then stopped and gathered me in his arms. "With God's help, we can do this. Look at all that has happened. Now, it's time to go home."

"Next week will be Mid-Winter Bash," I said but didn't feel like celebrating.

"Bash?" Martin asked.

"To make the winter months a little brighter after Gifting Day, they have continued with Mid-winter Bash. You know: gifts of candy, jewelry, lite entertainment." Then I thought about that word. "They are so rarely entertained, or have the capacity to enjoy life at all."

"When is the Bash?" he asked.

"February 14—wait, that's in a couple of days. I guess it will be nice to be home after all."

"Christy," Rebecca began with a crooked smile on her lips, "February 14 is Valentine's Day."

"Valentines? I've read about Valentine's Day," I gasped.

"Yes, Dear," she chuckled. "It's the day of love. The gifts they share are to show their loved one that they care." She patted my hand.

"Wait right here, Christy," she said as she stood up. "There is nothing I can give you since you would have no way of explaining where it came from. You must travel with nothing in your pockets, not even an extra wrap. But, I want you to have my grandmother's necklace. It's a cross and you can hide it under your clothes. If there is any danger that they could catch you with it, you have my full permission to cast it aside. It is only a symbol." She turned to go. "I'll be right back."

"You don't have to give me your grandmother's necklace, Rebecca," I called after her.

"Of course she doesn't Christy," Martin agreed. "And ... of course she does, My Dear." Martin got up and followed his wife in the house.

"I'm going to run in and get my own shoes, Honey," Jason said. "I still have on the boots they loaned me."

"Here it is," Rebecca said as she returned, holding her hand out reverently. "It's simple because I was very little, maybe five years old. Later, I had a longer chain made for it." She dangled the beautiful gold cross in front of me. "Let me fasten it for you."

I turned and lifted the back of my hair so she could secure the clasp. Once fastened, it dropped into place, long enough for me to see it and to hide under my clothing. I ran my fingers over the delicate design. "Rebecca, it is beautiful. I will cherish it."

"I know you will—that's why I gave it to you." She smiled and kissed my cheek. "Bless you Christy. May the Lord keep you safe."

"Thank you my friend," I whispered.

"I'm going to run in and make sure you haven't left anything in the house." She went back in the house, but I knew the goodbye was hard for her. It was difficult for me, too.

Alone on the porch, I looked beyond the valley to where we had been, to where the setting sun met the distant ridge—and suddenly I had hope. It felt like the lunar glow was resting on my face. Everyone had sacrificed so much for me I could do no less than return the trust. Hope never sleeps. We form our lives around it. It may nap for a while, but it always makes its way to the brim of the Eastern hill and soars in the spirit of the new morn. We were going home, to whatever new challenges awaited us. I refuse to be afraid.

Reference:

Other Books by Doris Gaines Rapp

<u>Novelette:</u>

News at Eleven (Glo Magazine Jan, Feb, March, and April 2015
Expanded to: *News at Eleven – A Novel* (Release April 2015)

<u>Novels:</u>

Length of Days – The Age of Silence
Escape from the Belfry
Smoke from Distant Fires
Hiawassee – Child of the Meadow

<u>Collection:</u>

Christmas Feather, one of eight short stories in a wonderful collection titled, **Christmases Past**

<u>Children's:</u>

Lincoln's Christmas Mouse

<u>Non-Fiction:</u>

Waiting for Jesus in a Can't Wait World – Advent 2014
Prayer Therapy of Jesus
Promote Yourself

Internet Presence:

www.prayertherapyrapp.blogspot.com
www.dorisgainesrapp.blogspot.com
Facebook: Doris Gaines Rapp – Author Page

About the Author

Doris Gaines Rapp, Ph.D. is a writer by birth, psychologist and teacher by education and experiences. She creates fictional characters that live in several centuries and loves the stories she tells. As a psychologist, she understands the people who appear on her computer screen; she laughs with them, cries with them, and triumphs over adversity with them. They are real and full of life. All of her works have at their heart a Christian world view.

Rapp also writes on the non-fiction topics of Self-publishing with an encouragement to promote yourself and your work, as well as Prayer Therapy, learning to pray specifically so God can answer prayers specifically.

She speaks on several topics:
Voices of Assertiveness within My Novel
Prayer Therapy
Promote Yourself
Know Your Own History

Dr. Rapp is a former counseling center director of Taylor University, Upland, and Bethel College, Mishawaka, IN. She currently writes and speaks full time. She and her pastor husband have survived rearing six children. They live in Indiana.

9 780099 150335 3